The Day the Leash Gave Way and Other Stories

©2009 Trent Zelazny

This is a work of fiction. All the characters and events portrayed in this collection of stories are either fictitious or are used fictitiously.

All rights reserved. Printed in the United States of America. No part of this book may be used or reproduced in any manner without written permission except for brief quotations for review purposes only.

Fantastic Books
PO Box 243
Blacksburg VA 24060
www.wilderpublications.com

ISBN 10: 1-60459-884-0
ISBN 13: 978-1-60459-884-1

First Edition

The Day the Leash Gave Way and Other Stories

by Trent Zelazny

Publishing History

"Hooch," 2005, unpublished; "Acupuncture," 2001, first appeared in *Shadow of the Marquis*; "Harold Asher and His Vomiting Dogs," 1999, first appeared in *Scavenger's Newsletter*, taking second place in the annual Killer Frog contest; "Competition," 2002, first appeared in *House of Pain*; "Found Money," 2006, first appeared in *Futures Mystery Anthology Magazine*; "On My Feet," 2002, first appeared in *Deviant Minds*; "Mourning Road," 2005, first appeared in *The Ethereal Gazette*; "The Day the Leash Gave Way," 2005, first appeared in *Aphelion*; "Caught in Etcetera," 2002, first appeared in *Psrhea Magazine*; "The House of Happy Mayhem," 2006, unpublished; "Two-Thirty-Six," 2006, first appeared on a short-lived mystery website, under the pseudonym J.T. Deckard; "A Dead Man's Burrito," 2002, first appeared in *House of Pain*; "Hope is an Inanimate Desire," 1999, first appeared in *Cemetery Sonata*; "Davidividavida," 2006, first appeared in *Susurrus: The Literature of Madness*; "Lovely Day for Beating an Old Guy," 2002, first appeared in *Random Acts of Weirdness*; "Opportunity Knocks," 2003, first appeared in *Penumbric Speculative Fiction*; "Bathing Beauty," 2002, unpublished; "The Disappearance of Experimentation," 2001, first appeared in *Shadow of the Marquis*; "An Angle for the Angels," 2006, first appeared in *The Ethereal Gazette*; "How to Write a Short Story for Publication in The New Yorker, by Everette Sage Brown," 2006, first appeared in *The Santa Fe Literary Review*; "End of the Rainbow," 2002, first appeared in *The Swamp*; "The Music," 2002, first appeared in *Horrorfind*; "Sparkle Head," 2005, unpublished.

This collection is dedicated to two very important people.

For Gerald Hausman, wonderful dear friend, and the one who said time and time again for years that I should put together a collection of my shorter works.

And for Joe Lansdale, who has always been a tremendous support, a good friend, and the writer I mimicked most as I learned how to write.

I truly and dearly appreciate you both. Thank you so much.

Contents

Hooch	8
Acupuncture	18
Harold Asher and His Vomiting Dogs	22
Competition	24
Found Money	27
On My Feet	46
Mourning Road	49
The Day the Leash Gave Way	55
Caught in Etcetera	64
The House of Happy Mayhem	68
Two-Thirty-Six	79
A Dead Man's Burrito	82
Hope Is an Inanimate Desire	88
Divadavidavida	96
Lovely Day for Beating an Old Guy	97
Opportunity Knocks	104
Bathing Beauty	114
The Disappearance of Experimentation	122
An Angle for the Angels	125
"How to Write a Short Story for Publication in the *New Yorker*, by Everette Sage Brown"	141
End of the Rainbow	144
The Music	152
Sparkle Head	153

Hooch

If only Tim had gone to the goddamn store like his mother had asked him, none of this would have happened. Mom had wanted some goddamn lettuce so she could make a goddamn salad for goddamn dinner tonight. Tim might not have been so pissed at her for getting upset with him because he'd stumbled into the house drunk last night and wandered into her bedroom where she was sleeping, and thrown up on her. Maybe is she hadn't taken a curtain rod to his hung-over body in morning as he slept it off—in his own bed, mind you—he might have gone to the goddamn store and gotten her the goddamn lettuce she wanted. But no, to hell with her. People make mistakes. That didn't mean they should be bludgeoned to within an inch of their life, especially not with a goddamn curtain rod.

Instead, when Mom gave him the money for the lettuce, he took it and went over to old Crabtree's place. Ox Crabtree was an old bastard with a mouth like a sour turd and limbs so thin one always thought they were going to snap. His glass eye left most anyone that ever visited him unsettled but he was also the only guy in town from whom one not yet of legal age could acquire something to drink. Something harder than Dr. Pepper, that is. Ox Crabtree had no qualms about such things. He'd sell a kid right out of the womb a Mason jar full of Everclear if they had the money; he didn't give a fuck.

So that's where Tim went, instead of to the goddamn store.

Crabtree's house was a crumbling old adobe fucker with cracked windows and overgrown weeds in the yard that looked like ratty hair on the head of someone feverish. There was half a bucket and lots of garbage strewn throughout the yard, too, and every time Tim walked through the busted gate he immediately felt dirty, as though a sort of film not dissimilar to sewage had suddenly caked onto his flesh from out of nowhere.

Inside he could hear the television. It sounded like a game show, "Wheel of Fortune" or "Jeopardy" or some shit. When he knocked there came the raspy bark of Nail, Crabtree's pig-fucker of a dog. Little white bitch about the size of a couple potatoes and not too dissimilar in appearance due to some fucked-up disease the pooch had that wilted its flesh and covered it in scabs.

The door opened. Crabtree stood there a moment. He blinked his real eye several times, then said: "Ain't you the little shit that was here last night?"

"I came back to buy some more hooch," Tim said, and reached into his pocket, from which he produced the five-dollar bill his mom had given him.

Crabtree reached out and took the money. "Lesson one," he said putting the five in his pocket. "Never wave money in front of a man sells hooch." Then he stood aside and made a gesture with his head for Tim to enter. "Your bitch is in the kitchen," he added.

The Day the Leash Gave Way

Not sure what Crabtree meant, Tim was surprised to find Harry standing by the sink swigging out of a Mason jar. The way Harry stood always made him look like he'd forgotten to wipe and was trying to compensate somehow. He had this sort of duck walk too, a waddle, and when he smiled his front teeth looked like two enormous Tic-Tacs set an inch or so outside his lips.

Harry took his mouth away from the jar and coughed, then wiped his face on the back of his hand and looked at Tim. "Hey," he said, and smiled. "You getting yourself some hooch?"

Tim said that he was, and almost asked why else he would be here. He told him about his mom being all pissed at him and beating him with the curtain rod, and this being the reason why he felt he deserved a drink. "What you up to?" he asked.

"You know Darlene," Harry said, "from school?"

"Sure."

"She agreed to let me put it in her for ten dollars."

"Shit," Tim said. "Doesn't Darlene have some sort of disease?"

"That's just a rumor," Harry said.

"I hear that down between her legs it's all covered in scabs and shit."

"That's not true," Harry said. "I been down there once before. She let me feel around but that was about it. I didn't find no scabs or nothing."

"Hey bitch," Crabtree said as he entered the kitchen scratching himself. "You got your goods. Why the fuck you still here?" Then he turned to Tim, shook his head and got together a jar for him. "Now get out of here. Go love each other somewhere else."

"Thanks, Mr. Crabtree."

"I said out, fudge-packers."

They left the house. Nail snarled and showed his teeth as they made their way out. When they got to the sidewalk they stopped. Each unscrewed the lid of their sacred nectar and took a sip, and as they screwed them back on Harry said, "You wanna come along? Darlene mentioned she thought you were kind of cute. Hell, she might let you put it in her for less than ten. Give her some hooch she might do it for free."

"Wouldn't be free if I gotta give her hooch," Tim said. He couldn't get the image of scabs out of his mind. He wondered if Darlene maybe had the same disease that Crabtree's dog had. This of course led to a joke in his mind about doing it doggie style. He laughed a bit to himself.

"What's so funny?" Harry asked.

Tim shook his head.

There ensued a lengthy pause as each of them considered their Mason jar.

"That Ox Crabtree sure is an asshole," said Harry.

"Aw, he's okay," said Tim. "He sold us hooch, didn't he?"

"True enough." They unscrewed their jars, clicked them together and had another swig.

It was dark out and with the clouds and the way the moon was shining, it looked like there were mud streaks smeared across the sky. Tim wondered if it was true what Harry was saying about Darlene. About her thinking he was cute. If it was, then maybe there was a chance that he could get laid before he would technically be graduating high school, not that he ever would, seeing how he dropped out.

"I still can't help being uncomfortable," Harry said, "when he looks at me with that glass eye."

"It's a damn weird thing," Tim said, looking down the street one way then the other.

"I heard his dead wife scooped it out with a spoon after she caught him looking at another woman."

"That's the way I heard it too," Tim said.

"Hey!" Crabtree's voice rang from the house. "I told you dick slits to get out of here!"

"We're going, we're going."

They began walking along. Tim went with Harry, given that Harry had someplace to be and Tim didn't know what the fuck he was doing. It was a quiet night, sort of peaceful. If not for the mud streaks in the sky it would have been downright beautiful.

"Did you mean what you were saying," Tim said after a time, "about Darlene thinking I'm cute?"

"That's what she said," Harry told him. "We're only about a block away from her house. You wanna come along and see?"

Tim thought about the scabs again. It was a mighty unpleasant image but he told himself, It's just a rumor. Harry said it himself that he'd felt down there and there hadn't been nothing like that. "Aw hell," he said, "why not?"

They walked down the block. Darlene's house was beat up but nothing like Ox Crabtree's place. Ox Crabtree had the shittiest house in town, even worse than Harry's which had never completely recovered from the fire. The front porch light of Darlene's was on but all the inside lights were out.

"Is anybody even home?" Tim asked as he unscrewed his hooch.

The second he asked this a window on the side of the house opened up. A raggedy head popped out, then popped back in. A moment later, two legs came dangling out, followed by the rest of Darlene. She dropped to the ground, eased the window shut, raced across the yard and joined them on the sidewalk. She was wearing this tight sweater and these tight jeans that, even in the dark, made her look a little uncomfortable.

"I was listening for you," she said to Harry. "I was hoping you'd show up. Dad got drunk early and beat Mom until he knocked her out, then he passed out on the TV and broke it."

"Hi, Darlene," Harry said and smiled, then gestured to Tim. "You know Tim, right?"

"Now we got no fucking TV," Darlene said. She looked at Tim and smiled. "Hey, Tim."

Tim smiled back and took another swig of hooch. Dammit, Harry might have been right. Way she looked at him just then, he sensed that she was wet for his meat. As long as there weren't no scabs down there in the nether region or anything like that, Tim felt that he would be more than happy to oblige.

"So, where you all gonna do this?" he asked while giving Darlene the once over. Maybe it was what Harry had said or maybe it was just the light, but at the moment Tim thought Darlene looked like one sweet piece of ass.

The Day the Leash Gave Way

"I was thinking the playground over at Briar Park," Harry said. He looked at Darlene. "Might be kind of cool on the merry-go-round."

"You got the ten dollars?" she asked.

This threw some of the thunder out of Harry. He looked down at his hooch, then down beyond to his shoes. "Yeah," he said, "I got it."

"All right, then. Cause there ain't no such thing as free tang." She twisted her fingers in her ratty hair and looked Tim up and down as she said this.

"I know," Harry said, humble as a pillow. He unscrewed his lid and offered the jar to Darlene. "You want some hooch?"

"Well, maybe a little." She threw back a sip and coughed. "Whew! That's like drinking fire!"

"Me and Tim drink it all the time."

"Probably why you're so stupid." She fished a pack of Marlboros from her pocket, lipped one and lit it.

"Hey, Darlene, give us one of those."

"All right," she said, and passed them out. "Good thing Mom smokes so much she never knows how many she has. There were, like, five packs by the bathtub."

They made their way to the park, smoking their cigarettes and drinking hooch. Tim noticed that he was now stumbling a little bit and thought about how this night was turning out much better than last night. Last night he'd sat outside on the sidewalk all by himself and drank until he puked. Then he'd gone inside and...well, he didn't want his mind to keep repeating *all* that had happened since.

When they got to the park Darlene immediately sat down on one of the swings. Tim sat on another and Harry staggered around in small circles like a dog chasing its tail in slow motion.

"It's a nice night," Darlene said, pushing herself back and forth a little with her feet.

Harry looked up to the sky. He uncapped his hooch and took another gulp then set the jar on the merry-go-round and got back to his circles. Tim noticed that his waddle was a little different than usual and wasn't sure if it was the hooch or something else. He himself began thinking about what his mother was going to do when he came home, drunk again, later than fuck and with no goddamn lettuce. He knew there was gonna be hellfire and brimstone throughout the house, but at the moment he just didn't care. Hell, even if he didn't get to stick nothing into Darlene, he was just having fun hanging out. It was worth the trouble that would come later. This didn't stop him from reaching down and touching his dick, though.

"So," Darlene finally said. "We gonna do this or what?"

"Yeah," Harry said. There was a tremor in his voice. "Let's get to it."

"All right, but I don't want Tim watching." She looked at Tim. "Be a gentleman and go stand behind a tree or something."

"Why don't you guys go somewhere else? You all are having the fun. At least let me ride on the swing or something."

"Come on, Tim," Harry said, then gestured to the merry-go-round.

"Well," Tim said, "all right." He got up from the swing, took his jar of hooch and made his way through the playground over to the soccer field. There weren't any lights about other than the glow of the shit-stained moon and it shrouded the dead grass with an eerie sort of light that reminded Tim of Halloween.

This place held a lot of memories for him. He remembered when he was a kid—maybe seven or eight—and he used to play junior league soccer. It was on this exact same field, actually. Tim was the only kid all year to score against his own team. He could remember people yelling at him but that was about it. He wondered if Scott O'Farrell ever got yelled at in his younger days. Scott was captain of the high school varsity soccer team, a chick magnet, and the nicest guy in the world. It would be impossible to hate the guy. Called the shots right nearly every fucking time like some sort of magician or child of God—at least the god of soccer, if such a god existed.

Off in the distance behind him he heard the bewildered voice of Harry asking, "Now what?" as he walked clear to the other end of the field, where a park bench sat next to a scoreboard that looked like someone had recently taken a baseball bat to it.

He sat down and unscrewed the lid of his hooch but didn't drink any. Goddamn, it was weird. What with Harry saying how Darlene thought he was cute and all, and then the way she had looked at him while they were all standing outside her house—and then they get to the park and it's almost like he doesn't exist. What the fuck was that all about? Was it all a lie? Was Darlene just some sort of goddamn slut? He didn't know what to think. If she really had interest in having his meat inside her, then why the fuck did she want him to leave?

Around him he could hear the subtle movements of wildlife. It spooked him a little, not knowing what was out there in those trees. Just a stupid rabbit or something, he told himself. Then he heard Darlene say "Ouch!" and Harry said, "I'm sorry." Tim stared through the darkness across the field, trying to catch a glimpse of them. As he did, it suddenly came to his attention that some of the wildlife had moved closer. At least one piece of wildlife had, and it was coming in his direction.

It sounded like feet—human feet.

Tim shot up from the bench and spun around, knocking over his hooch and spilling it into the dead grass. The second his focus trained into the darkness the movement stopped. Everything was as silent as a deaf man's world.

"Who's there?" he said, knowing he wasn't going to get so much as a fart in response.

Then off to his left he heard a similar sound, though it came and went so fast Tim had a hard time convincing himself that he had actually heard it at all. He looked down at the now empty Mason jar in the grass, and as he turned to head back towards the playground he heard another similar sound from somewhere else.

Goddamn shit was scaring him now. He tried to walk at a leisurely pace but found his feet moving him faster and faster against his command. As he went he noticed that the sounds seemed to pace him on either side. He stopped and they stopped. He walked slow for a couple seconds and they seemed to as well. And when he got moving fast again so did whatever it was out there.

The Day the Leash Gave Way 13

When he got back to the playground Darlene had her pants off and she was on top of Harry on the merry-go-round. Harry's pants were around his ankles.

"Let me know when you're gonna come, all right?"

"I, uh...just did," said Harry.

Before any reaction could come from Darlene, Tim said, "Hey, guys, there's something or someone out there."

"What?" Darlene jumped off of Harry and grabbed her pants. In the dark Tim couldn't tell whether she had scabs or not.

Harry pulled up his pants and got to his feet. "What are you talking about?"

Before Tim could answer he came to the unfortunate realization that they were surrounded. A tense, awkward silence passed. The three of them looked around and found shapes closing in all around them.

"Well slit it up the middle," came a voice, "if it isn't Scabby Bitch and her two lesbian lovers." They all recognized the voice. It was Alec Pearce, the dumb fuck son of a bitch that lost out as varsity soccer captain to Scott O'Farrell. A walking 165-pound jar of bitters. Guy was a stinking boozer when he wasn't on the field. He was a mean bastard, too. If he wanted, the guy could probably eat a baby's rattle and shit you a handgun.

He turned to Tim. "Why were you running, Drop Out?"

Tim heard stupid laughter from Alec's stupid friends. He looked around and counted six shapes, including Alec's, whichever one it was. Damn, they were outnumbered worse than a female Red-Sided Garter snake at mating time.

"I asked you a question," Alec said, and took a step forward, allowing Tim to realize which shape was his. "Why were you running?"

Tim looked around, trying to see if there was a way out, what the best route to make a run for it would be. They couldn't stay where they were. They'd be squashed like a stale turd under a hard and spiky shoe.

"Drops out of school and becomes dumb as a mute," Alec said. Then he turned and looked at Darlene, who was standing there clutching her pants in her hands. "How do you like that?" he said. "I always wondered if what they said about the scabs was true. And here she is, standing with her beaver already out as though she knew I was gonna show up."

"Look," Harry said. "We don't want any trouble."

"I didn't ask you what you wanted," Alec said. He moved toward Harry and pushed him. "Moreso, I don't give a shit what you want."

Tim watched Harry quiver in the darkness. He wondered if Alec had made it as captain of the soccer team, would he still be such an asshole? He didn't know; but there was a part of him now that didn't think being beaten with a curtain rod was all that bad—at least not in comparison to what he was pretty sure was in store here on the playground.

"You gonna fuck her, Alec?" one the cronies asked.

"Hell no! And catch some sort of goddamn disease that puts scabs all over my dick? I'd rather have my eyes scooped out with a spoon."

Alec's pals all laughed. Tim, Harry and Darlene thought about Ox Crabtree and him looking at a woman the wrong way. Tim looked up to the sky. There seemed to be more shit smeared on the moon than before.

"Tell you, I'm thinking," Alec said, "we should at least find out if the rumor is true."

It was then, while Alec's buddies grumbled and laughed in agreement, that Tim saw something just beyond the swings he and Darlene had been sitting on. He hadn't seen it before, but now it stood out so prominently to him it almost seemed to be waving hello. It was a little farther away than he would have liked but he felt he had a good chance of getting it, if only a little luck would be with him. He focused on his breathing and knew that he had to wait a little longer before he could make any sort of move for it. He prayed that he wasn't hallucinating. He also prayed that none of these drunken jock assholes would find it first.

"Let's see," Alec said.

Next thing Tim knew someone had knocked him to the ground. When he stirred he saw that Harry was on his knees, holding his stomach and gasping for breath. It was also at this time that he heard Darlene scream. Alec and the boys had gotten a hold of her, and they were dragging her struggling, bottomless body back over to the merry-go-round. Her pants were lying in the dirt.

"Anyone got a lighter?" one of the guys asked. "We gotta be able to see good."

"Yeah," someone else said. "And if there's any bleeding we might need to cauterize it."

This was followed by more laughter.

This was also the moment that Tim got to his feet and raced beyond the swings. No one seemed to notice that he was moving, or if they did they didn't care. He reached down and found that what he'd seen was real. He picked it up and tested its weight, wondering if it was the same bat that had smashed up the scoreboard across the field. He didn't waste any time thinking about it. Instead he moved right over to the crowd and swung as hard as he could at the nearest son of a bitch, connecting with their ribs and sending them down. Before anyone knew what was going on he'd already taken out another.

Alec and the others moved away. Darlene got up off the merry-go-round, grabbed her pants and shoes and ran. Harry was only just getting to his feet.

"You gonna take us *all* on, you stupid goddamn drop out?"

Tim didn't know why he did it. Some kind of dumb reaction of some sort, but in response to Alec's question he flung the bat at him. It whirled through the air and connected directly with Alec's face, making a horrible cracking sound when it did. Alec screamed and dropped to his ass with both hands on his face and sounds gurgling from his throat like a cat throwing up a hairball. As Tim backed away he saw Harry, rather than making a run for it like he should have been, making his way over to the merry-go-round, where his jar of hooch still sat unharmed.

Before Tim could ask, "What the fuck are you doing?" the three uninjured boys were on top of Harry, beating him down as though they were working on the railroad and really hated the railroad. Tim continued to move away, saw one of the boys pick up the bat and go at Harry with it. The further away Tim got, the less Harry seemed to move and the

The Day the Leash Gave Way 15

fewer sounds he seemed to make. *Nothing can be done now*, Tim thought, and spun around and ran.

He cut through the trees but in the general direction of the street, tripping and almost losing his footing over something he was pretty sure was a goddamn rabbit. Reaching the street, looking one way then the other, he decided the best thing to do was to head towards Darlene's house. There were streetlights now, which was good because the moon was completely covered by those shit-colored clouds. With what had happened and all, he discovered that he had sobered up plenty from the hooch he'd drunk.

Goddamn, he thought. Poor Harry, getting beaten like that, all on account that the idiot had to have his fucking hooch and was willing to risk his goddamn life for it. Guy could be dead by now, for all Tim knew. The way those guys were going at him it wouldn't be a surprise in the least. Tim felt bad for leaving him there, but what the hell could he have done? He'd been stupid enough to throw the bat. Practically handed it over to the opposition, like when he'd scored against his own soccer team nearly ten years ago. Some things never change, he thought, sensing the threat of a tear at the edge of his eye.

Rounding the corner onto Darlene's street he saw someone up ahead carrying what looked like pants in one hand and shoes in the other.

"Hey Darlene," he called out.

Darlene stopped and spun around. When she realized it was Tim she came towards him, sniffling and blubbering and carrying on like some stupid hysterical bitch in one of those cheap horror films with bad special effects and lots of tits. Tim wanted to slap her like they did in the movies but felt that it would be un-gentleman like. Instead he told her to calm down about fifty fucking times, and when she had finally relaxed he put his arm around her and they slowly walked to her house.

"Harry...he's dead, isn't he?"

"I dunno," Tim said, squeezing her shoulder. "Looked mighty bad, what I saw of it."

They arrived at her window. Tim had seen a light on inside the house, at the other end from Darlene's room. A moment later he thought he heard something that might have been a door.

Darlene wiped away tears with her pants and said, "Thanks, Tim. Thanks for saving my life."

"Yeah," Tim said, wishing he could have saved Harry too.

"Y'know," Darlene said, "I always thought you were cute."

Tim lied his ass off and told her that he'd always felt the same about her. He still hadn't gotten a good look at her pussy, and there was this nagging—almost obsession now, with wondering whether what they said about the scabs was true or not.

"Maybe you and I could hang out sometime," Darlene said.

"Yeah," Tim said, "maybe." If she didn't have any kind of disease then he kind of just wanted to fuck her and get things over with. The idea of talking to her too much left a bad taste in his mouth. Sure, she'd been walking around without pants for the past half-hour but his dick wasn't made of steel. It wasn't gonna wait five, six, seven days and he didn't have ten bucks to hurry the process along.

He was about to try inviting himself in through the window when a hand grabbed him by the back of the shirt and flung him to the ground, giving him some sort of whiplash and scraping up his hands. Before he could get oriented a hard boot cracked him in the face.

"Papa, no!"

"You get on in the house right now, you filthy slut. I'll deal with you soon enough."

Tim felt the boot kick him hard in the stomach. Hard enough for bile and hooch to squirt up through his throat. He was pretty sure his nose was broken too.

"Papa, please stop. You don't understand."

"I understand just fine," Papa said. "You standing outside the window with your goddamn pants off. This dumb-fuck clinging to your ass like some sort of fucking turd."

He kicked Tim again. Tim wasn't sure if he was seeing stars or sleeping. He tried swatting his hands out in defense but Darlene's papa merely smacked them away. Already this was ten times worse than being beaten with a curtain rod. Hell, he'd be happy to let his mom beat him all she wanted, just so long as he was at home. He'd even take whatever disease it was Darlene had. Gobble it up like it was goddamn ice cream and ask for seconds. Fuck, God could put all the scabs on his dick He wanted, just so long as He got him out of this jam.

"You are one low piece of shit," Darlene's papa said, picking him up by both his shirt and his hair and dragging him like a rag doll out towards the street.

"Daddy, you're drunk. Why can't you just listen to me?"

"I'm through listening to you."

Tim wished to hell and back that he hadn't sobered up. What he wouldn't give to find out that this was just another drunken dream. To wake up to his mom beating him with a curtain rod—that would have been just fine about now.

He could feel the blood from his nose running down his face and neck. His brain felt like it was spinning around inside his skull and he was pretty sure a couple of teeth had been dislodged. For whatever dumb reason he wondered what Ox Crabtree was doing at that moment. Was he still watching his fucking game shows? Sitting and drinking hooch and picking scabs off his bitch of a dog?

The world flipped upside down. When he caught a glimpse of the moon he saw it had reverted back to how it had looked earlier, like an infant had reached into its diaper and finger-painted all over it. The dirt beneath his dragging feet solidified into cement.

"Now get the hell out of here and don't come back," Darlene's papa yelled, and Tim felt himself hoisted through the air and flailing into the street.

"Papa, no!"

The timing couldn't have been more for shit. First he was hit by headlights. Then he was slammed by the front of a truck. He flipped through the air like a handicapped trapeze artist, still feeling things breaking inside him, and landed on his back with a loud crack. The first thing he realized was that he couldn't move at all and he couldn't see out of his left eye. The right eye wasn't seeing too good but the left eye was done and gone and he thought briefly about how this must be how Ox Crabtree sees all the time.

The Day the Leash Gave Way

He heard the squeal of tires as the truck slammed its brakes. Along with this he heard Darlene screaming out in horror, and her papa, clearly as surprised about the timing as Tim was, saying "Holy shit."

Then the sight zipped out of Tim's right eye and his entire fading world suddenly became smeared in shit. Everything drew away from him as though he was falling down a dark black sewage tunnel. The entire world got smaller and smaller, dwindled to almost nothing; then his mom hit him once with a curtain rod and the world disappeared all together.

That sucked. It sucked real bad. The worst part about it all was, he never got to find out if what they said about Darlene having those scabs was true or not.

Acupuncture

Remember me?

We met about two months ago at the Johnson's house—the party for Phil because of his great promotion. Yeah, we met that night and a few days later you started fucking my wife.

You know my wife, right? The cute brunette with the great smile? You even commented on her smile that night, said it reminded you of sunshine. And then you started fucking her, I bet getting that smile—sunshine—more and more every time.

So you don't need to deny it. I even watched you through the window one night. Said I was going out to a lecture, and instead went to the Circle K nearby and got a coke, sat in my car and drank it. Then slowly, taking the long way, seeing some of the sights I don't appreciate these days, I drove back and parked at the end of the street. Actually I parked right behind your car, and I walked to the house and watched through the window as the two of you fucked like rabbits, and she took you into her smile.

So you don't need to deny it. I saw you guys, even heard her call out your name. And you fucked and fucked until you couldn't fuck no more, then you left in a hurry, practically walked right by me, bolted up the street to your car as quickly as you could—and, stupid man, you didn't notice that my car was parked right behind yours. Of course, I'm not sure you ever saw my car before, so I guess you wouldn't have known what it looked like. I'll give you that, okay.

Does that hurt?

I don't really know anything about acupuncture. I know you're supposed to use a different kind of needle but sewing needles are easier to find—can get them just about any fucking where. Got these at the arts and crafts store. They had a lot of different sizes... I thought these would work well.

You doing okay? I know you're not supposed to bleed like this, but I've never done this before. Hopefully I'll get better with practice. Maybe you won't bleed this time.

Whoops! Well, yeah, looks like more blood. Oh well...

Anyway, what I wanna know is, you're a married man, aren't ya'? Is there something she doesn't give you at home? Why do you wanna be fucking around? Why do you wanna cheat on your wife? She was very nice and quite attractive—smart, too; so why'd you need to fuck mine? And the other thing I'm wondering is why my wife decided to cheat on *me*? Did she tell you anything? Anything I should maybe know? Was it just something the two of you couldn't fight?

Ah, it doesn't matter. I'll talk with her later, when she gets home. What's done is done—you poked my wife so now I'm poking you. Fair is fair, right?

The Day the Leash Gave Way

Those ropes are tied good and tight, aren't they? Can't move your arms. Can't move your legs and I did a good job up here because it seems that you can't turn your head. You look uncomfortable. Is it because you're tied down naked in front of another man? Don't worry. I don't swing that way. Me, I'm born and bred to love women. I just hope your nose doesn't plug up cause with that gag in your mouth you won't be able to breathe.

Another question. I guess the only way you can really answer me is with your eyes, like a dog. So, I'm wondering: would you mind if I fucked your wife? After all, you got to do mine a number of times. How do you feel about me doing yours?

You wouldn't like that, huh? I can see it in your eyes.

Well, I might poke your wife, but I wanna finish poking you first. In a sense this is almost orgasmic for me, you know that? In its own way, of course.

I'm gonna put a needle into your nipple now. Your left one. I want you to focus on that nipple. At the moment nothing else exists. I'm gonna stick it in slowly, like you stuck your pole into my wife. Think of the faces and sounds she made. Think of her when she'd come. And think of your nipple. Think. Focus...

Wow. Holy shit. Got more blood than I thought.

Don't do that.

If you think those tears are going to help you, you're wrong. Actually, I like it. It lets me know I'm doing a good job. I wanna do a good job. My boss tells me I do a good job at work. Just got a raise, in fact. Of course, while I was busy at work, you were doing a good job—a better job than me obviously—at satisfying my wife. Wish I could have been better at that. I really do. But I guess there are a lot of things I wish I were better at. Guess I'm not doing a very good job with this acupuncture thing. Oh well, I've never done it before. Didn't even bother reading a book on it. You a reader?

Ah, who cares.

This nipple's bleeding less than the first one. What'd you think? Maybe I'm getting better at this. One can only get better with practice, right? Maybe I'll have this down by the time I'm finished. Get into a new line of work, maybe, and maybe my wife will love me again, like she used to. Get myself a new job and maybe she'll stop fucking other people. What do you think? I've been doing the same damn thing for years now. Just got a raise but any job gets old.

Is that what it was? Was she just tired of me? You tired of your wife? Need someone new to look at? Someone new to fuck? I think it probably happens to everyone.

Anyway, back to reading. I once read that if you puncture the eye, there's a moment when you see an Inner Light. I don't recall where I read that, whether it was fiction or not; but if you go deep into the eye, there's a light that you see, if only for a second—then probably you don't ever see anything at all, ever again.

I want you to see that light. I want you to witness your own inner light—the light of your soul—and try to find the answer as to why you had to fuck my wife, not just once, but several times. See if you can find the answer. Take a good look, if you can.

Since we did your left nipple first, we'll do your right eye first, this time. You left-handed or right-handed? Which hand do you jerk off with? Oh, well, you don't need to jerk off like *some* people.

So, now, nothing exists but your eye—and this needle. I wanna know if it hurts. The more it hurts the better I feel. Let me know how much it hurts, okay? You owe me that much, I think.

Focus, now.

No, open your eye. Hey, open your eye. Watch the needle as it comes closer and moves in, so small and pointy. Sharp. You looking? Look now. I said look. Here it comes. Watch it. Watch it. I'm gonna try to get it right in the center. Keep it open. Open. A little more. A little more…

Oh…

There, I'll push slowly. How is it? Does it hurt? I guess so from the amount of noise you're making underneath that gag. Good. Oh, so sweet, yes, and there's blood—just a little, though.

Do you see the Inner Light? Am I there? Have we reached it? I'll keep going. Maybe, if you haven't seen it, you will when we do the left eye. I want you to see it. Even if you don't tell me, I want you to see it, and know for yourself.

Do you see it? Do you? I can't really go any further in. Like a dick, a needle is only so long. What about it? What about the light? Do you see it? Can you see it, motherfucker?

I'm sorry. No need for me to shout. Everything is under control. Everything is being taken care of.

How do I look? With one eye things are more two-dimensional, huh? I'll have to tell you how close I am with the next one, so you know just where we stand.

Yes, good, keep crying. Keep screaming. It makes me feel so damn good; better than I've ever felt in my life. Yeah, good, yeah. Cry. Cry, because soon you'll never shed another tear. You'll never see another color. You'll never see anything, ever again.

Here we go. Watch. Watch it. Watch the silver little point. I said watch it, you bastard. Asshole, keep that eye open. It's coming—closer, closer still. About an inch. Almost there. Watch it—here we go.

There!

Let me know if you see the light. Well, I guess you can't. With your eyes gone you're not even good enough to be a goddamn dog. No damn way for you to let me know. I saw you do it doggie style with my wife that night. *I saw you*; but you, you'll never see again. Never ever. Maybe you'll see within your soul, find reasons and meaning—but out here, never ever again.

Okay.

I'm sure it must be odd, only my voice, not being able to see anything at all. Only my voice and nothing more—nothing except feeling…you can still feel. And so can I. That's right. I feel this, too. I feel all of it, dammit, every bit of it. So, wait, here, let me move in and get close so I can whisper in your ear. Ah, there we go. Listen to me:

I'm gonna castrate you, slowly, then I'm gonna bash your fucking head in with a hammer, you piece of shit. I want you to hurt and hurt bad.

I only hope you've seen the Inner Light. Maybe you can find some sort of redemption, wherever it is you find yourself next. If not, then I didn't do my job well enough. That being the case, it's my fault. I try to do a good job, I really do—but I've learned, partially

The Day the Leash Gave Way

thanks to you, that doing a good job, no matter how hard you try or how well you do, isn't always enough, you no good shit-for-brains bastard!

Right, right, no need to shout, right, I'm sorry.

I just hope you've seen things in a different light, and you know where we stand.

All right, now, where were we?

Harold Asher and His Vomiting Dogs

Harold unlocked the cages and brought the dogs out into the courtyard for a final rehearsal. Back in high school he sang tenor, and had also been a member of the drama club. After graduating he decided that, in one way or another, he wanted to stay involved with performing arts.

"All right," he announced, "we've got a little over forty minutes before show time, so what I wanna do is run through it one more time, then we're off to the theater." He clapped his hands together twice.

One of the dogs was throwing up.

"Poochie," Harold said, "hold back a bit, okay? We've gotta make sure you've got enough for the show."

Disgorging one small final batch, Poochie ceased.

"Now," clapping his hands together again, "are we ready? 'Singin' in the Puke,' from the top! One, Two, Three—!"

In perfect time, the dogs began puking.

"Uh-huh," Harold said, swaying his head back and forth, tapping his foot to the spewing rhythm. "Yeah. Yeah." The smell of the dog vomit hit him, and he regurgitated a hearty sum onto himself. He was used to that, however, both from dealing with vomiting dogs and from bulimia.

Suddenly he was stricken with utter horror—one of the dogs was off key. It was Spot, the tenor, at least half a key off from everybody else. Spot looked weak and weary-eyed but Harold didn't take notice of that.

"Dammit!" he shouted, stomping his foot, this time out of anger. "We've gotta be at the theater in half an hour, and we sound more like shit than puke!"

The dogs all looked down with embarrassment, vomit dripping from their mouths.

Harold wiped away the ring of barf on his lips then clapped his hands together. "All right, you dogs. One more time. Singin' in the Puke, from the top."

Again, the dogs started puking.

"Dammit! Remember, it's a swing, not a samba. Now let's try it again."

He closed his eyes and listened. Yes, yes, now they were getting it. The regurgitating melody began gliding through his ears, into his nose. "Uh-huh," he said. "Better...Better. Yeah. YEAH! Puke it, baby, yeah!"

Suddenly, the music was interrupted by a gagging sound—gagging, choking, and Harold's eyes opened just in time to see Spot throw up a lung. The dog howled, then collapsed to the ground in a puddle of blood and puke. The other five dogs continued barfing their tune.

The Day the Leash Gave Way

"Hold it!" Harold shouted, waving his arms above his head, quieting the other dogs. He approached the animal, a knot developing in his stomach, his chest tightening. "Spot?" he said, scooping the dog's head into his lap, stroking the caked fur, examining the lung sitting six inches away. The dog turned its eyes up to Harold, gagged, threw up on his legs and shoes, then was still. "Oh, Spot…" A tear escaped him. He wiped it away. Then reality hit him.

"Dammit! I've lost my tenor!" He stomped back and forth, vomit and dirt jumping around his feet. "I've lost my goddamn tenor!" The other dogs watched him in silence, barf on their tongues, on their noses, in their teeth.

Then it came to him, and Harold knew what he had to do. He ran into the garage and began unpacking boxes of old clothes. A sigh of relief when he found it, remembering when he was in his high school's production of The Phantom Tollbooth.

Clyde Barnes, the man in charge of booking shows at Media Convention Center, was tapping his foot anxiously. He chain-smoked one cigarette after another, nervous as hell, and with good reason—it was a sell-out crowd. People couldn't wait to see Harold Asher's Vomiting Dogs. But here it was five minutes to show time and the performers were nowhere to be found.

He smoked another cigarette, hoping it would be the one that killed him.

Thirty seconds to curtain a knock came at the backstage door. Clyde opened it to see six dogs—all of which smelled very foul—standing, ready and waiting.

"Where the hell have you guys been? Where's your owner?"

"Sorry we're late," one of the dogs said, a dog who stood upright and had a clock sewn into its belly. "Harold's out in the audience."

Clyde couldn't remember ever hearing a dog talk before, at least not so well, but he didn't have time to think about it at the moment. "Well, go on, go on, get out there and do your thing!"

Harold Asher's Vomiting Dogs were a complete success, though everyone agreed (and it was written in the review the next day) that the tenor was the weakest part.

Competition

Damn I love the Chiffons. I love the song "He's So Fine." It's the only song I know by them but I love it. I fucking love it. George Harrison got sued for stealing the music. I like the Chiffons song better. It's on the radio right now as I drive out towards Espanola, but I'll be taking a right turn before I get there. There's this little road not too many people know about, and the people who do know about it don't really care because why should they? All it does is go on for a few miles and then stop. A dead end, without any signs or warnings or anything. It's a bumpy dirt road and I'm sure it's muddy as all hell when it rains. But it isn't raining. No, it's a lovely evening, just lovely. The sun is almost completely gone and there aren't many cars on the road and the guy in my trunk stopped kicking and screaming a few minutes ago. I've got his wrists tied tight with duct tape and his ankles too. I put a piece over his mouth but I think it's probably hotter than hell in there and with all the sweat or something it must have peeled away because he started crying for help. So I turned up the music really loud and nobody seemed to notice. I wonder if he passed out or just got tired. Anyway, he's not complaining anymore.

That turn's coming up in a just a minute now.

The guy in my trunk. I don't know his name. Only seen him around town but I've seen him around town for years. I never liked the way he looked. He always looked sleazy to me, the kind of guy that would dick you over if given half a chance. But I'd never thought much of him until yesterday, when he told my wife that she was pretty. That got to me but not as much as when she smiled back and him. The way she smiled at him made my heart feel like lead. The only time I could ever recall seeing her smile like that was at me when we first got together. The first few months of our relationship she had that same smile because I was cute and sexy and she was falling in love with me. But she hadn't smiled like that in a long time. Not to me or anybody else as far as I'd seen. Only yesterday when we were at the video store and so was he and we got behind him in line to rent our movies. The guy looked at me, then looked at her and smiled and she smiled back and I didn't think anything of it until he just right outta the blue told her she was pretty. And there came that smile.

Here we go. The road's even bumpier than I remember. It's been a while since I've been out this way. The trees are looming like shadows of monsters. I hope it being so bumpy doesn't get him all screaming again. The tone of his voice is fucking irritating.

This is a good song, too. The Hollywood Argyles—"Alley-Oop." Sort of fitting since we're going up and down so much on this road.

As fate had it, just a little while ago, as I drove to return *The Hudsucker Proxy* to the video store, I saw him walking in the same direction, a video in his hand. I pulled over and said we were in line behind him yesterday and it took him a moment but then he smiled

The Day the Leash Gave Way

and said something like, Oh yeah. I'm sure it took thinking about my wife to get him to remember me. But he remembered me and I said it looked like he was going to the same place I was, and if he wanted a ride I'd be happy to give him a lift. He looked up the street, then back to me and shrugged his shoulders and said something like okay and he got in. We drove to the store but when we got there I kept going and hung a left, and when there wasn't anybody around to see anything I cracked him in the face with my fist and got blood on my hand from his nose. He screamed, and so I asked him if he still thought my wife was pretty. All he could do was say huh. I cracked him again and he crouched over and started crying.

I looked but there was nobody around so I pulled over and climbed out of the car and went around to his side and opened the door. There was all kinds of blood and snot dripping from his nose. I pulled him out by the collar of his shirt and threw him to the ground and kicked him and kicked him until he stopped moving. Then I looked around again to make sure there wasn't anybody in the area.

I popped the trunk and found a roll of duct tape back there. I always keep shit like that in my trunk just because you never know when or where you might need it. I wrapped his ankles first, then picked him up and put him in the trunk, and once I had him in I wrapped his hands and put a piece over his mouth. Right when I finished putting the piece on his mouth he woke up and started crying so I closed the trunk and made my way out of town. Then the tape came off his mouth and he screamed and I turned up the music and then he stopped after a while and here we are.

I love my wife so much. I don't know what I'd do if she ever left me. Sometimes she complains that I don't show my affection but it isn't because I don't love her. I just don't really know how, I guess. But if there's any kind of competition, who's to say she wouldn't just up and leave me? If I don't always make her happy then why would she wanna stay when there's some new guy telling her she's pretty and she can't help but smile that way like she used to smile at me.

I bring the car to a stop at the end of the road. There's nothing to see for miles and my guess is someone was going to build a house way out here but never did, for whatever reason. But here we are and there's no one else around and so I turn off the car and climb out and walk around to the trunk and unlock it and open it up and there he is. His face is covered in blood and snot and the duct tape is hanging just a little bit from his left cheek. I'm a relatively strong man. I hoist him out and throw him on the ground. The duct tape falls away from his face and I pick it up and toss it into the trunk, then I kick him in the guts and go to the glove compartment, where I always carry a nine-milimeter. About a year ago there were a bunch of these convicts that escaped from prison and they found a couple of them around where we live, so I started carrying the gun just because I didn't wanna run into some psycho and not have any way to protect myself.

I tell him to get on his hands and knees but he can't quite do it so I lift him up and set him that way and he slowly inches along the ground, hurting—I can tell he's hurting. I fire a shot into the air just to scare him and he topples over to one side. I kneel down and remove the tape from his ankles and tell him he's got 'til the count of five. I hoist him to his feet and start counting. He runs and I can hear him panting. I can't help laughing a little. Not that it's funny. Anyone who might try and steal my wife is no laughing matter. But he kind of looks like a rabbit out there, maybe because of the way he's sort of limping, I dunno.

I finish counting to five and shoot but I miss him. He screams out for me to please stop, so I run after him and I can run much faster, partly because I'm in pretty good shape and partly because he has this sort of limp going on his legs. I catch up to him fast and push him down and there he is crying again.

I ask him if he'd be crying if my wife was here but he doesn't understand or he's too scared or something. I ask him if he thinks all women are pretty or just my wife and he gives another huh and says he doesn't know what I'm talking about—but he knows, all right. He knows, so I ask him if he wanted to fuck her and he asks who, and I say my wife, asshole, and he says again that he doesn't know what I'm talking about.

Enough games. I shoot him in the face. He gets blood all over the ground and on his clothes. There's blood all over my hands and my pants and my shoes. Jesus, there's blood fucking everywhere. I take the duct tape off his wrists and I walk back to the car. I get in and drive home and listen to the Fireballs sing "Sugar Shack."

On the way I see I have the movie he was returning in the car with me. I've wanted to see it, so I take it home. My wife can watch the movie with me and there won't be any worries—at least for a while. I'm feeling much better now.

Found Money

Earlier Nick had sold his grandfather's watch to a pawnshop in order to get enough money to buy some food, and had then lost the money on his way home when some guy with a pompadour had bumped into him. Upon realizing what had happened, Nick tried locating the guy with the pompadour, but to no avail. The dude was long gone.

Nick then made his way home for real, where a block from his house he found a blank envelope containing three thousand dollars.

Other than Nick and a couple of birds, the street was empty. The street was always empty, especially at this time of day. He didn't really know why but people just didn't go for walks in this area. He stuffed the envelope into his pocket and went the rest of the way home.

Inside his small third story apartment he locked the door, removed the envelope from his pocket and opened it again. Three thousand eighty-seven dollars to be exact. Wow. More money than Nick had seen in a long time. Or ever. He'd never actually had more than a thousand dollars to his name, and most of that had gone away to unpaid bills. One doesn't get rich being fired from a bookstore, heaven knows, and it doesn't help when one is fired for theft, and it helps even less when one never committed said theft in the first place.

For a while he sat on his bed, the envelope beside him, the money beside the envelope, and considered a few things. People don't typically drop that kind of money. Heck, people don't typically *carry* that kind of money. It was possible that someone had cashed their paycheck at the bank and then lost it. That kind of thing can happen to anyone. But your average person would deposit most, if not all of it. Carrying around that kind of cash can be dangerous. Also the envelope wasn't the type any bank Nick knew of used for cash. It was a standard business envelope, 4 by 9 ½ inches with printed security lining and the sort of flap you have to lick instead of the self-adhesive kind. Banks always use the self-adhesive kind.

He considered turning it over to the police. If there was some way to track this money down he didn't want to be the guy caught with it. He'd already gotten in trouble for this kind of thing once and didn't want it to happen again. While at the same time, even though it was a lot of money for Nick, in the grand scheme of things it wasn't much at all. Anyone who could afford to carry around $3,087 probably wasn't going to miss it if they lost it.

Someone knocked at the door. Nick collected the money, stuffed it back into the envelope then stuck the envelope between his mattress and box spring. He approached the door cautiously, overtaken with a new sense of paranoia.

"Who is it?"

There was no answer from the other side. Momentary quiet ensued then the knock came again.

"Who's there?"

Again, no answer.

Slowly, carefully, Nick turned the bolt, then turned the handle and eased the door open the couple of inches the security chain allowed.

It was Carl from the bookstore, Nick's only friend. In his hand he held half a sandwich, and in his mouth he held the other half.

"Oh, for crying out loud." Nick shut the door, undid the chain and opened it again.

Carl entered, still chewing, and after about fifteen seconds he swallowed, cleared his throat and said, "Hey, man. Sorry I didn't answer. I stuffed way too much of this baby into my mouth at once. It was either silence or have half-chewed food all over your door." He sat down and made himself comfortable, continuing with his sandwich, making sure to take smaller bites. "I came to see how you're doing. I'm sorry about what happened at Page Turner."

Nick looked at him and saw he was sincere. "Those are the breaks, I guess."

"I don't believe you stole that money," Carl said. "You're not the type."

"You're right," Nick said. "I'm not the type. I didn't steal that money."

A small piece of bread fell from Carl's mouth when he asked, "What are you gonna do?"

"I'll find something else." He glanced toward his bedroom.

Carl finished his sandwich, got up and went to the refrigerator. "You're out of beer."

"I know." Beer had been one of the main things on his grocery list before the man with the pompadour had bumped into him. "I'm out of pretty much everything."

Carl inspected the fridge, eased it shut, then turned to Nick. "I'm sorry, man. How about I take you out for a beer?"

Brutto Ed always hated his name. His first name was Italian for ugly and his last name was an abbreviated first name. Ugly Ed is what the kids had called him in school, and he'd never had a girl so much as spit in is face without having to pay a pretty penny for it. If he'd had a normal middle name, things might not have been so bad. But given that his middle name was Grasso, Italian for fat, he realized there just wasn't any way to win. And even eliminating the first and middle name was terrible. He hated being addressed as Mr. Ed. He wasn't a goddamn talking horse. But out of all the options, this was sadly the best of the bunch. If only his Italian mother hadn't been so cruel maybe his life would have been different. As it was, though, he was currently sitting in the modest extravagance of his modestly extravagant home waiting for some guy who was neither modest nor extravagant named Steve to call him up and tell him that the job was done.

Brutto had hired this Steve to take care of a man named Jason Bishop. Mr. Bishop had done a job for Brutto a couple months back but had clipped an additional $3,087 for himself on top of what Brutto was already paying him. In the grand scheme of schemes, what Jason took was nothing, but that wasn't the point. The point was that Brutto didn't like being screwed with. Forget the money. In fact he'd offered Steve the exact amount stolen from him for Steve to set things right. It somehow seemed to add a nice irony to the whole thing.

"An odd amount," Steve had said, "And I'm not sure that's enough for me to knock someone off."

"All right, I'll double that. $6,174."

"That sounds a little better," Steve had said. "Though it's still a strange amount."

"I have my reasons," Brutto told him, wondering himself why he was so fixated on that number. "I'll give you half before, and half when the job is done." He supposed he just liked the irony bit.

"Deal," Steve had said.

Utilizing his many connections, Brutto had learned of Bishop's whereabouts. He'd given Steve all the information, and explained that he didn't care how it was done, so long as it was done. Sooner was better than later.

Brutto had never met Steve in person and didn't plan on ever meeting him. In order to protect both parties involved, all business was to be conducted by phone. What Brutto had done was set up a time for Steve to get his first half of the money. The plan was that at four o'clock one of Brutto's men was going to drop an envelope at the corner of Garson Street and Juniper. Inside that envelope would be $3,087. At five minutes after, Steve was to round the corner and pick it up. The corner of Garson and Juniper had been chosen because of its extremely low foot traffic, especially at that hour. Nobody really knew why, but people just didn't go for walks in that area. From there Steve was to then take care of Jason Bishop. Once it was done he was to call Brutto on the phone, let him know that it was done, and the two of them together would make plans for the drop-off and pick-up of the second half of the payment.

At four forty-five the phone rang. Brutto picked it up with stumpy fingers.

"It wasn't there," Steve told him.

"What do you mean?"

"The envelope," Steve said. "It's wasn't there."

The Cat 'n' Scratch was quiet this evening. The lights were down lower than usual but the eighties pop music was at its regular volume, and right now "Rosanna" by Toto was playing.

"And so I said," Carl said, now having five beers in him, "no princess could have such delicate skin that she could feel a pea in her back through twenty mattresses and twenty featherbeds."

Nick didn't actually know where this conversation had begun. For the last forty-five minutes he'd been thinking about the money he'd found, hearing only inane snippets of what Carl was saying.

"And even if she could," Carl went on, "why would any prince want to marry her? I mean, you couldn't touch her without puncturing her. And forget about getting some of the good stuff at night, if you know what I mean. Pin her to the goddamn floor."

Nick let out an incredibly fake laugh and looked down at his second beer, which was at the halfway mark. He wondered if it was half empty or half full, realized it didn't much matter either way, and drank down the rest of it, deciding he would hang onto the money for two days. If nothing popped up in the newspaper or anything like that, he would keep it. If something did come up, then he would return the money to its rightful owner. That seemed the best thing to do.

While on the other hand, what if it took the owner of the money a little longer to discover it was gone? What if after two days nothing had come about, Nick went and spent it—even some of it—and then on the third day someone came along looking for it? With this possibility, maybe he should keep it for three days. Of course then there was the fourth day to think about. Maybe he should keep it for an entire week. Wait, no, maybe an entire year, just to be on the safe side.

Oh hell, he didn't know.

"Carl?"

Carl looked at him with half-closed eyes. Maybe they were half open.

"How drunk are you?"

"I can drive, if that's what you mean." He pantomimed driving a car and knocked over his beer. "Aw crap."

Nick ordered him another, as well as another for himself, and when they arrived he said, "I'm just wondering how well you might remember things tomorrow."

"You're not gonna try and take advantage of me, are you?"

"No, nothing like that. I just have something I wanna run by you, and I think, at least at this time, I might prefer if you didn't remember it so well in the morning."

"You *are* gonna try and take advantage of me," Carl said, his right eye opening wide, his left eye closing a little more.

"Carl, for the love of God, I'm not gonna try anything like that."

Carl looked unsure, but after a while he settled down and drank his beer.

"I was just hoping to maybe get some advice."

"Advice?"

Nick told him about the envelope he'd found. He didn't tell him exactly how much money was in it but the point seemed to get across just fine, even in the state Carl was in.

"So you wanna know if you should keep it or not."

"That's right."

"You realize that you should be paying for these drinks, right?"

"I don't have any of it on me," Nick said. "It's not like I found a dollar and no one is gonna miss it all that much. This is serious."

"Yes, yeah, yes, this serious," Carl said. "What I suggest is…I suggest…" He looked at Nick for a long time. Nick was starting to wish he'd kept things to himself. "I suggest you… keep it."

"Really?"

"I suggest you keep it."

In all reality it probably was the thing to do. No one could prove that it was his or her money. And even if they could, there wasn't a soul in the area when he found it. Nobody saw him pick it up. There wasn't any way anyone could ever figure out that he had been the one to find it.

The Day the Leash Gave Way 31

The waitress came to check on them.

"I suggest you keep it," Carl told her.

Brutto Ed called Lenny and Krude—Lenny being Lenny's real name, Krude's real name being Ed. "What the hell are you guys doing?"

Lenny adjusted his cell phone against his shoulder. "Having a burger at the Burger Bowl," he said.

"What about Operation…whatever the hell we were calling it?"

"Operation Drop-Off?"

It was such a terrible name for an operation that Brutto understood at once why he'd chosen to forget it. "Did you drop off the envelope?"

"Of course we did."

"Where the hell did you drop it?"

"At the corner of Garson and Juniper, like you told us to."

"Well, Steve said it wasn't there," Brutto said, almost shouting. He didn't like to shout. He prided himself on being someone who could keep his voice level and calm, but found himself breaking now. "Go back there and see if it's still where you dropped it."

"But Steve said it wasn't there."

"Maybe he didn't see it because you put it somewhere he couldn't find it."

"We left it right on the sidewalk next to those rose bushes, just like you told us to." Brutto heard the last remnants of soda being sucked through a straw, then Lenny said, "How do you know this Steve guy isn't pulling a fast one?"

"Because what I know of him after speaking with him three times, and what I know of you guys after having you both work for me for years, I can safely say that Steve is far more reliable."

"That hurts, boss."

"Just go back and look." He hung up then, and rose from his seat. He shut his eyes and conjured Lenny and Krude's faces in his mind, and once they were firmly in place, he did it.

He shouted.

Nick looked at Carl, who was passed out face down on the table. Nick himself seemed to be seeing the world through an amber fog but was able to hold his own. Not that he wanted to drive Carl's car, or any other car for that matter. It would be bad for him to get behind the wheel of an automobile for a couple of reasons, one being he had consumed a fair amount of alcohol and another being he had never driven a car in his life.

Get a taxi? Maybe; he didn't know how much money Carl had on him, and he knew he sure didn't have any unless he counted what he'd found, which was at home in any case. It was only six blocks from the Cat 'n' Scratch to Nick's apartment. Probably shouldn't have even bothered driving at all. They could hoof it. At least Nick could, if things went that way.

The waitress returned and asked if Carl was all right. To which Nick smiled the smile of a drunk man, gave an overly elaborate nod and said, "Oh yeah, he's fine. We're not driving or anything."

The waitress let their check flutter to the table and then vanished. Nick didn't bother to look at it. He shook Carl on the shoulder until the man stirred, grumbled, stirred again, and finally rose.

"Let's get out of here," Nick said.

"Yeah, sure." Carl sat upright, reached into his pocket, left a handful of crumpled bills on the table, then clambered to his feet. He took three steps forward, then took three steps back, sat back down at the table and said, "Let's maybe wait a few minutes, if you don't mind."

Nick sat back down. "You want some water or something?"

"Yeah," Carl said. "I'll take either one."

Both Krude and Lenny had gone over the spot at least a dozen times. The rose bush had also pricked both of them more than either cared to admit. The street was silent with only the sound of their humming car and the distant wash of traffic several streets over.

Lenny had originally been the one to drop the envelope but Krude had been behind the wheel of the car and had seen him drop it. They both knew it had been there.

"Well damn," said Krude.

"This is a bummer," Lenny said as he reached into his pocket for his cigarettes. Once he had one lit he looked at Krude. "You know what I think happened? I think someone else came along, saw the envelope and picked it up."

"Well damn," said Krude.

"I know. How often do people actually walk around in this area? I mean, even the mailman doesn't get out of his truck unless he absolutely has to."

"Damn," said Krude.

"Well, no point in standing around here all night waiting for it to come back."

They climbed back into the car, Krude behind the wheel, and Lenny dialed Mr. Ed.

With the car still in park, Krude looked down the empty street and shook his head. "Damn," he said.

"Hey, boss."

"You find it?"

"No. There's nothing here. Either this Steve guy is pulling a fast one, or someone came along and picked it up, but either way it's not here now."

"So you're telling me," Mr. Ed said, "that if I want Jason Bishop taken care of, I now have to pay out an additional $3,087?"

Given Mr. Ed's tone, Lenny felt the best thing was to not say anything. What he did, so he wouldn't feel completely left out, he nodded while looking at the phone.

Krude shook his head. "Damn."

"I now have to pay...whatever $6,174 plus $3,087 is?"

"I'm sorry, boss." Lenny tried doing the math in his head. He was pretty sure it came to $12,000. "Is there anything we can do?"

"You could find my money."

"I dunno how we can do that. Only thing I can think of is to find this Steve guy and put a lot of heat on him, find out if he really got it or not."

The Day the Leash Gave Way

"That sounds like a waste of time. None of us even know how to locate Steve and I'm sure he doesn't have it anyway."

Lenny almost asked why, then remembered what he'd been told earlier. It still kind of hurt to know that's how the boss felt about them.

A long and frustrated pause ensued. Then Mr. Ed said, "Dammit, whose stupid idea was it to just leave the envelope on the sidewalk like that?"

"I don't recall, boss," Lenny said, his throat drying up.

"I want you guys here first thing tomorrow morning," Mr. Ed told them. "We're gonna set up a new plan for getting Steve that money. Something a little better than Operation…"

"Drop-Off," Lenny offered, tossing his cigarette out the window.

"I want Bishop dead by five o'clock tomorrow."

"Sure thing, boss." The phone connection was broken. Lenny turned to Krude. Krude had his hands clasped in his lap and was twiddling his thumbs. "He wants us there first thing in the morning."

"Did he say what time?"

"No, he just said first thing in the morning."

"Yeah, but, like, seven, eight?"

"He didn't say."

Shaking his head, Krude brought his hands up to the wheel. "Damn," he said.

Lenny agreed, then reached for another cigarette and said, "Let's go get a beer."

For the last twenty minutes Carl had been asleep with his head on the table while Nick used bar matches to melt cocktail swords in an attempt to shape them into cartoon characters. The only one (out of about ten) that even had a vague resemblance was Daffy Duck, though on that one Nick had been trying for Charlie Brown.

He thought about his grandfather's watch, a 1945, 14kt Rose Gold Tropical Model Rolex, currently sitting at City Pawn. That thing was worth a lot. Certainly a lot more than Chris—City Pawn's owner—gave him. "I'll give you two hundred for it," Chris had told him, which had seemed extremely low, probably because, in all actuality, it *was* extremely low. The reason Nick hadn't bothered to argue was that he needed whatever he could get, and worried that haggling would get Chris upset enough to call the whole deal off. Chris seemed the type of guy to behave that way. Still, two hundred bucks was two hundred bucks, for all the good it did him now, thanks to Mr. Pompadour.

Carl raised his head from the table, where there now sat a small patch of drool.

"You about ready to go?" Nick asked.

"I suggest you keep it," Carl told him.

"Right." Nick got up. He moved around the table and helped Carl to his feet. They made their way to the door, Carl with his arm slung over Nick's shoulders, Nick giving self-conscious smiles and nods to various staring patrons.

"It's all right," Nick told them. "He just got a divorce."

"Why would any prince want to marry her?" Carl said.

This seemed to put things right by everybody.

"You touch her, you puncture her," Carl went on. "Forget some of the good stuff."

"That's right," Nick said. "You're far too good for her. She's nothing."

"I can't believe...you found money."

"Jeez," Nick said. "A little louder, please."

"I said—!"

"I know what you said, Carl. Let's get you home."

When they reached the door it opened from the other side. Two men in suits entered. The second man held the door for Nick and Carl.

"Thanks," Nick said.

"I've been there myself," said the man holding the door.

"An envelope," Carl said. "An envelope with all kinds of money in it."

"You're dreaming," Nick told him, trying to get him outside.

"No." Carl burped, looked at the man holding the door. "My friend...my friend Nick, he found..."

"All right, let's get going." Nick yanked him through the door.

"But you found an envelope with money in it."

"Forget about it," Nick said, and began schlepping Carl the six blocks to his apartment.

When Krude let the door close something simultaneously clicked in is brain. He looked at Lenny, who appeared to have just had the same low-grade epiphany.

"Did that guy say what I think he said?" Lenny asked, pointing at the closed door.

Krude looked at Lenny, looked at the door and narrowed his eyes, then looked at Lenny again before looking down to the floor. "Damn," he said.

"He said, 'An envelope with all kinds of money in it,' didn't he?"

"Damn," said Krude.

Brutto was throwing darts at a picture of his dead Italian mother when the phone rang.

"Yes?"

"Mr. Ed?"

God, he hated being called that. "Yes. What?"

"Krude and I are at the Cat 'n' Scratch. Some guys just left, one of them carrying on about his buddy finding an envelope with money in it."

Brutto's eyebrows climbed up his forehead. "Oh really?" Now how about that? he thought. What are the chances?

"They only left a minute ago. I don't think they were driving. They probably aren't far."

"Then why are you standing there talking to me?"

"Well because, well, I thought, y'know..."

"Go catch up to them."

"Right."

Brutto hung up. He looked at the picture of his mother full of holes and said, "Things are looking up. I'm getting back on top of things, Mom."

"*Mio figlio ha no genitale*," his mothered seemed to say.

He threw another dart. The moment it struck, the phone rang again.

The Day the Leash Gave Way

It was Steve. "I'm curious," Steve said, "as to how serious you are about this whole deal?"

"What do you mean?"

"Well, if you want this guy knocked off so bad, what's the holdup? Shouldn't I have my three Gs plus eighty-seven singles by now?"

"I assure you, Steve, you'll have your money tomorrow."

"Tomorrow? Correct me if I'm wrong, Mr. Ed, but didn't you want this guy knocked off as soon as possible?"

"I did, but—"

"*But*? But what? You're not backing out on me, are you? I don't take kindly to that. I get a real itchy trigger finger with people who back out on deals."

"We still have a deal," Brutto assured him, feeling moisture develop at his brow. "It's just that we had some trouble."

"Not as much as you might have."

Was that a threat? Brutto wondered, and decided not to ask verbally. "You'll have your money as soon as—"

"We're not going with the same exchange plan as we did today, are we? Whoever came up with that one should be smacked real hard in the back of the head."

Brutto gripped the phone. "No," he said, "we'll figure something else out."

"I just wanna make sure everything is on the up and up."

"It's on the up and up and going more up," Brutto said, and thought, Huh?

Steve said, "What?"

Brutto cleared his throat, trying to think of what to say.

What he finally said was, "I gotta go. I'm waiting for a call. I'll be in touch."

"Yeah."

He hung up. This time, rather than throwing darts, he paced back and forth rubbing his chin in a thoughtful manner (which was something he always did when he paced), and wondered how Lenny and Krude were making out.

Nick had managed to drag Carl one entire block so far. It would have been easier had Carl not been trying to sing. Nick didn't know if it was better or worse that, in the state the guy was in, Carl sang very quietly. His voice didn't draw much attention from other people on the street, but Nick couldn't shake this feeling that Carl was whispering sweet nothings in his ear. Right now he was attempting to sing "Last Train to Clarksville" to the tune of "Wake Me Up Before You Go-Go."

Nick rolled his eyes. He just wanted to get home. It had been a long day.

"I'm sorry, Nick," Carl said. "I'm sorry that you got fired from the store."

Nick replayed in his mind the moment when Mike Williams, the manager at Page Turner, had let him go, explaining that they knew that he had stolen the money, though he never offered up an amount or how Knigk had done it or anything like that. Nick was just somehow guilty. Though because Nick had worked there for such a long time, Mike and John Bishop, the owner, had agreed not to press charges so long as Nick never showed his face at the store again.

"Like I said," Nick said to Carl. "That's how it goes."

"I don't see how anyone could steal that kind of money there," Carl said, then stumbled and almost fell. "And how it got pinned on you, I'll never know. That doesn't make any sense. Me and some of the other guys were talking about it at work. You couldn't have done it. Impossible. You didn't even have access to the safe."

That was true. It had occurred to Nick before but he hadn't really given the matter much thought. He'd been so wrapped up in the fact that he was losing his job and avoiding prosecution that he hadn't considered too many of the specifics. He didn't have access to the safe at all, nor did he know the combination. He hadn't even been back in the accounting area at all the day the money vanished. And certainly no one could have stolen that kind of money from the register.

"To think," Carl said, "how someone could waltz in, not be noticed, and tango out with $3,087. I mean, like, yeah, right."

$3,087!

Nick quickly stopped and turned to Carl, which forced Carl to stand up on his own, which was difficult for him to do. "What was that amount again?"

"Come on, Nick, you should know, you stole it."

"No, I *didn't*."

"I know." Carl laughed—apparently he thought it was funny—then said, "$3,087."

The exact amount Nick had found in the envelope on the sidewalk.

Before he could think about it, however, he was suddenly shoved into Carl, who was shoved into a wall. And when Carl hit the wall Nick was shoved into the wall also, barely able to get his hands up in time to keep his face from smashing into it.

Shaking away their surprise, Nick and Carl turned around. It was the two guys in suits from the bar that had entered as they'd left. They didn't look nearly as good-natured as they had in the bar light. The one who had held the door open for them now held a knife, which was pretty scary but not quite as scary as the other guy, who held a pistol. Cutting his glance quickly around the area, as Nick should have expected, there had been other people around until this very moment. Now they were all alone.

"All right," the guy with the pistol said. "Where is it?"

"Huh?"

"The money, duck-face. The envelope with the money."

Carl turned to Nick in shock. "You told *them, too?*"

Boy, Nick thought, what an asshole.

"Look," he said. "I dunno if I understand what you're talking about."

"Earlier today you found an envelope at the corner of Garson and Juniper," the man with the pistol said. "It contained $3,087, none of it belonging to you."

"Well, I..."

There all of a sudden came a ringing sound from the man with the pistol. "Wait, hold on," he told Nick, and reached into his pocket, from which he extracted a cell phone. He looked at the phone, then at the guy with the knife. "It's the boss," he said.

"Damn," said the guy with the knife.

The Day the Leash Gave Way 37

The man with the pistol answered. "Hello?" A pause, then, "I'm working on it right—huh? Well, we're trying. If you'd just..." He looked at the man with the knife and flailed his gun hand to the side in frustration, momentarily forgetting where he was and what he was supposed to be doing because he then dropped his gun hand down to his side and let it just hang there. When the man with the knife saw this he too let his guard down, apparently understanding whatever was going on with the person on the phone but not fully understanding his own purpose in the current situation.

Fortunately, Nick had just enough presence of mind to see the opening. He grabbed Carl and rushed at the two assailants while both assailants were focused on the phone. The dangerous, but necessary collision sent the man with the knife down onto his back, while the man with the pistol staggered several steps backward into the street, dropped both pistol and phone and nearly got hit by an oncoming car.

Nick fell down as well but immediately shot up to his feet, and he and Carl raced down the street, turned the next corner, then the next corner and the next, until they finally felt out of harm's way.

"Wow," Carl said. "I think I'm sober now."

What Brutto heard through the phone was a static-laced crunch, followed by a *clink-clink-clink* and then someone saying "Ouch!" then someone saying "Jeez!"

"Lenny?"

In the distance he heard a car horn honk, then someone said, "Watch it, you creep, I could have killed you," and a moment later Lenny, suddenly out of breath, said, "You still there?"

"What the hell just happened?"

"They caught us off guard," Lenny said. "It seems that we underestimated them. They moved so quickly, we didn't have time to react. From that move, I'm thinking they might even be professionals."

"Are you kidding me?"

"Well, it seems, if you ask me, they...what's that, Krude? Oh really?" Then Lenny giggled like he was eight and had just heard a really good dirty joke.

"What are you laughing about?" Brutto demanded. "Go on after them."

"I don't think that's necessary," Lenny said.

"Why?" Brutto asked. "Did they leave the envelope behind?"

"No, but they left the next best thing."

"Just the money, without the envelope?"

"One of them dropped their wallet," Lenny said.

"Is the money in it?"

"Uh...no."

"Dang."

"But his I.D. is."

Steve X sat in his living room flipping through a girly magazine while the TV was on in front of him displaying girls in bikinis. Naked girls and almost naked girls were just about the only thing in the world that calmed him down when he was angry. And right now he was fairly angry. He didn't like the way Mr. Ed was handling their arrangement. He should have told Mr. Ed outright that leaving an envelope with that kind of money in it on the street in broad daylight was a terrible idea.

He set down the magazine, leaving it open to a page he especially liked, and got up. The more he thought about it the less he liked the way things were going. He hadn't trusted Mr. Ed from the beginning, and given the incident earlier today, Steve began to wonder if he was somehow being taken for a ride. He didn't really know how, but something about the whole deal was starting to smell incredibly fishy. And this made Steve even angrier.

He went to the bedroom he had converted into an office, into the closet and the file cabinet therein, where he kept his classified files. He pulled out the file on Mr. Ed that Mr. Ed didn't know Steve had on him. He studied it for a brief moment, then decided it was time to get out of the house for a while, just to make sure everything was really on the up and up and going more up.

When they got back to Nick's apartment, Carl, who had started feeling the effects of alcohol again, immediately staggered into Nick's bedroom and flopped onto his bed.

"This is turning out to be a crazy night," Carl said. "And I have to be at work at eight tomorrow morning." A moment later he was asleep. Nick figured, for the time being anyway, it was probably for the best.

He left Carl on the bed and went to the kitchen to make some coffee, realizing with great disappointment that he was out of both coffee and coffee filters. He got himself a glass of water then paced around, attempting to bring clarity to all that had transpired. The money he'd found versus the money he'd allegedly stolen from the bookstore, both in the amount of $3,087. What was going on with that specific amount? And what an absolutely bizarre amount. It seemed that there should be some sort of tie-in between the two, but what? He was accused of stealing the first $3,087, and the next day he just happened to find $3,087 on the street. Was it the same $3,087? Was it just random chance? The two men in suits knew about the second $3,087, and they wanted it back. If only Nick hadn't been frightened out of his mind, he probably would have told them to come on over and take it. This was more trouble than it was worth, and it really wasn't very much money. Sure, it was more than he'd ever had, but this was way too much trouble for a measly $3,087.

Someone had to have answers, though who it was that had these answers, he didn't know. And for all he knew maybe it was all over. Maybe he would never see those two guys in the suits again. Any which way, he decided that first thing tomorrow he was going to put that money right back where he'd found it.

Carl mumbled, stirred, and sat up. "Where am I?" he said, then saw where he was and said to Nick, "I had this crazy dream that you and I were accosted by two guys on the street."

"Really?" Nick said, wanting to smack him.

"You had found some envelope with money in it, and these guys wanted it back."

The Day the Leash Gave Way 39

"Huh," Nick said. "Sounds like a crazy dream."

"The thing that gets me about it," Carl said, "is that we managed to get away. We knocked them over and took off, but when we knocked them over you also fell down, and dropped your wallet." He couldn't help chuckling a little at that. "It's weird. I dunno why on earth I dreamed that."

A chill tingled down Nick's spine as he checked his pockets.

"Aw crap."

For the past fifteen or twenty minutes Brutto had been playing solo games of Tiddly Winks, each time hoping that red would win but finding green constantly in the lead no matter how hard he tried. He didn't like that. It was a bad sign. Brutto was accustomed to getting what he wanted; and when red refused to win, against his wishes, he knew there were greater forces involved.

He wondered just what exactly had gone on while he was speaking with Lenny on the phone. Lenny had suggested that these guys they'd found might be professionals, but somehow Brutto just wasn't able to believe it. What kind of professional blurts out their findings at a bar?

He was debating calling Lenny and Krude again to check on things and was just about to pick up the entire Tiddly Winks game and dump it onto the floor when a strange man with an out-of-style haircut walked into his office and said, "Hi, Mr. Ed."

Brutto straightened in his seat. "Who the hell are you?" he asked, sliding Tiddly Winks to the side with one hand while his other hand slid down below his desk to the drawer in which he kept a small .22 caliber. "How did you get in here?"

"I'm Steve," said Steve, "and I let myself in. I'm good at things like that."

"Steve?" Brutto said. "As in *Steve*?" He tugged at the drawer. It was locked, and the key was nowhere to be seen. Damn cleaning woman.

"Yes, Steve," said Steve. "The guy who didn't get his money today."

"We were never supposed to meet in person. Everything was to be discussed by phone. How in the world did you—?"

"Don't bother yourself with such trivialities," Steve said. "You know why I'm here."

"No," Brutto said. "As a matter of fact, I don't."

"I came by to check the score," Steve said, then moved to the desk and began playing Brutto's game of Tiddly Winks. He was pretty good at it, and of course he had opted to be green. "We made a deal," Steve continued. "Then right away you flake out."

"I didn't flake out," Brutto said. "I told you, you'd have your money first thing tomorrow."

"But I was supposed to have my money at four o'clock today."

Brutto almost told him that he was supposed to have it at 4:05 but decided not to bother with such trivialities. Instead he cursed the cleaning woman again and leaned back in his chair. "I thought we had already discussed this," he said.

"Last thing you said to me was that you'd be in touch," Steve said. "And you haven't been, so I figured I'd get in touch with you." He landed the last green wink disc into the one-hundred-point center of the tray and rose from the desk. "I wanna know what's going on."

"What happened was, the money was there, and then it was gone. Someone took it. I was about to write it off and start from scratch when a couple of my men—"

The phone rang. Brutto looked at Steve. Steve nodded and made a gesture for him to go ahead and answer.

"Hello?"

"Boss, it's Lenny. This guy, Nick Adams, he lives not even a block away from where we had dropped the money."

"You don't say."

"We're outside the apartment building now. He's up on the third floor. You want us to move in?"

"Lenny, hang on just a second." Brutto put his hand over the mouthpiece and said to Steve, "My men have just located your money."

"Hot diggety dirt," Steve said. "Let's go get it."

"They'll bring it back here."

"I'd rather not hang around here," Steve said. "Let's go meet them, wherever they are."

"I'm not sure that's a good…" Brutto's words trailed off as Steve removed a pistol from behind his back. He aimed it right between Brutto's eyes. "All right," Brutto said. He removed his hand from the mouthpiece. "Lenny, give me the address." He wrote it down on a Post-It, then said, "Okay, go ahead and move in. I'll see you soon."

"You coming down here?" Lenny asked.

"I am," Brutto told him. "I'd like to speak with the man who took my money."

"Eh-hem," Steve said.

Brutto covered the mouthpiece again. "Your money, yes, I know, *your* money."

"You okay, boss?"

"Fine," Brutto said. His voice cracked a bit. "We'll—I'll be down there soon."

"Sure thing."

He hung up and looked at Steve, who had put the gun away and was fixing his hair. "How much time do your men need?"

"They didn't say," Brutto told him.

"What do you think, fifteen, twenty minutes?"

"I don't know," Brutto said. "I just said I'd be down there soon."

Steve glanced at the Tiddly Winks game then shook his head. "No," he said. "I guess we probably shouldn't try to squeeze in a quick game."

"Probably not," Brutto agreed.

The Maison Cassée Residential Suites are located one block off Juniper down on Garson Street. It is a large three-story complex of outside apartments with flights of stairs on both the left and right and one in the middle. A black metal guardrail runs along the walkway of both the second and third stories.

By this time every outside light was turned off. With the exception of the dingy emerald glow from the rundown fountain fifty yards out front and the interior lights of

The Day the Leash Gave Way

three separate residences, two on the second floor, one on the third, the place was almost as dark as the night surrounding it.

"I bet you," Lenny said, "that light on the third floor is our boy Nick."

"I bet you," Krude said, "that light on the third floor is the light of our boy Nick's apartment, in which lives our boy Nick."

"Shut up," said Lenny.

They climbed out of the car.

What to do, what to do?

Nick raced over and looked out the window.

"You mean to tell that wasn't a dream?" Carl asked rubbing his eyes. He was still drunk, but thank God he was finally sobering up.

"We should call the police," Nick said, and moved over towards the phone then stopped. "No, we should turn out the lights." He retreated from the phone and made his way to the light switch then stopped again.

Someone was coming up the stairs.

"Oh jeez," Carl said. "What kind of trouble have you gotten us into, Nick?"

Nick wanted to say "Me?" but didn't feel it was the time. Instead he moved the rest of the way to the light switch.

"This is the one," a voice from outside said.

He turned the switch off. Darkness consumed everything.

"Aw crap," a different voice said. "He went to sleep."

"Carl," Nick whispered, "get behind me."

Carl stumbled over and did as Nick said. "What have you gotten us into?" he said again.

Nick positioned himself at the door, one hand on the knob, the other hand on the deadbolt latch. "Be ready for anything," he told Carl, who, if Nick could have seen it, rolled his eyes.

Three loud knocks thumped upon the door. "Open up, Nick," the first voice said. "We wanna make a deal with you."

"A deal?" the second voice said. "We don't wanna make any kind of deal with them."

"Do me a favor," the first voice said. "Don't ever talk again."

"Damn," the second voice said.

Three more knocks wrapped upon the door. "C'mon, Nick, we know you're in there."

"They know we're in here," Carl said. "All they're gonna do is break the door down."

That's what Nick was hoping for.

He briefly let go of the handle as it jiggled. When the jiggling stopped he took hold of it again. "Get ready," he told Carl.

Crunch! From the sound of it both men had just simultaneously rammed their shoulders against the other side of the door. The sound reverberated through Nick's apartment and Nick wondered if it was going to wake up any of his neighbors. *Crunch!* A second time, and through his concern for his neighbors, Nick had counted three seconds, which he counted again, finding yet another spot in his mind for prayer.

Just before he reached three, Nick undid the deadbolt and opened the door.

The two men ran into the room through the darkness and smashed against the opposing wall, one of them hitting his stereo, both turning it on and cranking the volume in the process.

"This is KZBF, radio free America!"

"Rosanna" by Toto began.

Nick found Carl's arm and yanked him out the door. Unfortunately, with the darkness and Nick's own anxiousness, he smacked right into the guardrail four feet from the door and collapsed backwards into Carl. The two of them fell back, while at the same time the two intruders raced back towards the door, where one tripped over Carl's head and the other tripped over the guy who had tripped over Carl's head.

What happened next was a flurry of shouts and limbs. Nick got his right foot stuck between posts in the guardrail while Carl shouted protests at being kicked in the head. At this same time the guy who had tripped over Carl's head dropped to his knees. When he tried to rise, his buddy fell on top of him, and not knowing who it was on his back, the guy who had tripped over Carl's head forced himself up to his feet, which sent the man on his back up and over the guardrail.

At the last second, the man that had been flung over the guardrail managed to grab Nick's foot, which fortunately did not break the foot, but rather pulled Nick down through the rail until his crotch insisted that no more of him was going to go through that small space. It was considerably painful.

The man who had tripped over Carl's head, while flinging his buddy over the guardrail, had also achieved throwing out his back. He collapsed to the floor in a splayed heap, saying over and over again, "Damn."

Brutto hated driving. He hated it almost as much as he hated his name. He was so used to having someone else drive him around that he almost didn't know what to do. If only the damn cleaning woman had put his car keys where she'd put the key to his desk, or had she not put the key to his desk somewhere he couldn't find it in the first place he wouldn't be in this mess.

When he pulled into the parking lot of the Maison Cassée Residential Suites and killed the headlights he told Steve, "Other than this ugly emerald glow, I can't see a damn thing."

"Just get out of the car," Steve told him.

The two of them got out. There was one interior light on what looked like the second floor, far to the left. As they made their way towards the building, Brutto wondered if it was the place. As they drew nearer he learned that the light was in fact on the second floor, and Lenny and Krude had told him their man was on the third. From somewhere up above he heard music.

"Where the hell are the stairs?" Brutto said, and, squinting his eyes to help along his night vision, he turned slowly around in a circle. He stopped and looked directly at the vague shape of Steve and realized his eyesight was improving.

The Day the Leash Gave Way

Or not. Lots of interior lights were suddenly coming on. Voices were asking what was happening. Someone shouted to turn down the music.

Right behind Steve, Brutto saw the outline of the stairway and was just about to tell Steve as much when a man fell from out of the sky and knocked them both out cold.

Once the man had let go of Nick's foot, Carl had helped Nick get his leg out of the guardrail posts, and had then gone back inside to call the police. The man who had thrown out his back kept trying to get up but each time he got to his knees he collapsed again with a crash and a "Damn."

Enough lights were on now that when Nick looked over the edge of the three-story drop-off he saw not just the guy who had fallen, but two others, all clustered together like a stack of dead fish. He stretched his leg and rubbed himself for several minutes before trusting himself to walk anywhere.

"Police are on their way," Carl said, then the two of them carried the guy with the bad back downstairs, where they set him beside the pile of other guys.

"Boss?" the guy with the bad back said, looking at one of the two unconscious guys the other guy had fallen on top of.

Nick had to sit down. His leg was still aching like crazy. People were wandering around aimlessly, some carrying valuable possessions, maybe thinking the place was on fire. Nobody seemed to pay much attention to Nick or Carl or the pile of people.

"Well," Carl said, rubbing the side of his head, "we can't say this night has been boring."

One of the people in the pile began to stir. Slowly, he eased up, groaned, and squirmed his way out from under various limbs on all fours.

Nick studied him, then studied him more closely. He looked familiar. Then the light hit the man's head just right and Nick understood why. It was the guy with the pompadour.

"You son of a..." Nick got up, limped over to him, and kicked him in the face. The man flung around and landed on his back though did not again lose consciousness. Because of his leg, rather than kneel above him, Nick sat down next to him and grabbed him by the shirt. To make up for Nick's inability to do so, Carl kneeled over the guy, and together, for their own sake as well as a way to pass the time until the police arrived, the two of them began questioning him.

Two days later Page Turner was out of business. Neither Nick nor Carl had ever liked the owner's son Jason. He had been a shady dude from the start and it came as no surprise that he had worked for this Mr. Ed guy. It also came as no surprise that he had *stolen* from this Mr. Ed guy.

"Amazing," Nick said to Carl as the two of them filled out applications for Sam Goody while sitting in the food court at the mall. "I still can't believe that John Bishop not only knew his son had stolen from him, but he then fired me in order to cover it up, and had actually plotted the whole scam with Jason."

"At least he didn't press charges when he fired you," Carl said. "You could have been in a lot more trouble."

"True."

"John just didn't have the money personally, I guess. When he learned what kind of trouble his son was really in with this Mr. Ed guy, they had to come up with something."

"Probably would have worked too, had I not found that envelope and those guys learned about it," Nick said, still wanting to curse Carl for letting it slip in the first place. "I wonder where in the world that got off to."

When Nick had explained what had happened to the police and told them about the envelope, he'd taken two officers up to his bedroom and lifted the mattress, where he'd found nothing but a penny, a broken pencil, and a drugstore receipt. He'd checked all around and under the bed, but neither the envelope nor the money was anywhere to be found. Nick had been the only person who knew where it was. He hadn't told a soul where he'd put it until the police had arrived.

"Oh well," Carl said. "Small price to pay in the end."

"What gets me more than that," Nick said, "is that guy Steve. Jerk stole two hundred dollars from me earlier in the day. We bust him on something else, but I'm never gonna see that money again."

"I'll lend you the two hundred, Nick," Carl told him.

"How? You don't have a job right now either, remember?"

"I've got some cash socked away." Carl smiled sheepishly then looked away. Nick tried to meet his eyes but Carl avoided them at all costs.

"Carl?" Nick kept trying to find his eyes. "Carl, how do you have cash put away? You didn't a week ago when you locked yourself out of your house and couldn't pay a locksmith."

Carl squirmed around in his seat, filled out something on the Sam Goody application then said, "Well, when we got back to your house after our run-in with those two guys and I passed out on your bed."

"You found it?"

Carl nodded. "Just before I passed out. You left the room and I just, I dunno, grabbed the mattress for some weird drunken reason. You didn't stuff the envelope in very far."

"So you stole the money," Nick said. "You had it before those guys even showed up."

"I didn't actually remember I had it until those guys started pounding on the door. And by that time I guess I figured, if we ran out of the apartment, there was a good chance those guys were gonna stay around and rip the place to shreds looking for it." He took a sip of his soda. "I was gonna tell you, I swear. But y'know, that money has been considered lost. No one is looking for it anymore. We can split it."

More than any other time during this whole ordeal Nick wanted to punch Carl right in the eye. Then, as he tried to let his anger subside, he realized that what Carl had just said was true.

"You really planned on telling me?" he asked.

"Of course. Why would I have offered you the two hundred in the first place?"

"And we're gonna split it?"

"Fifty-fifty."

"Why fifty-fifty? I'm the one who found it."

The Day the Leash Gave Way

"Yeah, but you got me into a whole heap of trouble because of it."

Nick wanted to punch him again. Then, to his surprise, he started to laugh. "All right," he said, "But I get to keep the odd dollar."

"Fine," Carl said.

On My Feet

Hello, my once upon a time darling:

I'm writing to let you know that I got back on my feet. All those years of you and me, and then right when that ended, hours and hours every week of working, working, working. Got to the point where I couldn't do anything when I got home, couldn't think, couldn't feel, and was disinterested in even trying. That's what all that time did to me. Not that this has been an entirely bad thing. Most of my life I'd always been overly sensitive, taking offense too easily to the smallest things and allowing matters of little to no importance to rule my days.

So I'm thankful for that much, because there's more to life than worrying and feeling, which was all I did. Not that I wouldn't like to feel again. Emotion is a powerful part of the human soul. It's what gives artists, for example, the means by which to express themselves—it's the doorway *into* the soul. But like anything else, too much is not good, and I had too much. So when you ended what we had, at first I was worried that all I was going to do was feel. That I would feel and feel and think and feel and never get anything done, allow myself to get trapped, like I always did.

But when it ended, yes, for about a day I felt like you wouldn't believe. The feelings bubbling inside me were so strong they were nearly out of control. But only for a day, yes, only for a day.

After that first day everything disappeared. My heart became stone. I cared not one bit. The only thing that made this difficult was that you kept calling me, trying to be my friend, trying to tap into those "feelings," which I now put in quotes because they were not there. Why you felt it necessary to call me day in and day out is still beyond my comprehension. It was over, and it is over, and I've moved on, like it or not. Whether *I* like it or not, I've moved on.

I get this feeling that you think I've done nothing with my time since our parting, assuming things about me that even in all the years we knew each other better than anyone else in the world, you still could not see. It was not long before I started dating someone new, and came close to falling in love with her. She was considerably younger than myself, though age is merely numbers and little more, and the connection we had was one of great significance. The problem was that even though we had this connection, the timing was wrong. She had to leave for school, and therefore it had to end. The other problem was that I did not have enough emotion to really care. Stone-hearted, I could not allow myself access to the deeper levels, which, on reflection, probably would have been quite astoundingly beautiful. A part of me hopes what she and I found will resume at a later date, as she was a fascinating and wonderful person. But I digress.

The Day the Leash Gave Way

After you and I broke up I dove into work. I took a second job and kept myself as busy as humanly possible. Interesting enough, this was not to avoid feeling. It was to take advantage of the fact that I was not feeling. Without any feelings, life gets boring, reading becomes a chore. Expression has no point. With all the debt I'd accrued being with you, a lot of it thanks to you, I took advantage of the time and worked, worked, worked, saving what I could and bringing myself this much closer to financial freedom once again. Did pretty well, too. And now that I am through with working so much, sticking with only one job as a way to keep things together, my soul is resurfacing, little by little. I still find it hard to care, and I know I will never care the same way I did before and while you and I were together. But I do feel enough to where I can write this letter, as impersonal as it may sound in some ways.

I feel no anger towards you, as I assume you probably expect I do. I had little interest in seeing you at all until only recently, and now, as I sit down with pen and paper, I feel a little moreso. You hurt me, yes, but life moves on for most of us. Frankly, I couldn't help wondering if you calling me day in and day out to be "friends" was either a way to fuck with my head, or some unconscious means by which you could monitor my behavior and self-reliance, and if and when satisfied, make an attempt at reclaiming me. Which, if the case, you never would have been successful. Like touching a hot stove. Burn your hand on a stove you instantly discover you don't ever want to touch that stove again—of course it does not mean you want to blow up the stove. You just may not want to have anything to do with it anymore. And maybe you stop cooking all together for a while. So I see you as nothing more than a stove I touched when I wasn't paying attention, that is all. I have no interest in cooking on that particular stove, not much interest in cooking at all—though, like everyone, I do get hungry from time to time. And when I get hungry, I no longer crave the taste of you. There are others who are tastier. So I have moved on, and as much as you'd tried convincing me with each and every phone call that you had moved on too, I still find it a little difficult to believe. If you had moved on, you wouldn't have called so often, wouldn't have called for stupid, needy reasons, like Diane Keaton did to Woody Allen in *Annie Hall*. Even after you had found someone else. You would have just let it go and moved on, enjoyed your new man and let things go.

But whatever, whatever, all that is behind us, and I should wrap this up. I don't know if this is something you will be able to read. Honestly, I'm not sure that I care. The dirt is still fresh where they buried you, so I should have little to no trouble delivering this letter, and even less trouble burying it with you and what we once had. A part of me wishes I could feel sorry for what happened, to you, to us, to me; but what we had turned me to stone, and the feelings I have about what has happened to you are weak. When I try to picture it in my mind, imagine what you looked like the moment everything stopped, it matters little to me. A shame you had so much money that you hadn't earned yourself. Hell, a shame you had so much money at all, and a shame that the new man you chose to be with had his own agenda, and that he let too much of that be known to others. A shame he is now in prison for the rest of his life and deserves what he gets, yet funny that with all he was, he was completely innocent.

It's amusing to me that what happened did. That you left this world, and your sweet and wonderful new darling is for the rest of his life condemned, and that I, the one without feeling, without emotion, can sit down and write this letter, and can take the time to deliver it properly, and can chuckle at the fact that what I did has had little to no effect on me.

Maybe someday I'll feel again, though I'm not really sure that I care.

Sleep gently.

Signed,

Your Demise

Mourning Road

When he'd caught sight of the scene through his windshield, Ted Bishop had been thinking about something entirely different. Now, given what he had seen, he couldn't remember what he had been thinking about at all.

It was in front of the high school. The prairie dog was on its back, head pointed behind itself, all four limbs upright, like the posts of an elegant bed frame, its tiny mouth open in a big, gaping animal yawn.

This was not what got to Ted. What got to him were the other two prairie dogs standing with it. One stood watching, wringing its front paws, while the other shook the dead animal as if to wake it, as though his companion had merely chosen a bad place to sleep.

Once he'd driven past, all Ted could see was the prairie dog shaking his dead friend—his brother, his sister, his mother—and all he could feel was the moment in which the reality of the situation would dawn upon them.

Road kill was common, especially out along the highway. Ted didn't know how many times he'd seen it, nor how many times he hadn't given it a second thought. Typically he averted his eyes, changed subjects in his head because he didn't like to remember. Remembering brought up guilt like so many sharp-stabbing needles in his heart.

Never before, however, had he seen a situation in which the animal's family or friends were present, standing around, disillusioned, afraid, trying to comprehend. This made it personal. It was any family in the world. It might as well have been his family. It was the thing that forced him to remember. It was what brought the tears to his eyes.

It was why he drove out of town and along the highway.

The amber-lit stretch was empty at this hour, save for the memories of others. Others who, like the prairie dogs, had lost loved ones to the road. The roadside memorials were as frequent as the mile markers. As were the squirrels, the cats, the dogs, life knocked out of them, broken, smeared across the highway like butter on toast.

It wasn't long ago when he and Aaron were drunk and the dog had come from out of nowhere. When it had happened so fast he'd never gotten a chance to hit the brakes. When the loud crunch had struck the right front of his car, and Aaron, in the passenger seat, had screamed, "What the hell was that?" They'd pulled over in the midnight darkness.

"Dude, you hit a dog."

But Ted had already known this. In the split second of the crunch, he'd seen it: large, black and gray, a collar around its neck. A collar, with tags. This dog belonged to somebody. This dog had somebody who loved it, and now it had just been taken away from them forever.

This dog was dead. And it was Ted's fault that this was so.

He'd put the car in gear and left.

"We can't leave it there," Aaron had said.

Ted had trembled, his hands shaking so bad he had to grip the steering wheel with all his might. "It's dead," he told Aaron, his voice wavering like paper in the wind.

At the next memorial he came to he pulled over. He did not get out of the car, just studied it in the light of the setting sun, read it over and over like a sentence he didn't understand.

IN LOVING
MEMORY OF
J.J. VIGIL

Speeding? Drunk? Wrong decision at the wrong moment? Whatever the reason, it did not change the fact that this person was no longer living. It did not change that this person had died upon the road.

Ted reached for his cigarettes, remembered he'd given them up and bit lightly on his knuckle.

Dude, you hit a dog…

He imagined what J.J. Vigil's family and friends did when they learned of the accident. He tried to put himself in their shoes, to feel their disillusionment, their fear—

And suddenly he owned the dog. He was the one worrying, pacing all night, imagining the worst possible thoughts, then discovering them to be true.

That's when he pulled back onto the highway, found the next exit, turned around, and went home.

The following morning Ted went to both the hardware store and the craft store. He bought several items at each, then went back out to the highway, studied the shrines and thought his thoughts until he came upon his first mission.

The cat's eyelids were scrunched down, as if from terrible pain. Its back legs, just over the line into the road, were crushed and imbedded into the asphalt, its crusted blood maybe a day old.

Ted went to the trunk of his Honda and first removed a garbage bag, then a shovel. He wrapped the animal, took little notice of the car that passed and ignored him, then set to work, digging a hole in the dirt, just off the road.

When the cat was buried he took pieces of wood from his back seat, constructed them into a cross, and with paint he wrote upon it:

ANOTHER CAT
KILLED IN THE ROAD
AND LEFT BEHIND

The Day the Leash Gave Way

He fixed this into the ground, along with some plastic flowers, and moved on.

For several weeks Ted traveled roads, buried animals and built memorials. There was a squirrel so utterly destroyed it took him half an hour to collect all the pieces. There was half a bird skeleton. A dog with no head (he was never able to retrieve it). He wrote the epitaphs accordingly.

Along the way he took deep interest in the memorials left behind for people. People who died in cars. People who died in things created by people.

What of all the animals? The black roads that broke through and crumbled their environment? Our world was forced upon them, and it picked them off along the way, one by one. And the worst part about it: it didn't care. Any time Ted bagged an animal, dug a hole, built a cross, these thoughts ran through his mind. How we cared so much about and covered up our own stupidity and carelessness, wrongly made such a big deal about our own failures in something we never should have had the right to understand, let alone turn into power.

And yet a world is invaded, innocent victims are murdered, and other than the prairie dogs, nobody cares.

It made him sick, down to the core.

Dude, you hit a dog...

Yes, he had done that. He hated himself for that. If he could take it back, he would race the animal to the vet, take the number off the dog tag and apologize, do anything in his power to make things better.

But he couldn't, and he hated himself because of it.

This was the only thing he could think to do.

And still, every time he drove away from a gravesite, Aaron's voice rang through his ears. "We can't just leave it there."

During this time, when he wasn't on the road trying to make right what others had broken, Ted began getting involved with his local animal shelter. He donated towels and blankets and office supplies, pet food and cleaning products. He frequently donated small sums of cash. Twice a week he spent two hours working one-on-one with cats and dogs, walking them, grooming them, socializing. He distributed and retrieved donation boxes from around town, and from time to time he did light repairs and general upkeep. The tasks were not always easy, but they were always rewarding. The only times he found it difficult were when animals were brought in injured due to car accidents. Any time he saw or heard about them, he would hear the loud crunch, see the collar, see the road before him as he'd driven away. On occasion he would see the files, learn where the animals had been found. In the instances in which the animals wound up dying, Ted was always half tempted to swipe the animal from the shelter, drive it back to where it had been found and bury it there. He never did this, however. That was not what it was about. What he did was go out to the location at night, and set up a cross.

Grieving for animals is no different than mourning the death of a person, he would think. The difference is in the value placed on the animal.

So many abandoned. Left to die. People inflicting, people witnessing, people doing nothing to change it. The value was not the same as the value people place on themselves.

Ted couldn't understand this. At one point he had been the same way. Had been like everyone else. He would look the other way, deny what was there. Deny what had happened. Deny what he had done.

He hated himself for that, and he wanted to do right. Regrets can linger forever, and this one probably would. But at least maybe he could find a pathway to redemption.

He hoped.

After a month, driving in the late afternoon light, Ted spied a small moving shape on the road's shoulder. As his car brought him closer, he saw that the dog dragged itself with its front legs; its back left leg broken at an impossible looking angle, right leg gone at the knee.

Ted pulled over. The retriever whimpered softly, almost inaudibly. For a time Ted stood and watched it. The animal pulled itself to a shallow ditch, stopped, and collapsed its head on its front paws.

With slow, gentle steps, Ted approached the animal. The dog looked up at him, cried weakly as Ted eased his hand in front of its nose. Two sniffs, even in the poor animal's state, was enough to earn trust. Its whimper was a little louder this time.

Around the animal's neck was a collar. The tag read: KING LEAR, followed by a telephone number.

Ted went back to his car, made room in the backseat by moving his pre-made crosses to the front. He spread out the jacket he always kept in his car year-round, then went back to the battered animal, allowed it to sniff once more, and then scooped it into his arms. For the first time the dog made more than a whimper. An agonized howl of madness bellowed forth.

He placed King Lear on the jacket in the back of the car and drove back to town. Several times he tried to calm the dog with soothing words. In response King Lear whimpered and howled, and twice he thrashed about.

Hearing these howls, Ted saw behind his eyes the prairie dogs the instant in which comprehension set in.

In town he raced to the Emergency Veterinarian Clinic. He handed them his credit card, telling them to do whatever it took. They told him it would probably be pricey. Ted didn't care. He explained the situation, and asked that when they contacted King Lear's owner, not to give out Ted's name.

Three days later, as Ted covered up a squirrel, he was startled at the sound of a young voice.

"What'cha doing?"

A boy, eight maybe, red and white striped shirt, shorts, stood at the top of a small hill. In his hand he held a stick he'd found, and he tapped it against the skin of his leg, scratching it a little but not seeming to mind.

"Where did you come from?" Ted asked.

The Day the Leash Gave Way 53

"I live not far from here," the boy said.

"Don't you know you shouldn't talk to strangers?"

The boy thought on this a moment, then repeated his introductory question.

"There was a squirrel," Ted said. "It had been killed by a car. I'm burying it."

"Why?"

"Because it's dead."

The boy joined Ted and watched as he put down the last shovel-full of dirt. He watched Ted put the shovel back in his car, and remove a cross from the backseat.

"What's that?"

"A grave marker," Ted told him.

The boy took a step back, tapping his stick upon his leg. He watched Ted open a jar of paint and dip a brush in it. He asked Ted what it was he was going to paint.

"An epitaph." He looked at the boy. "Any suggestions as to what it should say?"

The boy shook his head, dropped his stick and quickly snatched it up again.

Ted asked him if he had any pets.

"I have two cats and three dogs," the boy said.

"Have you ever lost one? Has one ever run away or died?"

The boy nodded. A car drove by without slowing.

"What was its name?"

"Mopsy," the boy said. "She was a cat."

"Did you like her?"

The boy, confused, looked at him. He tapped the stick against his leg and told Ted, "I loved her. She was the best in the whole world."

Ted put that down on the cross.

Yet another dog—Charles, the tag said—his tail long departed from the rest of his body, back broken where the tire treads planted themselves, now finally buried and remembered as:

ANOTHER DOG
CHARLES
SOMEBODY MISSES HIM

Ted put the shovel back into his car as the sun crept slowly behind the distant mountains. A long day, a lot of work. Everything was now motionless. If there were any other animals out they didn't let themselves be known. It almost seemed as though the world itself was dead, a shell of a land that once breathed.

Then came the horrible specter inside him that whispered in his ear, spoke words that frustrated him, that told him things about himself he didn't want to hear. He tuned it out—like always—but with difficulty, and found that he was walking away from his car, up the highway, toward the sinking sun. Peace and quiet, get away, meditate…he knew it would do him some good.

He looked at the ground before turning his gaze up to the shimmering sky, then directed his attention to the road, away from the sun, looking back the way from which he had come. Seeing the new cross, planted beside his Honda, both now several hundred feet away.

There was a flicker in the distance beyond. Ted squinted as the light blinked away and he saw it was a car. A truck, coming up the highway, hauling ass. The sun prickled off the windshield like glitter in a child's hair. The truck had to be doing at least eighty-five but more likely it was going faster than that.

What of all the people over the course of time who have died without acknowledgment? he wondered. What of the people hundreds of years ago who died crossing the country, alone, with no one to hold them, to comfort them, to bury them? No one to leave a marker, not even a rock with a name scratched in it? Are they remembered? Are they worth anything? Did they ever exist at all?

Ted looked at the ground once again, saw that he was standing right next to an anthill, and that no matter where he stepped he was going to be killing them. He took a long step out, away, thinking how one's place in the universe is interpreted in terms of what one sees and experiences. How the universe operates in very specific ways, yet for each individual it operates differently.

He set his foot down upon asphalt. Upon the shoulder of the road. His attention returned just in time to see a split second of the shape before it crunched against him. He felt himself instantaneously broken, ruined, drifting through the air like a lazy cloud then thwapping against the dirt, flipping and tumbling.

"What the hell was that?" Aaron's voice demanded from somewhere Ted couldn't see.

He came to rest on his back, his lap twisted to the right of him, eyes inadvertently rolling around in their sockets, his cheek pressed firmly against his shoulder. Somewhere around him he heard the fading sounds of the truck as it continued on its course.

His roaming eyes took in flashes of his Honda, of the cross he'd set up for Charles only minutes before. The cross…a grave marker. A symbol which states that you are remembered, that the living acknowledge you were here, you were worth something.

This was not what got to Ted. What got to him were the others. The other people standing around, wringing their hands, shaking him, telling him the side of the road was a terrible place to sleep. Through his pain he sensed the moment in which the reality of the situation dawned upon them.

What got to him was they were not there.

Another car sped by.

The Day the Leash Gave Way

Sam was surprised twice over when he pulled into the driveway of the Kelly residence. First of all there was an old car parked out front that would have been better off compacted into a cube. A leash was attached to the rear bumper, old and weathered and ready to fall to pieces and with what had once been a dog tucked in the loop of it. Mostly bone now, part of the dog's skull and one of the front legs was covered in light blue paint, like the skeleton had been painting a swimming pool locker room. Sam half expected to see a cigarette in the pooch's jaws but what he saw instead was a boy, somewhere between eight and ten with his teeth clamped down on one of the animal's back legs. From time to time the boy grunted as though he might be a reincarnation of the dog, shaking and wiggling and refusing to let go, yet not willing to pull that bone free, which he most certainly could have done. Sam wondered if the leg came free if that boy would have anything to do at all, cause other than a dead dog, a dead car and some garbage, the place didn't seem to have much going for it in the way of entertainment.

Sam stopped the car and climbed out, watched the boy a minute then said, "Afternoon, son. Your mom or daddy home?" Sam had always kind of wanted a boy of his own, but knew it would never happen. Not the way his life had gone.

The boy quit struggling and with that leg still in his mouth looked at Sam, who saw that the boy had real sweet eyes. There were little cuts all over his face, too, as though *he'd* been dragged from the back of a car.

After a moment's contemplation, the boy went back to the dead dog and at the same time Sam heard the front door of the house open. A man came out with a shotgun in his hands and a half-smoked cigar in his mouth. Sam could see from where he was that the stogy was getting a lot of use as a human chew-toy. The man held the shotgun casually aimed at Sam, relaxed enough but ready to shoot if Sam so much as breathed wrong.

"What business you got on my property?" the man asked, the cigar bouncing from one side of his mouth to the other with each word.

Adjusting the collar of his sport coat, a passing thought zipped through Sam's mind about how he wished he could be wearing a sundress, it being such a lovely day. But how Mr. Franzheim and Mr. Beckett and all the rest would frown seriously upon something like cross-dressing, especially in a business-like situation. He cleared his throat and ran a hand through his hair. "I'm looking for a Mister Kelly," he said. "Dirk Kelly?" When the man didn't respond, Sam asked, "You him?"

"Maybe, maybe not," the man said, and tightened his grip on the shotgun. "Who wants to know?"

"My name's Sam McKenna. I'm from..." Sam lost track of his words when the boy slid down his dirty pants and peed on the ground. Not just a little, like a boy that age would give off, but like a garden hose turned on high.

"Pay my boy no mind," the man said. "Etchy's just got character and any boy of mine can feel free to go where he wants." He raised the gun. "Now you was saying about yourself?"

Sam couldn't help watching the yellow flood that was finding its way towards his shoes. Mostly he was unsettled, but he couldn't deny that there was something intriguing about it. He never would have admitted it but he kind of hoped some of the boy's pee would touch his shoes. "My name's Sam McKenna. I'm from Arkham and Ketcher." He reached into his pocket and withdrew an envelope. "Six months ago you filled out a..."

"Now wait just a minute." The man raised the gun. "You come here to sell me something? Cause if you did, I'm telling you to get right back in that car of yours and pull on outta here before that head you got on your shoulders explodes and blows up into more pieces than you can count."

Sam quickly raised his hands. "No, sir, no, I'm not here to sell you anything. I'm here because you filled out an entry form sponsored by Arkham and Ketcher, to win your choice of a brand new Subaru Outback or twenty thousand dollars cash."

"Yeah. So what if I did?"

The boy's pee had now touched upon the toe of Sam's right shoe and a tingle of excitement oscillated through him. "Mister Kelly, I'm here because I'm pleased to say that you won the drawing. It says here, where you were asked to choose which prize, you preferred the cash, so with me I have a check for twenty thousand dollars and zero cents, made out to a Mister Dirk Kelly. So, sir, if you are indeed Dirk Kelly, then..."

Kelly extended the shotgun up into the heavens and fired at the clouds. "You mean to tell me I won? I won twenty thousand dollars, all for writing my name down on a piece of paper?"

Sam laughed a tad, sensing he was moving out of harm's way, even though the man had just fired the gun. "Yes, Mister Kelly, that's just what I mean."

"Well why didn't you say so right off?" The cigar dropped from his mouth but he didn't bother picking it up. "Come on in."

Sam watched the shotgun ease down. Once satisfied that it wasn't going to come up again he nodded and made his way to the house, glad things were turning in a friendly direction but a little disappointed that he wasn't going to get more of the boy's pee on his shoe. Kelly held open the front door for Sam. "Etchy, you quit playing with Jethro and come on in here like a good boy and get your daddy and his friend a beer."

The boy pulled up his boxers then pulled up his trousers, his teeth still steadfast to the dead dog's leg. After he buckled his belt he let go and stood up and ran inside, past Sam and into the kitchen.

Mr. Kelly came in and closed the door behind him, set his shotgun beside the door and led Sam out of the foyer and into the living room, where Sam saw Mrs. Kelly sitting on the couch. She didn't seem much interested in what was going on. In fact, she didn't seem to move at all.

The Day the Leash Gave Way   57

"That's my cookie," said Mr. Kelly. "Don't you worry none about her. I got papers on her. She's all good and legal."

Sam didn't understand. He moved around to the front of the couch to introduce himself and to explain why he had come when he saw that her eyes were gone and her gaunt, wrinkled skin looked tough as leather.

"She ain't got no brains no more," Mr. Kelly said. "Nothing upstairs but saw dust." Then he straightened up proudly, as much as his hunched back would allow. "Did her myself. Didn't take too long neither." He motioned for Sam to sit in a chair across from the missus, and sat on the couch himself and put his arm around her. "I know she ain't pretty to look at. Never was, truth be told. But a boy needs to have his mother around, and when she grabbed her chest that day and keeled over, I thought to myself, 'Oh boy, what's a kid to do without his dear old loving ma around?' So I went to the preacher and told him the story and asked him what I should do about it, on account that I have trouble as it is doing the daddy part and I sure as shit can't be his mama and his daddy both. Preacher told me that his mama would never truly leave him, even though she'd moved on up into heaven. Way I seen it, if she's in heaven then she sure as hell can't be here, so when you get down to it, she *did* leave Etchy and me both. I knew she was gone and, not to sound disrespectful, but in many ways I'm glad; but that boy there"—he pointed towards the kitchen, where Etchy was still fetching two beers—"he didn't know his mama was gone. He thought she was sleeping on the kitchen floor. So I send him out to go play down in the road while I pick her up and haul her into the bedroom, getting my last time with her and thinking what to do. And I remember my buddy Vince has this book on how to stuff dead animals, so I finish with what I'm doing and call Vince, who lends me the book. It was tough to read cause there were more words than pictures but I managed okay. Once I knew what it was I was supposed to do I called up the courthouse and asked to speak to Jed, who's the one they got in charge of mortal remains down there. We went to high school together and he'd always had a thing for Daria. So I explain it to him and he fixes it so we got this gravestone out in the cemetery with her name on it and all, but here she is with Etchy and me, and here it is she'll stay. Preacher said it was a good way to hold on to some otherwise lost family values."

Something tickled the back of Sam's throat. He swallowed it down then straightened in the chair, which was covered in cigar ash and smelled a little like spoiled meat. Even though Mrs. Kelly didn't have eyes Sam couldn't shake this feeling that she was watching him. He didn't dare say anything, but the fact was she made him downright uncomfortable.

The boy, Etchy, came into the room, a bottle of beer in each hand and a cracker in his mouth. He gave both beers to his daddy then disappeared. Mr. Kelly rose from the couch and passed a beer to Sam. The bottle was warm and the beer inside was hot. To be polite Sam took one sip then set it down on the floor beside the chair, hoping to never see it again.

"So you still got that envelope in your hand," Mr. Kelly said. "That my check?"

"It is," Sam said.

"Well, hand it on over." The man reached his hand out expectantly, his lower lip trembling and his right eyebrow twitching. It was sort of odd. Sam thought he looked more like a man going to the electric chair than he did a man who'd won a contest. In the time it took Sam to think this thought Mr. Kelly lost his patience. "Well c'mon, c'mon. Ain't got all day."

The envelope jittered against Sam's leg. "Yes, Mr. Kelly, well, you see…" Letting out a sigh he opened the envelope and removed the contents: a check made out to Dirk Kelly for twenty thousand dollars and zero cents, and two sheets of paper. Legalities. Sam worried about the legalities. It wasn't that there was anything underhanded or sneaky about them, but Sam knew a man like Dirk Kelly wasn't the type to want to cooperate, even with the simplest of procedures.

"I see?" said Mr. Kelly. "I'll tell you what I see. A check in your hand with my name on it—and there's a problem with that. It's got *my* name on it but it's in *your* hand. That don't make no sense to me." He extended his hand a little further, eyes narrow, foot tapping, breaths sucking up his nose and pushing out again with a little high-pitched whistle sound.

Sam looked over at Mrs. Kelly sitting there all dead and stuffed and with no eyes and it was just the thing to focus him back on the papers in his hand. "Yes, sir," Sam said. "Essentially this is just a release form. It merely states that you filled out the entry form, confirms your address and says you're responsible for the taxes."

Mr. Kelly thought on it a minute. Sam could tell the man thought he still had the cigar in his mouth by the way he moved his lips. After a moment he shook his head. "Dunno if I like the idea of signing nothing."

Sam wanted to tell him that was fine because he was actually required to sign *something*, but he let it go, crossed his right leg over his left and straightened the papers in his hand. Before he could say a word, Etchy burst into the room from out of nowhere, the cracker now gone from between his lips but still in his mouth all chewed up and caked on his tongue and teeth. He was crying and in his hands he held a bone that Sam immediately recognized was from the dog outside because of the teeth marks on it.

"Daddy! Daddy!" Etchy cried, dripping cracker from his mouth and tears from his eyes.

"Etchy, boy!" Mr. Kelly rose to his feet. "What in God's name…what happened? What'd you do to Jethro?"

Etchy sniffled and whined and tried to get himself under control. "Dare's a bad guys outside, an-uh, an-uh, one of them called me farts and pulled the leg off doggy." He erupted then, collapsed to his knees, that bone in his hands which he brought to his forehead. Weird as he thought it was, Sam couldn't help feeling sorry for the boy who, so far as Sam could see, other than biting a dead dog and peeing in the yard, hadn't done anything to anyone.

"What you talking, bad guys?" Mr. Kelly asked, straightening where he stood. Way the man was standing Sam was real glad not to be wearing a sundress.

"Two bad guys in black," the boy said. "Says they here to take mama away, an-uh, an-uh"—he started losing it again and more wet cracker spewed from his mouth—"they pulled leg off doggy!"

The Day the Leash Gave Way

Mr. Kelly placed a hand on his boy's shoulder. "Now don't you worry, son. Jethro's got three more where that came from. Now go on into your room and play like a good boy. Go on now."

Etchy woefully climbed to his feet and slumped away, Jethro's leg in his hands. Sam thought about when Etchy's pee had touched the toe of his shoe; but before the thought could manifest into fantasy, Mr. Kelly adjusted himself, cleared his throat and told Sam to excuse him while he dealt with some business outside.

Sam looked at Mrs. Kelly there on the couch. He didn't like the idea of being left alone with her but told the man that was fine and watched him disappear into the foyer then listened to the front door open and close. A moment later he heard some muffled shouting but couldn't make anything out. All he could think about was dead Mrs. Kelly sitting across the way from him with no eyes, scrutinizing him, her hands at her sides. If she didn't have such a pretty sundress, Sam knew he would have been downright terrified. It sure was a pretty dress, no doubt about that and, most likely, no one would argue it. Looked about his size and would have fit well into the wardrobe he kept in the trunk under his bed—but then he looked up and saw that face again. If he ever wore that sundress himself, he thought, it would have to go through the wash first. Sam wondered if she always wore the same dress or if Dirk and Etchy changed it each day.

The muffled shouting got louder. Sam heard what sounded like a cardboard box being dragged along cement, then the shotgun went off. There was silence for a moment, then came what Sam interpreted as someone being beaten. Sam wished he were home, in his back yard, basking in the sun with a Corona in his hand, wearing the J. Crew sundress with the daffodils on it he'd picked up on sale last fall. He had his dead father's wedding ring, which he put on when he bought such things, so people would think he was buying them for his wife that he didn't have.

He heard the boy grunt.

The front door slammed open. In the time Sam could have counted to three Mr. Kelly entered the living room with a shiner and a busted nose and his shirt torn somewhere it hadn't been before. Protruding from his back was the shotgun. Then as he stepped further into the room Sam saw that it wasn't sticking out of his back, but rather it was pressed into it, and attached to the trigger end was a man in a cheap black suit. Behind this man came another in a cheaper black suit. He was balding and about forty pounds overweight and sweating like a pig. Both men wore sunglasses.

Sam rose to his feet solely out of reaction. The chubby man told him to sit back down, which he did, worried that the one with the shotgun might take it upon himself to start shooting at anything that moved. At least Mrs. Kelly would be all right, he thought.

The chubby man came around and looked at Mrs. Kelly there on the couch. He placed his hands on his hips and sighed. "Sorry, Dirk," he said, "but you know keeping a woman six months in the grave outta her grave ain't right."

"I told you I got papers on her," Mr. Kelly insisted, holding back tears, trying to stop the gush of blood pouring from his nose.

"According to those papers," said Chubby, "she's snug as a bug in a rug six feet underground in Sweet Home cemetery. But here she is in the middle of your living room without a bug on her. And y'know, I bet'cha there ain't any inside her neither." With that the man bent over and lifted the woman's skirt, stuck his hand up between her legs and felt around a moment. Once satisfied, he removed his hand, studied his finger and said, "Nope. That's where they'd be, and nary a bug could I detect. Least you're keeping her clean."

Sam saw that Mr. Kelly was raging inside. Had that shotgun not been pressed against his back, things likely would have been working differently. But as it was, Mr. Kelly looked down at his shoes and said, "Please, Garth, don't take her. Don't take her away from Etchy and me. She's all we got. How's I supposed to explain it to the boy when he comes in here and realizes his ma ain't no longer sitting on the couch? Just what the hell am I supposed to tell him?"

"You can tell the little fart that playing with dead things is bad for his health, and if he really loves his mother then he'd let her rest in peace, for crying out loud, and stop humiliating her corpse and treating her like she were the deer I got over my mantle. That's what you can tell him, Dirk. You can tell him that creatures should have been squirming in her months ago."

Still studying his shoes, Mr. Kelly said, "You're still jealous."

"Huh?" said Garth. He brought his hand to his ear and leaned over. "What was that?"

Mr. Kelly shook his head. "Nothing."

The man with the shotgun, who hadn't so much as breathed loud, poked the barrel hard against Mr. Kelly's back. "Answer him," he said.

"Yeah," said Garth. "You was brave enough to say it once, you can say it again."

Mr. Kelly looked up from his shoes, glanced briefly at Sam, then looked Garth right in the eye. "You're still pissed on account that she took me over you in the end." The blood had stopped running from his nose and even though he hadn't put anything up there, it looked like he had two blood soaked tissues shoved way up inside. "You're mad because I got the woman you had, and the woman you always wanted. You can't just let things be, Garth—you never could. Even after the woman's dead you still gotta keep chasin' after her. She ain't causing no trouble here. Hell, Preacher thought it was healthy for Etchy to have his ma around."

Garth scratched his thin-haired head then wiped a large rinse of sweat from his brow. "You got it all wrong there, Mister Dirk Kelly. I'm here on account that Jed gets himself caught down by the river with his twelve-year old cousin and we haul him in, and while me and Smitty here's interrogating him, he confesses both to stealing Dilbert McClinton's old Ford and driving it into the lake, as well as fudging certain papers down in his office so your wife could appear to be with the worms, when in fact she's here on the couch with a Reader's Digest at her side and no eyes in her head." He made a tsk-tsk sound. "You wanna get mad at someone, get mad at Jed. He's the one blew your cover."

Sam could tell by the look on Mr. Kelly's face that he thought it only partially true. Mr. Kelly tightened his hands into fists and trembled, closed his eyes and said, "Then you're gonna take her back to your place and fuck her dead sawdust brains out."

Garth sighed, then nodded to Smitty. Smitty tilted the shotgun up to the back of Mr. Kelly's head and pulled the trigger. There was a loud, echoing boom and Smitty jolted back as Mr. Kelly's head disappeared into an explosion of blood, brains and skull fragments. They sprayed against the wall and some got onto the ceiling.

Sam recalled this being the first threat Mr. Kelly had made to him, to blow his head off with that very same shotgun that had now done him in. A moment later his knees buckled and he dropped down, collapsed forward onto the floor behind Mrs. Kelly and the couch.

Mr. Kelly wasn't ever going to get to enjoy his twenty thousand dollars and zero cents, and now that boy no longer had a mother *or* a father. And these two guys, they were going to do him in just as they'd done Mr. Kelly, fire a big hole in his chest or blow up his head. He couldn't help finding it odd that he'd be getting paid the moment he died—at least he'd be getting another eight dollars and fifty cents when that shotgun blew him to pieces.

Sadly, it wasn't much comfort. All he'd wanted was to deliver the check, shake the man's hand and maybe have Etchy take a picture of the two of them. But that wasn't going to happen. Even if the two men let Sam and the boy live, the photograph wouldn't hold much appeal to Arkham and Ketcher customers when the man who'd won the drawing didn't have a goddamn head to smile with and no eyes to light up in shock and excitement.

Smitty, with a side-of-the-mouth smile, pumped the shotgun.

Garth took three steps over to Sam and leaned close. "Now, I know you wouldn't say nothing about what happened here. I'm right, am I not?"

Sam heaved but nothing came out.

"That's what I thought," said Garth. "But we can't have any witnesses, even though I believe you. And I want you to know I do. I really do believe you. I think you'd keep a secret. Bet you got plenty of secrets of your own. I remember my daddy slipping it to me when I was a kid and I kept that a secret for a long time; but I digress—what's your name anyway?"

Sam tried to speak but all that came out was a long string of stuttering. "S-s-s-suh-suh-muh-muh…suh-muck-uck-uck…"

"That's an interesting name," said Garth. "Almost sounds nigger but it might also be Polish. And given that you're paper white and don't speak the name with rhythm, I'm gonna go with the latter." He straightened up and wiped his brow, then turned to Smitty. "That reminds me, Smitty—why did the Polak cross the road?"

Smitty shrugged.

"He couldn't get his dick out of the chicken."

Smitty grinned.

Sam was not about to say he wasn't Polish.

"Y'know, Smitty, even dead, Daria's still one lovely lady."

Smitty didn't say anything.

Sam heaved again. Mr. Kelly's blood and bits of his brain and skull slid down the wall like chunky red drops of rain on a window. Sam studied the vomit in his lap as Kelly had studied his shoes, felt shivers ripple up and down his back as tears danced at the edges of his eyes, which he closed; but even with them closed he still saw Mr. Kelly's head splattered against the wall.

Lifting the sleeve of his cheap black coat Garth looked at his watch then wiped sweat from the back of his neck. "Think we're wasting our time here now, Smitty. We've got other things to do." He adjusted his belt. "Let's get this over with and get the hell outta here."

Sam's heart jumped in his chest. He watched Smitty snicker, then bring the gun around and aim it right at his face. About to scream like an eight-year old girl on a roller coaster ride, Sam saw a large hairless dog sweep into the room and attach its jaws to Smitty's leg. Smitty swayed backwards with a horrible scream and the gun went off, shooting Garth square in the chest and the report knocking the off-balanced Smitty down to the floor. It all happened in a flash—Garth's back jumping out and taking most of his torso with it while Smitty dropped to the floor and the dog jumped on top of him and started tearing at his throat.

Blinking twice, Sam saw that it wasn't a dog. It was Kelly's boy, Etchy, growling and grunting like a dog, biting like a dog, but nothing like a dog at all when it came to physical features. No muzzle and no fur other than what he had on top of his head. The pants and T-shirt should have given it away immediately but everything was happening so fast that Sam wasn't entirely sure his head hadn't blown up and was in the process of scattering around Dirk Kelly's living room.

Smitty kicked the boy off him, got enough of a breather to pump the shotgun but was once again pounced upon, at which time the gun went off, this time dissolving Mrs. Kelly from the breasts up and ruining her dress.

The boy tore into Smitty again. Blood washed over both of their faces. Smitty tried crying out but Etchy's teeth had shred his vocal cords and all that came out were high-pitched squeaks that made Sam think briefly of mice on fire.

Just when he thought things couldn't get any worse, Sam wet his pants. At first it was warm but after a minute it got colder and less comfortable. Had he been wearing a dress, he thought, it would have been easier to dry because he could have fanned it out, but that was beside the point and something he just had to deal with.

Smitty stopped struggling about this time. Once he was still Etchy backed away, called the dead man a fart and started crying. Both his mama and his daddy had blown up, and there was nothing left for him other than Jethro, who now lacked a leg and wasn't much with conversation to begin with.

Etchy kicked a dirty sneaker at Smitty and landed it square in his groin but the aftereffects of death had caused the man to lose mobility and reaction along with a lengthy string of other devices useful for the living. Even so, Etchy seemed to achieve a certain level of satisfaction. Not enough to settle the tears, but there was an unspoken assertion after that moment, and Sam almost clapped and giggled but managed to refrain.

Instead, he looked around the room at the gore and the chaos and the carnage. Garth with his chest gone and his tongue lolling out. He looked like he was still sweating. Sam looked away and over to where Etchy and Smitty were, Etchy standing there with blood all over him, crying and staring like a rabid dog. Even ravaged the way he was, Smitty looked cool with his sunglasses on, though he matched Etchy when it came to the blood part.

All he could see of Mr. Kelly were his shoes, save for his head which was on the wall. The rest of him was behind the couch.

The Day the Leash Gave Way 63

A strange sort of sadness he hadn't yet experienced came over him when he looked at Mrs. Kelly. He was thankful that those eyeless sockets of hers were no longer watching him, but that had been a really pretty dress. And now it was destroyed. Couldn't even put it through the wash now. Still, he was thankful for the cessation of scrutiny.

Etchy turned to Sam and wiped the blood from his chin then the tears from his eyes, smearing blood along his brow. "Everybody," he said, whimpering, "—everybody blowed up, an-uh, an-uh, now there's no mama an-uh no daddy." His lips curled back and displayed his crimson teeth as he cried.

Sam looked at the boy. Etchy was an odd kid, no doubt about that, but it didn't change the fact that Sam had always wanted one of his own. He beckoned the child over, felt a bit ashamed having thrown up on himself, not to mention he'd wet his pants, though Etchy didn't seem to mind or even take notice. There was plenty of other disconcerting stuff around the room that Sam's appearance was, by measure, small potatoes.

Not at all sure that it was wise, Sam couldn't shake this feeling that what he had in mind was right—beneficial for both of them, if not additionally liberating for Sam himself. He reached out and messed up Etchy's hair and said, "Now don't worry, son. You're not alone." A tremor of arousal shuddered through him—"Way I see it right now, you've lost your mom and daddy; and I'm real sorry about that. I really am. But I was thinking, well, I know you don't know me from Adam. All I did was bring your daddy a big check that he can no longer use. Hell, I think I even threw up on part of it. But back to what I was thinking. You see, I've always kind of wanted a boy, obtuse or simple or otherwise—and if nothing else, I can promise you this: I've trained myself in the art of both masculine and womanly attributes."

Etchy looked at Sam with complete confusion.

"What that means, son, is I have the ability, or gift, rather, to be both your mama and your daddy all rolled into one. That's where you'd have it good, son—two complete parents encapsulated into one body. You can come live with me in town where I got a modest house and you could have your own room and, hell, even Jethro could come along if you like, but he'd have to stay in the back yard." Sam straightened proudly in his seat and looked the boy in the eyes. "What'd you say?"

Etchy thought on it a minute, then crumpled his face and started to cry. Sam could not interpret the reasoning. If it was because his folks were dead, that was one thing; but if it was something else…

After a minute passed, Sam rose from his seat, stuffed Mr. Kelly's check for twenty thousand dollars and zero cents and the legalities into his pocket, then scooped the boy up into his arms and carried him outside, distressed at picking up a child while covered in his own vomit.

Etchy didn't fight, just kept on crying.

Sam walked past Jethro, the leg the boy had been chewing on earlier now gone. Opening the passenger door of his Chrysler he placed the boy gently inside, told him everything was going to be all right, then closed the door and went to the driver's side.

A moment later they pulled out of the driveway, got onto the road, then onto the highway, and made their way into town at a calm and leisurely pace.

Back at the Kelly's house, the rotted leash connecting the old car to the dead dog finally gave and fell into two pieces.

Caught in Etcetera

It was happening. The day was coming to an end, and as he did his evening chores it kept happening, all the things he had done that day, from waking up in the morning to putting his head down soon, and all points and tasks in between—etcetera, etcetera, etcetera.

He was trying to relax now. He wanted to relax before he went to bed—unwind, forget about his day; but he was in it, doing it all over again. And again and again.

He was climbing out of bed, stretching, yawning, etcetera. Then he was brushing his teeth, making coffee, etcetera, etcetera. Driving to work, punching in at nine. Etcetera, etcetera, etcetera.

Work was boring—both the first time and the next. The same as any other day, it was filled with harsh, tedious monotony.

All he wanted to do was relax but he was going to lunch at the same place he went every day, ordering the same food from the same menu—

Then he was back at work, looking at the clock, waiting for it to be five, though he knew that it didn't matter. He knew he would be here again later on. So he kept on working: typing on his computer, making meaningless phone calls to people he didn't care about, etcetera, etcetera.

He drove to the bar and met his girlfriend. She was in a bad mood and had been drinking without him, and he was forced to listen to her rants again. Etcetera, etcetera, etcetera.

He was trying to relax but he couldn't. The day was there with him, trapped inside him, again and again, and he was there again.

His girlfriend got drunk as hell and began telling him what was wrong with him, etcetera.

"You never stand up for yourself," she told him. Then, "You act like a big baby a lot of the time."

Etc.

Etc.

Etc.

Their date ended in a fight. The usual shouting, insulting, etcetera, etcetera. He always hated it when they fought.

She left. He stayed a while and had a few more drinks, considered what happened, what to do about it, etcetera.

When he got home he washed the dishes he had been neglecting for so long, then did his laundry, yadda-yadda, etcetera, etcetera.

He felt numb from all the alcohol but decided to fix himself another.

The Day the Leash Gave Way

It had all begun shortly before lunch. It seemed to be starting sooner each day. Just before he went to eat he was waking up, stretching, yawning, brushing his teeth, making coffee, etcetera, etcetera. It always happened that way.

When he left work he was having lunch at the same place he always went, having the same food he always got, etcetera.

While at the bar he was working, waiting for the clock to hit five, typing on his computer and making meaningless phone calls, etcetera, etcetera, etcetera.

As he did his dishes and his laundry he was drinking with his girlfriend, fighting, drinking alone.

He knew that when he fell asleep it would all go in reverse. It would be sooner than before and he knew it. Maybe he could make things right next time. He wanted to make things right.

He set his head down to rest a couple of times, then fell asleep.

He was drinking alone, fighting with his girlfriend, drinking with her, etcetera: driving backwards to work, unmaking meaningless phone calls, untyping on his computer, etcetera, etcetera. He undid the work he had done that day, watched the clock tick away from five. Then he was coming back from where he was going to lunch, and he un-ate the same food from the same menu at the same place. The he arrived at work, getting ready to go to lunch. The earlier part of the day was filled with harsh, tedious monotony, etcetera. It was boring—boring as hell. He unpunched his time card at nine and drove home backwards. He unmade coffee, unbrushed his teeth, etcetera. Then he was yawning, stretching and climbing into bed.

He woke up, climbed out of bed, stretched, yawned, drove to work, punched in at nine; and as he punched in at nine he was waking up, climbing out of bed, stretching, yawning. It was starting much sooner today. As he worked his boring, tedious, monotonous job, he was driving to work and punching in at nine.

Maybe if he quit he could break out of it, though there was a chance that he'd trap himself deeper.

Getting ready to go to lunch, he found his work to be harsh, tedious and boring. As he waited for five o'clock to roll around, knowing that it wouldn't matter, he was ordering the same food from the same menu at the same restaurant.

As five o'clock came around he was typing on his computer and making meaningless phone calls as he drove to meet his girlfriend at the bar, where she had started drinking without him.

Closer and closer.

His girlfriend was telling him what was wrong with him, reiterating it as she went on. "You never stand up for yourself," she told him, then said it again as she said: "You act like a big baby a lot of the time." Then again.

Etcetera, etcetera.

Etcetera—

And again.

He wanted to apologize. He knew he should, though for what he had no idea. Maybe if he did, however, he could make things right; and he wanted to make things right. But what good would an apology really do? Most likely nothing. Possibly it could change everything—alter his entire existence. Maybe. Possibly. But he didn't apologize and he kicked himself for it, thinking he should have at least tried.

She stood up and left, then stood up and left again. He sat and drank then redrank the same drink again.

He went home twice and washed his dishes, did his laundry, washed his dishes, and did his laundry. He wanted to relax, then thought about how he wanted to relax.

He knew that when he fell asleep it would all go in reverse.

And it did ti dnA.

When he woke up it was only off by a split second.

He climbed out of bed, stretched, yawned.
    he climbed out of bed, stretched, yawned.
He brushed his teeth, made coffee, etcetera.
    He brushed his teeth, made coffee, etcetera.

Work was boring, harsh, tedious.
    Work was boring, harsh, tedious.
He was going to lunch at the same
    He was going to lunch at the same
place he went every day, ordering the
    place he went every day, ordering the
same food from the same menu.
    same food from the same menu.

Then he was back at work, and back at work again, looking at the clock, waiting for it to be five. Then again. He knew it wouldn't matter—twice—and continued working, typing, calling, etcetera, etcetera, etcetera.

Five o'clock was approaching.

Five o'clock was approaching.

He continued working and every minute and minute again that passed twice was filled with the same: etcetera, etcetera, etcetera.

He drove to the bar, then did it again, met his girlfriend twice. She was in a bad mood and had been drinking without him, then drinking the same drinks again without him cause she was in a bad mood. He was forced to listen to her rants, then reiterate them. Etcetera. She began telling him what was wrong with him, then she would tell him what was wrong with him.

Etcetera,
    Etcetera,
        Etcetera.

The Day the Leash Gave Way

The same date ended in a fight both times. The usual shouting, insulting, etcetera. He hated it when they fought, and hated it when they fought. He wanted to apologize, then wanted to apologize but didn't—he didn't and kicked himself.

She left, then left again. He stayed awhile and had a few more drinks, then had them again.

When when he he got got home home he he washed washed his his dishes dishes and and did did his his laundry laundry, etcetera etcetera, etcetera etcetera.

He eh knew wenk when nehw he eh fell llef asleep peelsa it ti would dluow all lla go og in ni reverse esrever.

And it did.

When he woke up he climbed out of bed, stretched, yawned; and then he paused.

It was gone. He wasn't repeating. He was no longer caught in etcetera.

Of course this wasn't true. He knew it. He was still there. He was still hooked in—trapped there every day of his life. Just like all the others who were caught in the tedium, the harsh monotony. Like every other he was repeating it, over and over again, etcetera, etcetera. And still at night it would all rewind and wait for him—wait for when he woke up, so it could start over and over again and he could wake up, climb out of bed, stretch, yawn, brush his teeth, make coffee, drive to work, clock in at nine, be bored and frustrated with tedious work, go to lunch, wait for it to be five, type, call, leave work and do it again. Over and over again.

Etcetera, etcetera, etcetera.

The House of Happy Mayhem

I like coming to the park.
It isn't a heavily populated park, nor is the acreage it covers much worth mentioning. There is a small river on the north side of it, with a street beyond (you have to cross a short bridge to get to the parking lot), and the east and west sides are flanked with houses. The west also has picnic tables and grills, the east a small basketball court, a jungle gym, and a couple of swings. The south side, where I like to spend my time, crests upward and has a chain-linked fence on the west end with an open entryway that leads to another, smaller street. The rest of it is trees, piñons, mostly, and it is in the shade of these trees that I like to sit. The fence, of course, extends all the way across the south side, but it is almost invisible amidst the trunks and branches and occasional large sitting rocks, though patches of light bleed through and you can see the little street with the little houses—cozy houses, safe and comfortable. The right kinds of houses for the right kinds of people, and all of the right people live in them.

Sitting on a rock in the shade, I watch the people, always with a paperback stuffed into my back pocket, resting in my lap, or on the ground at my feet. I don't ever read the book, but feel it's good to have one with me.

There aren't many people, the park is quiet this afternoon, but I relax and watch them. For a while I watch a man with his dog, looks like a Labrador, and he's throwing around a Frisbee for the dog to fetch. The man thinks more of his dog than he does any human being. My guess is that it's not because he has been mortally wounded by humanity; in fact, I bet he gets along quite well with most folks. But he's afraid of them, he's afraid of intimacy and the only intimacy he thinks he can afford—the only intimacy he knows is safe—is that of the black lab chasing after that sunny yellow Frisbee.

Far down to my right, on the jungle gym, two kids hang upside down and swing around and scream with childish glee while the mother and father lean against the side of the nearby car, both with their arms crossed. They're fighting. They hate each other and they hate their kids, and to me their kids are sexless. The parents are discussing divorce, or they've gone through divorce and are trying their best to get along for the children's sake, which contradicts the fact that they hate their children and are only here with prayers for the little runts to burn off enough energy on the fucking jungle gym so that they'll keep the hell quiet at home.

There's a guy shooting baskets, too, but I don't much care about his story right now. Instead I pull the paperback from the back pocket of my jeans and flitter-flutter the pages rhythmically. It's a novel by Louis L'Amour, not that it matters since I never read the books I bring with me. But I play around with it in order to give my hands something to do, and I watch the black lab jump high into the air and catch the Frisbee in its mouth.

The Day the Leash Gave Way

"Good boy!" the man calls out, and claps his hands twice.

I glance down at the paperback and see it has a cowboy on it and then I hear distant, unintelligible conversation to my left. A couple has just stepped through the entryway and they're making their way down through the grass and over to one of the picnic tables. I've seen this couple here many times before—I'm pretty sure they live in one of the cozy houses behind me—and as I look at them they look at their feet. They are a youngish couple. The man is good-looking and probably about my age, which would put him somewhere in his early thirties, and the woman is a little younger, mid- to late-twenties, I'd say, stunning, with long red hair that she doesn't take well enough care of. They step up and sit down on one of the picnic tables, their feet resting on the bench and all of a sudden the entire picnic table is an intimate square.

Some birds, pigeons, I think, fly by overhead. I give them a fleeting glance, then focus my gaze downhill to the couple. They are a happy couple, for the most part. Their heads hanging low as they walked was not the result of depression but rather of contemplation. I set the paperback in my lap as the man puts his arm around her, and for a brief moment they look more like father and daughter than they do boyfriend and girlfriend, or husband and wife, and I have a snapshot behind my eyes of getting water up my nose while in the middle of a swimming hole. Seeing the grassy bank off in the distance and then seeing the intimate square again, and I enjoy watching them, more than anything else in the park I enjoy watching this couple. They are well educated and make a decent living and I envy their happiness so I pick up the book again and flutter its pages once more.

They read all kinds of books. I bet they read all the time. Sometimes they come out to the park and lie in the grass and each of them has a book, sometimes small paperbacks like the ones I carry and sometimes large volumes one would think it would take a forklift to move. With the exception of the woman's hair not quite being properly cared for—and it isn't bad; it is still quite lovely—they are very clean, always well dressed, and both have a genial manner that implies they have many friends and acquaintances. Nearly always smiling faces, as though every moment in their lives is a happy moment.

I move forward, stick the paperback back into my pocket, then take it out immediately again and run my fingers through the pages as the man runs his fingers through her hair, and in watching this action an opinion does an about face. They might have a lot of friends, but now I wonder, and suddenly I feel bad for them. Maybe they're sad and don't have any friends. Maybe the smiles are masks, cover-ups, like make-up they put on movie stars to hide their blemishes. Suddenly I feel bad for them, I feel really bad and as I feel really bad I scoff at myself just as the sunny yellow Frisbee lands at my feet.

The dog stops a couple yards away, excited, panting, bouncing. I reach down and pick up the Frisbee and fling it in the direction of the poor, lonely dog lover. "Thanks," he calls out, and I reply with a wave and my hand is still in motion when I hear the girl scream. My attention jolts back to them and the man is tickling her and she's laughing hysterically.

I scoff at myself again, look down at my book, open it to a random page, skim a line and close it up again as I stand up from my rock. I stuff the paperback into my back pocket and walk to my left until the trees dwindle to fence and the fence opens up. Giving the couple one more glance, I step out of the park and onto the sidewalk. I debate going left or right, then decide to go right, as it is the quicker way home.

As I pass by the houses I think of how wonderful it would be to live here. Christmas pops into my mind, and I can see myself in a sweater with a glass of eggnog and a black lab that worships the ground I walk on. In my home are all kinds of people, friends and acquaintances, and there is a Christmas tree in the living room, lit up all bright and pretty. One of those Starbucks Christmas compilation CDs is playing and everyone is laughing and having a good time. And standing in the corner, by the tree, talking with some friends, is my wife, a beautiful redhead. I excuse myself from my own friends and acquaintances, sneak up behind her and tickle her. She laughs hysterically, and in my mind her name is Laura.

For the next several days I don't see them at the park. I see the guy shooting hoops again, and decide that he drinks too much and can't let go of his glory days as a high school or possibly a college ball player. He never made it to the big time, though, and he probably works construction or at Home Depot and has a wife and child at home who resent him. I decide that the Lakers are his favorite team.

I tuck away the Mark Twain book I have this time, make my way to the left to the fence opening, and just as I exit the park, the couple comes in, the man guffawing about something.

"Excuse me," he says as he sidles past.

"Excuse me," she says, and her voice is as lovely as she is.

I stand aside and let them through. Then I stand on the other side of the fence and watch them stroll hand in hand down into the park. I bat at an insect that buzzes by my ear and want to know what the joke was about. I want to know what she said that made him laugh the way he did, or what *he* said that cracked him up so. Instead I watch them for a moment, and this time make a left up the sidewalk, along the chain-linked fence, running my fingers on it, looking at the houses to my right. I take note again of how sweet and cozy they are. Probably fairly expensive from the looks of them, though not too large. Nice, modest homes—the right kinds of homes for the right kinds of people, and I determine that my couple must live in one of them because they are, without a doubt, the right kind of people.

When the fence and trees end, I reach the main street, at which point I make another left. Down the sidewalk and across a bridge, then a left curve and the river is on my left. I walk parallel with it until the bridge serving as the entryway to the park appears, and I walk in and enter the parking lot. There's a couple making out in a parked car and the other guy is still shooting hoops. I retrieve my Mark Twain book and take a seat on one of the swings and stare across the grass field at the couple, listening to the bouncy-bounce of the basketball and the rattling sounds the backboard or the rim make when the ball hits.

After half an hour or so the couple gets up. I climb off the swing and slowly make my way across the field, quickening my pace when it isn't obvious I'm doing so. Behind me another car pulls into the parking lot blasting some loud rap music.

The Day the Leash Gave Way

I watch the couple crest the tiny hill and see that they veered to the left. I race up into the trees and find one of the tree-free splotches that reveals the world on the other side, and hear them talking but I can't make out what they're saying.

They pass by my opening. I give it a couple of seconds and then move until I find another, and it's in this second opening that I hit the jackpot. It's an adorable little home, eight steps up to a short walkway, and the woman breathes in the fresh air with a smile on her face as the man unlocks the door and then they are inside.

Casually, heading back to the fence opening, I once again step through it and go left. Their yard is small but well kept, and potted flowers flank the steps and the walkway. I can't get it out of my mind what they are doing inside there, and I become overwhelmed with an almost uncontrollable urge to find out, right then and there. Instead, I remove my copy of *The Adventures of Tom Sawyer*, flutter its pages, turn around and make my way home.

The next afternoon, I walk up to the front door and ring the bell. When nothing happens I ring the bell again and follow it with a series of knocks. Still, no one answers. With the exception of a couple of birds—pigeons, I think—the block is empty. And once I realize the block is empty I do something I know I shouldn't do but I do it anyway. First I look under the doormat. Then I begin looking under the potted flowers, cautiously, checking for on-lookers with every pot I lift. There are twelve pots in all and nothing under any of them.

I approach the door and ring the bell again, having a stupid story in mind in case someone does this time decide to answer. A dumb story about losing a book in the park and if you've been to the park recently, might you have seen it? But no one answers.

About to give up and await my next sight of them at the park, I see a small assemblage of stones to my right. Another check of the street shows me that no one is around. I rummage through the rocks until I find it. It's lighter than the others when I pick it up, and when I turn it over it has a small plastic flap, which flips to the side and inside the small compartment is a key. I remove the key, set the fake rock back to the side, slide the key into the lock and turn. I hear the pop as the lock disengages, check once more for on-lookers, and step inside.

The house is cool. Clearly air-conditioned. It is also tidy, as though they either have a maid or are adamant about keeping their place clean.

I shut the door quietly behind me, and I'm in a nice living room, mostly contemporary southwestern style but with a comfort not usually found in such interior decoration. To the right is a large, comfy-looking couch, and across from it a large flat-screen TV. Directly beyond the right side of the couch is what appears to be a coat closet. Between the couch and the TV is a coffee table, a couple of coasters as well as a large book about painting throughout the ages set upon it. Hanging nicely all about the room are framed works of art. Ahead and to the left is a nice sized kitchen, packed with all the modern day conveniences and an enormous walk-in pantry. On the dining table is a stack of mail. I learn that their names are James and Lisa Cohan. Lisa, Laura, Laura, Lisa... wasn't too far off. At the back of the kitchen is a sliding door leading out into the back yard, which I don't bother to investigate. To the right is a clean bathroom with a beige, Native American motif, and in between the two rooms is a hallway. I walk down the hall. A room on the right with the door open—I peer inside and see an office, packed with bookshelves packed with books.

Continuing on, I come to the last room: the master bedroom. The curtains are closed and it's dark, but I can make out the bed, which has been nicely made, with a nightstand on either side. There is a dresser on the left of the room and a dresser on the right, and the one on the right also has a vanity next to it.

I sit on the bed briefly and stroke the comforter. It is soft and light and clean and feels good on my fingertips. They have many pillows at the head of the bed. There is a smaller TV against the opposing wall, with a small stack of rented videos on top of it. Getting off the bed, I smooth out where I sat, and see what they rented. *Jules and Jim*, *The Prize Winner of Defiance, Ohio*, *The Secret of Roan Inish*, and *Life is Beautiful*. I've seen all four of them, and liked them all. They have good taste in movies, I decide, and look to the right of the TV. A large bathroom and to the right of that is a large walk-in closet with lots of nice clothes hanging on hangers and the floor is a chaotic assemblage of shoes. They never have trouble figuring out what to wear, I think as I reach out and touch some of Lisa's dresses. I bring a red sleeve to my nose and smell it. The scent is as beautiful as her voice, which is as beautiful as she is.

Closing the closet door, I leave the bedroom, walk down the hall and into the living room. I look out the window onto the street and see no one. I open the door, step outside, lock the door and make my way back to the street.

Later that night, when all the lights are out inside the house, I replace the key into the fake stone.

For the next few days, instead of going to the park, I pass by the chain-linked entryway and walk up the eight steps. The movies they had rented have been returned and they haven't rented any others. I sit on the couch and watch TV on the big screen in the living room. I watch a surprisingly interesting A&E Biography on Tom Selleck. During one of the commercial breaks I use the bathroom. I imagine stepping out of the bathroom and James and Lisa are on the couch, each on one side of it, and they've saved the middle for me. There are three sodas on the coffee table. I sit between them and we enjoy the rest of the Tom Selleck biography.

When the show ends I switch off the TV and just as I do I hear a car door close outside. I hop to my feet and listen. I can hear footsteps coming up the steps, then up the walkway. I run into the kitchen but know I don't have time to go out the sliding door, so I close myself in the pantry, in which, in addition to food, there is a washing machine and dryer, as well as a large hamper piled with dirty clothes and more dirty clothes piled on the floor. I crouch behind the hamper, in the darkness, as I hear the front door close.

It's Lisa. I can tell by the way she walks. Dainty and beautiful. Even her footsteps are beautiful.

I hear a beep and I know she's checking her phone messages. I can't hear anything other than a tinny, sexless voice that rambles on for a minute, and then there is another

The Day the Leash Gave Way 73

beep followed by silence and I guess that's it for the messages. I hear a door in the kitchen open, hear it close, hear the pop of a soda can then the solid sound of it being set on the dining table. Then the dainty footsteps grow louder as they approach and before I know it the pantry door is open and there is Lisa, looking to the shelves on her right. She looks so beautiful, wearing a white cardigan and a black skirt, her hair pulled back into a ponytail as she reaches for a bag of chips. She doesn't glance anywhere near the hamper, and then she closes the door.

She opens the refrigerator again and makes herself a sandwich. I know she's making a sandwich because what else would she be making? And now she's sitting at the table, eating her sandwich and thinking her thoughts. Thinking about how she wants to renew her membership at the health club she used to go to, and how she misses playing tennis with her friend whose name is probably Valerie or Sabrina or some pretty name like that. Now she is contemplating the book she is currently reading, I bet, and it's probably *The Time Traveler's Wife*, or maybe *Reading Lolita in Tehran*. I wonder if she belongs to a book club. She probably does, or did at one time.

For a moment the entire house becomes a vacuum of total idleness. Then I hear her get up and hear the clink of dishes in the sink, and at the same time I hear the front door close and heavier footsteps enter the kitchen and James says "Hi, honey."

"Hi, sweetie," Lisa says.

And I think, It's only 1:30 in the afternoon. What are they both doing home at such an hour? They never come home for lunch. What day is today? Friday, yes, it's Friday. So shouldn't they be at work? Yes, they should be at work, they never come home for lunch and they should definitely be at work…Unless their jobs entitle them to a half-day on Fridays. That has to be what it is, that must be it, and now they're both home, and I'm stuck in the pantry amidst dirty clothes until they either leave again, or I can figure a way out without being caught.

I make a note to myself that, in the future, I need to leave by eleven on Fridays.

Then something interesting happens. Their voices become quiet and I can't make out what they're saying, and it goes on like this for a while.

Then James says, "Do you wanna hurt me?"

"James, what are you even talking about?"

"How do you think we pay for all this?"

And then I can't hear them again. Their voices have become like white noise with just the tiniest bit more distinction. The kind of a sound a ghost makes when it says something and can't make itself understood. It is mysteriously luring, and I'm compelled to listen, even if I can't make out what they're saying.

The spell is broken briefly as I recall my brother heckling me through my closed bedroom window. I tried to punch him and I punched the glass instead, shattering the window and cutting up my hand.

Then Lisa says, "Do you even believe what you're saying?"

A dismal and silent room, though soft words I can't make out are being spoken. These soft words are the words of James, and though I can't make them out, I know they are bitter and caustic. It's an odd feeling to me, thinking how right they were, how right they are, living in the right house and being the right people to live in this house that is so full of rightfulness. Yet here they are, and I can't determine if it's a fight, a spat, a quarrel, a contest, or merely a struggle.

Eventually James slams his hands down on the table and says, "That's it, I'm outta here," and I hear his footsteps retreat from the kitchen. I don't hear the front door open but I hear it close and it closes hard. A moment passes and, harping on what's happened, I hear Lisa cry. In my mind I can see her hands covering her face, I can see her using her palms to stifle screams. More than anything I want to step out of the pantry and comfort her, tell her everything will be all right—but I know I can't do that. I know that I have to get out. Maybe she'll go out after James and then I can slip out.

But she sits there crying for a very long time, and my feet have gone numb and I think, Hush, little angel. Everything will be all right.

Eventually I hear her get up. Her dainty footsteps, less dainty than before, retreat from the kitchen and then the front door closes again and as I step cautiously out of the pantry I hear her locking the place up. I give it a minute, peruse their CD collection and wait until her car pulls out of the driveway. After another minute has passed I make my way out of the house, locking it up behind me.

The next day at the park the only person I recognize is the guy shooting baskets. I want to tell him to go home to his wife and child, but know it wouldn't do any good and I might suffer a broken nose or jaw as a result. So I leave him be and sit on a rock and flitter the pages of a Tom Clancy book, which has a picture of a submarine on it and that's all I know. I think about what the Louis L'Amour book must be like and I wonder if Mark Twain is really as great as everyone says he is. I sit on a comfortable stone with a good view through the trees and the chain-linked fence to the Cohan residence.

I think about how my dad had beat me for shattering my bedroom window, calling me a "Little shit." Then I look up and see Lisa walking down into the park. Alone. She's alone and James isn't anywhere to be seen. She doesn't look happy and an idea crosses my mind.

I look down and force myself to commit the Clancy title to memory: *Submarine: A Guided Tour Inside a Nuclear Warship*. I heft the book in my right hand and then fling it out somewhere into the grass. Then I count back from ten and get up off my rock. I stroll down the slope, looking as bewildered as I can, and out the corner of my eye I see Lisa taking a seat on one of the picnic tables. She doesn't look happy. She looks far from it, but my bewilderment and stupidity catch her attention, though not enough for her to say anything.

Slowly and stupidly, I make my way over to her. I look up at her and say hello.

She says "Hi," but her voice doesn't have the beautiful magic it once did.

"I'm sorry to impose upon you," I say, and then I tell her that I've lost my book and ask her if she's seen a paperback anywhere around.

She tells me she hasn't, and I tell her it's a Tom Clancy book, and if she sees it, would she mind letting me know.

"Tell you what," she tells me, "I'll help you look." She climbs off the picnic table and starts searching with me. As she heads in the proper direction, I let her, and make a point of going the other way.

"Found it!" she calls out, and walks over to me and hands me the book.

I thank her, and for the first time I see the ring on her finger. I tell her I'm trying to learn about submarines and she says that's pretty cool and then tells me to enjoy it and to have a nice day. And then I watch her go back to the picnic table. She hesitates before she climbs onto it, and instead she makes her way back up the slope and heads for home.

I consider following her but don't, and then I don't see either of them for a few days.

The next time I see either of them I see James. I'm hanging out at a place called the Catamount Bar and Grill and I'm having a couple drinks and watching the Red Sox lose. I tolerate some drunk bastard ramble on and on about the government for about twenty minutes, and then I see James walk in and he isn't alone and the woman he's with isn't Lisa. The woman is a brunette, very pretty but lacking the charming presence Lisa possesses. To me, she looks like a slut.

I pretend to watch the game but really watch James and the brunette, and after they've had a couple of drinks James has his hand on the brunette's leg and he's keeping his face close to hers and they're whispering things into each other's ears. Something burns inside me and I get so mad. I get so mad because James is married to Lisa and he shouldn't be out with this brunette, no matter how pretty she is, and he shouldn't have his hand on her leg and his face shouldn't be so close to hers and there shouldn't be anything they have to whisper about.

I try to shrug it off. I try to let it go because I love them and even though I love them their lives are none of my business. What they do is what they do and even though I love them, and, in my own way, am a part of them, they are none of my business—until I think about Lisa crying at the kitchen table. I think about their fight that Friday afternoon and how sad Lisa had looked when she helped me find that book in the park.

I don't smoke but I ask the bartender if he has one. Begrudgingly, he gives me one but doesn't offer me a light, which is what I was hoping for. With three beers in me, I get up and approach James and the brunette and I ask if either of them has a light. They both tell me that they don't smoke and I tell them that's probably for the best and walk away, crumpling the cigarette as I make my way back to the bar. I watch the crumpled paper and tobacco fall from my fist into the ashtray and ask the bartender for my check. As he hands it to me I see James and the brunette kiss.

Two days later I'm at the park again, this time with a copy of *The Shining*. Lisa is sitting on one of the picnic tables with a book of her own, a hardback but that's all I can tell. I doubt it's a copy of *The Shining*. Me, I'm sitting on one of my rocks, fluttering the pages, acting as though I'm reading when what I'm really doing is watching her. After a while she looks up from her book, presses her fingers to her eyes and then stretches out her shoulders. When she does this she sees me. She's pretty far away but I can tell there's a little bit of a smile on her face. And then she waves at me with the same hand she'd used to sooth her eyes.

I wave back with the same hand I'd been fluttering the pages with. For a moment I wonder if we're gonna talk, but I realize quickly we're not going to and so I pretend to get back to my book. A minute later, when I glance up from page 347 without knowing what's going on in the story, I see she's buried back in her book, and so I don't care about page 347 or any of the pages before or after. I care that such a sweet, beautiful woman is being treated in such a way. That James is two-timing her, and that makes me angry. Really angry.

It's none of my business, I tell myself. It's none of my business even if I'm in love with her. But I'm not in love with her. I can't be in love with her because I don't know her. To me she is someone for me to focus all that pent-up energy on, even if I love her and care about her and want her to be happy. I'm not a Cohan, and wonder briefly if James is related to the composer, playwright, actor, dancer and singer George M. Cohan. James doesn't look like any of those things, other than maybe an actor. I guess he's a pretty good actor, given that he's getting away with what he's doing. I'm not a Cohan, but it hurts me, it pisses me off that he's treating her this way, the son of a bitch. Good actor, lousy bastard.

Another night passes uneventfully. I don't see Lisa or James at the park the next day, and that night I go back to the Catamount. I've had a few drinks but I'm still holding my own, watching a rerun of a sitcom on the television when I glance out the window and see James. He's smiling, gesticulating, and then he's throwing his head back in laughter. I don't see whom he's talking and smiling and laughing with until he passes by the window, and as he does, he places his arm around the shoulders of the woman I saw him with before.

The brunette.

I ask the bartender for another drink and he brings it to me. Then I drink it and watch the window, even though they are gone and not likely to return. My mind whirls about. I hear the laugh track from the television and I take it as a sign. Not that anyone is laughing at me, no, there's no reason for anyone to laugh at me. They're all laughing at Lisa. She's being two-timed and doesn't know it and it's like a comical situation in a Woody Allen movie.

A man at the bar turns to me. He's the same man that went off at me the other night about the government. He's drunk as all hell. "I'm supposed to believe," he says, "that the man who sat in a classroom reading a kids' book for seven minutes *after* he was told the country was under attack, who was warned is a domestic or international disaster, is a decisive man-of-action with the fortitu repeatedly about imminent threats against the country and chose to ignore them, who has traipsed off on vacation every time there de to run a nation!"

I try to ignore him but he is relentless. I look back at the window and wonder what James and Little Miss Brunette are doing now behind Lisa's beautiful and trusting back.

"I'm supposed to believe that the escalating violence, chaos and deaths in Iraq and Afghanistan are a sign of progress?" he goes on.

The Day the Leash Gave Way

I turn to him and tell him to shut the hell up and he gets all uppity and warns me not to tell him to shut up. So I tell him to fuck off, and suddenly both of us are shouting at each other. I've had a few drinks and I'm pissed off and don't want some goddamn psychotic liberal going off at me at the moment.

When we get too loud, before the bartender can say anything, a voice behind us tells us both to shut the hell up.

I turn around and see the guy who shoots hoops at the park. He gives me a look like he's trying to place me from somewhere, and I make the mistake of letting him know by telling him that he's a has-been, his wife and child resent him and that the Lakers fucking suck. I tell him that he drinks too much and can't let go of his glory days as a high school or possibly a college ball player. He never made it to the big time and he probably works construction or at Home Depot and he hates the world for cheating him out of his dream. And while I'm saying all of this he's getting to his feet, and then he's standing right in front of me and I call him a loser with no other goals than a goal long since passed.

That's when he hits me, and everything spins around and I suddenly find myself on the floor. I lay there for a minute, and think about Lisa at home, and James off with that no-good bitch of a brunette. Then I stumble up to my feet, spit out what I hope will be pain but is only spit, and ask the bartender for my check.

I pay the man and leave a good tip and then make my way to Wal-Mart. It's about a fifteen-minute drive and I take it cautiously because I've been drinking. I purchase what I need and then stop at a convenience store and get something else and then I go home. I pour some bleach into a glass and then add some ice. Then I add some more ice and then a small amount of nail polish remover and when I've added that I add more ice. Then I add some more ice and wait about twenty minutes until the liquid in the glass has clouded. I go through a couple more minor procedures and pour the liquid into a sports water bottle, then go into my linen closet and grab two washcloths.

The park is different at night. All the specters, the evil sides of children—the angry sides that punch through windows—come out at night. They are like demons and they force me to see contorted faces and frightening things. I sit on the rock best situated to view the Cohan household, and I see that there is only one car in the driveway. I know it's Lisa's car, and so I wait and wait, and think about Lisa, so beautiful, and James, a son of a bitch who doesn't realize that what he has is the greatest thing anyone in the world could ever have.

Eventually headlights spring up and sparkle into the street. I watch the car pull into the Cohan driveway and I see James get out. He looks tired and a little drunk but he has the aura of a man who has gotten laid. I wait for him to go inside, give it another minute, and then make my way out of the park and across the street. I watch the living room light go off, then I creep up the eight steps and sit in the yard, passing the sports bottle back and forth between my hands.

I let this go on for over an hour. Then I get up, walk slowly to the front door and let myself in. The house is quiet. All the lights are off but I know my way around well enough now that I can find my way.

The bedroom door is open. The curtains are drawn open as well, and moonlight is spilling in and casting gray light upon the sleeping couple in bed together.

I pop the stopper on the sports bottle and it makes a tiny hiss. Then I wait patiently for a while. When I've waited long enough I pull the two washcloths out of my back pocket, and douse them both with the homemade chloroform. Crossing to the left side of the bed, where James is asleep, I study both of their faces. Such a perfect couple, the right kinds of people and the right kinds of people for this right kind of house.

But they aren't right. James has done something very wrong and I know he's guilty. I saw it. I saw it with my own eyes. I don't have to witness it in detail to know what he's doing, and I don't know what he's told Lisa, but Lisa, such a beautiful, perfect woman, so beautiful my mind boggles and dazzles at the very thought of her, doesn't deserve to be treated this way. And so I take the washcloths and cover both of their mouths and noses.

They struggle, but both of them are asleep and their fights are both short-lived and futile. I stuff the washcloths back into my pocket and think of how beautiful they are. Both of them so lovely, yet James screwed it up. I had hoped to drink soda or even beer with him in front of his big-screen TV, but now that I know the kind of person he is, that will never happen. The way I see it, he forfeited his humanity card, and I clench my right hand into a tight fist.

My first punch doesn't do a whole lot more than jostle his head, but the next one makes a cracking sound, and with the next I can feel his teeth loosening, breaking beneath my blows. I punch him more times than I can count, again and again until I actually have a piece of one of his teeth lodged into the flesh of my knuckles and there is blood all over his pillow and in my mind I quote Shakespeare. *How sharper than a serpent's tooth it is to have a thankless child!*

Unconscious, in the moonlight, he looks like a very sorry, very sad jack-o-lantern.

I think of my father calling me a "Little shit" and beating me for shattering a window, and then I walk around the bed to Lisa.

She's unconscious but beautiful. I get water up my nose while in the middle of a swimming hole, and now it comes out my eyes. I allow myself to stroke her hair three times. I plant a gentle kiss on her forehead and whisper, "The monster's gone, Lisa. The monster's gone and won't hurt you any more."

Then I rise up, make my way out of the bedroom, down the hall and out the front door, locking it behind me.

I cross the street, run my fingers along the chain-linked fence, and then enter the park, so dark and gloomy, but with less antagonism than before. I make my way across the grass and think about the man with the black lab—the poor lonely bastard—and when I reach the river I toss away my copy of the Cohan house key, a key for the right kind of house where the right kinds of people live, and my Christmas dream evaporates into the darkness surrounding me.

With my mind I see that dog jumping high into the air to catch that sunny yellow Frisbee. In the dark, sports bottle in hand, I think about how I forgot to bring a book this time.

I wonder what book it would have been.

Two-Thirty-Six

It took me two minutes and thirty-six seconds to realize I'd been shot. The moment I heard the blast, the moment that searing heat cut into me and blackness rained into my eyes, a clock began ticking in my skull. One, two, three, and so on, and each time it reached sixty seconds there was a ding, like a dinner bell, accompanied by a deep, echoing voice, saying "One" the first time and "Two" the second. Hands fumbled around me, reaching into my pockets and taking things. Then there was just the counter, the metronome, the second hand, whatever.

At two and thirty-six my eyes crept open and the first thing I saw was my own hand covered in my own blood, both shrouded in the darkness of the night. The person I falsely accused of killing me—seeing how I wasn't dead—was long gone, but I was still aware of the pain in my side. I struggled up into a sitting position, took in the empty street around me, and tried to review my circumstances.

I was walking to my car from a restaurant at which I'd had a rather unfortunate blind date. Not that she was unpleasant, but there were too many secrets buried inside her, and it kept the conversation to below minimal. I spent a lot of time looking out the window, where a man in a baseball cap paced around for a long while, chain-smoking. Although I didn't have a good time, and although she didn't have a good time and insisted going Dutch, I refused and paid for both meals, which came to not an unreasonable amount. We ended outside the restaurant with a friendly handshake and good night, then I turned and was on my way to my car. I had parked a block away and when I rounded the corner it felt like a ghost town, only without all the western attributes. There was light and shadow, but it was mostly shadow, and then came a moving shadow and a gruff voice that said, "Matt Collins?"

When I said yeah, there was a momentary hesitation, and then the blast came. Only once, but it was enough to put me down and set the clock ticking in my head.

It took me a while, but I managed to struggle to my feet. Though I was no longer blind, blackness still spilled in and out of my eyes like quick rinses of unconsciousness, and the pain in my side flared like a bad hemorrhoid in the wrong part of my body.

My friend Steve had told me—he's the one who'd set us up—that Angela, the girl I'd just seen, had been through some rough times lately, and had recently gotten out of a bad relationship. Myself, I'd recently gotten out of a bad relationship that involved constant shouting, which then elevated to throwing things, which again elevated to throwing things at each other. She was a much better pitcher than I was.

Then something else went off in my head and my blood ran cold. I don't know why. It was so insignificant at the time. It still seemed insignificant, but, obviously, it wasn't. When I'd spoken to Angela on the phone that afternoon in order to make the night's arrangements, I'd glanced over at the red and white wall clock I'd bought at Target for $12.99. The time was 2:36. While at the exact same moment, like a split screen or an image-over-image cross-fade, I remembered being hit with a plastic drinking glass. The moment the glass struck me, the first thing I looked at was not the owner of the limb that propelled it, but rather to the digital clock on a nearby table. It was 2:36. Afternoon or morning, I don't recall, but it was 2:36.

Dizzy, aware that I'd lost a lot of blood, feeling it sticky in my clothes, I made my way back toward the restaurant, increasingly becoming aware that I wasn't headed for the restaurant. Actually, I didn't know where I was headed. In fact, after a moment, I didn't know where I was. The street was different, though it was a street I knew from somewhere, a familiar part of downtown, and I was not quite walking and not quite staggering east.

It seemed so random. From out of nowhere, suddenly I'm shot, mugged. The only thing that didn't seem random was that the killer—attempted killer—knew my name. Matt Collins, me. I'm not in the encyclopedia but I'm in the phone book and I work as a copy editor for the local newspaper, so I have a credit in there, too.

Pools of blackness filled my eyes then washed away. Was Angela's bad relationship one of intense jealousy? To the point of violence? What were all those secrets she had bottled up inside her?

The moment I came to a conclusion, a ticking started in my head. It was like the Scattergories timer being amplified through a loudspeaker. One, two, three, and so on, and I watched my feet move in front of me, become swallowed in black, then move in front of me again. I knew every second. Some odd part of my brain counted every click. And though I didn't know where or why, I kept walking. I remembered my ex calling me a bastard, remembered her tearing up my tax return check. And the seconds went on as I recalled the man standing outside the restaurant for a long time as Angela and I did what little conversing we did. Angela didn't seem to notice him.

There was a ding, like a dinner bell, and a deep, echoing voice said, "One." I felt more blood on my clothes, more pain in my side, and darkness swallowed me up then spit me out again. Steve had told me that Angela could be timid, and that she had been especially so since her break-up. Maybe for fear of her ex-boyfriend? There are all kinds of stories like that. They happen every day. I do the copy-editing on some of them. Crimes of passion, *Jealous Man Slays Lover*, or *Jealous Lover Suspects Infidelity, Murders Friend*.

Then the bell rang again, and the voice said, "Two."

I counted the seconds more consciously than before, wondering about the times, trying to piece it together while trying to piece everything else together at the same time.

Twenty-eight. Twenty-nine, and suddenly a car drove by me. Thirty-two. Thirty-three. The streetlight just ahead was green—thirty-four—and I watched the car begin to pass through the intersection—thirty-five—and get sprayed with light—thirty-six—then get slammed by a pick-up truck going way over the speed limit.

There was a bell at thirty-six, but no voice. The two people in the fast-moving vehicle got out, assessed the damage as I approached, then checked on the passengers in the other car. Of which there was one. His face was covered in blood but I recognized him. He was

The Day the Leash Gave Way

already dead. On the passenger's seat were a baseball cap, a pack of Marlboros, a pistol, and my wallet.

Darkness filled my eyes again. The dizziness became too much. My legs became rubber and then became jelly, then finally melted down to the asphalt. One of the two people was on their cell phone and the other had noticed me and saw that I was bleeding and asked me if I was all right. Things cleared again briefly and I realized where I was. Had I kept heading east, the direction my perpetrator was headed, we would have found ourselves at the same place.

The accident took place right down the street from my ex's house.

A Dead Man's Burrito

Ted kissed his date goodnight but didn't invite her in on account that he had somewhere else to be. Rose had been a fine woman and he wouldn't mind seeing her again. Maybe next time he'd have her inside. For now he watched her drive away and give a little wave, which he returned, then pulled out his keys and inserted the proper one into his lock. The moment Rose's Toyota was out of sight he removed the key, stuck it back into his pocket and took a short jog down to where the Nissan was waiting.

Once under the glow of the streetlight the back door opened and Ted climbed in. Jose and Markus were up front, Markus behind the wheel. Philip sat in the back next to Ted. Philip had his mask resting on his lap and a 12-gauge between his knees—barrel pointed up. Ted told him he should point the barrel at the floor. Philip said he knew what he was doing.

Jose turned around in his seat and extended a mask back to Ted, a cyclops with pointy ears he'd picked up at the drugstore last Halloween. A little P-32 was on the floor at Ted's feet and Ted wanted to voice that he didn't like the idea of Philip being the one with the shotgun, especially since the guy insisted on having the barrel pointed up. But he kept his mouth shut and waited for Jose to give instructions.

Jose didn't feel much like talking yet.

Markus steered the car onto I-25 and drove it a short while then took the second exit they came to, which brought them to the outskirts of Cerrillos and a stone's throw away from the state penitentiary.

"Ain't that where Jules is?" Markus asked.

"*Si*," said Jose, who rarely spoke Spanish but occasionally slipped a word or phrase in, usually when he was excited or nervous. "Guy keeps talking about breaking outta there."

Ted had only met Jules once, just before the guy got picked up for his loss of self-control at Taco Bell. If only there hadn't been onions on his burrito those pimply employees would still be alive and Jules wouldn't be behind bars, never to have another burrito as long as he lived, with or without onions.

About two miles down Markus made a left turn onto a lonely road where the streetlights disappeared and trees took their place. The house they were headed for was a quarter mile down—the first right after the first set of mailboxes.

Philip giggled. Ted always found Philip to be damn annoying and pretty irresponsible; and he really didn't like him being the one with the shotgun.

"Okay," Jose said, inspecting his Dracula mask in the moonlight, "we wanna be in and out in under five minutes. When we go in we have to go full force. Don is a short tempered man who sleeps with his wife beside him and his Uzi beneath him."

Ted briefly thought about having Rose sleep beside him—maybe next time.

The Day the Leash Gave Way

"So's we gotta be quick," Jose continued. "In and out, ASAP. We get what the bastard owes me, plus everything else he has as interest." Then he turned around in his seat again and shifted a cold, hard stare between Philip and Ted. "Just don't touch his wife unless it's in self-defense. His lady hasn't done nothing wrong."

Philip giggled again. Ted wanted to slap him across the face. Markus started whistling, as he always did just before an attack. Jose told him to shut up. Ted wished he'd tell Philip the same thing.

Don and Jose had pulled a heist together about two months back. Some sort of armored car deal they'd cooked up between just the two of them. They'd pulled it off well enough, but Don took off with all the money and left Jose in the dust. Jose didn't much care for that.

Making the right turn after the mailboxes the pavement was gone and the road got bumpy. Markus started whistling again but checked himself and stopped before Jose could say anything. In the near distance the porch light was on but other than that the house up ahead was dark. It was late but Ted didn't know exactly how late. He'd had a lot of fun with Rose and lost track of time. He lifted his wrist and tried aiming it so the moonlight could hit upon his watch. Just as he got it angled properly the car hit a deep trench and Ted's arm flew up then down and a thunderous boom exploded beside him. A good portion of the rear windshield was gone and most of Philip's head was gone with it, all except some chunky bits at the neck.

"What the hell was that?" Markus shouted.

"Philip just blew his head off," Ted said, half frightened, half pleased and completely disgusted. With the light the way it was it looked like someone had thrown a pot of chunky beef stew on the ceiling and seat. Philip's neck was still totally in tact, just splintered and shredded at the top with little bits dripping off it.

Panicked, Markus turned for a better look. Jose yelled for him to watch the fucking road. A split second later the left front tire hit a bump and the car lost control right in front of the house and slammed sideways into a BMW, pinning Philip's door closed. Jose called Markus an idiot then cussed in Spanish and climbed out. As he reached for his gun and mask the door of the house opened and a man in a nice bathrobe came out with a cigar in his mouth and an Uzi in his hands. Jose had told the others that Don was a shoot-first-ask-questions-later kind of guy. Proof was shown as the man emptied the entire Uzi into Jose, who collapsed to the ground with more holes than a fly swatter.

Ted aimed his P-32 through the seats, pulled the trigger three times and the man in the bathrobe lost his cigar and did a sort of spastic dance before falling backwards and cracking his head on the ground.

A woman came out with her hair up in curlers. Seeing both Don and Jose, she let out a Yoko Ono-esque scream and raced back into the house.

Markus reached across and pulled Jose's door shut, then hit the gas and steered the car back up the driveway, hitting bumps and trenches but keeping it on the path.

"She's gonna call the cops," Markus said, more to himself than to Ted or Philip, not that Philip could hear him.

"Just keep your cool, man," Ted told him, trying to find the cool within himself.

They got to the paved road. Markus didn't stop or even slow down. He hung a left and pressed the gas pedal to the floor. Just as he did he saw a large construction cone with arms and a head directly in front of him. Slamming the brakes he was too late. The cone flip-flopped over the windshield and roof, then the car came to a complete stop and Markus climbed out, for some reason cursing his mother.

"What the hell are you doing?" Ted shouted.

"We're leaving a trail, man. Gotta cover our asses. Gonna be something every five feet if we're not careful."

"Dammit." Ted climbed out, glad to at least be away from Philip's headless body, and joined Markus twenty feet back at the construction cone, which was moving and coughing occasionally. Then he realized it wasn't a cone at all.

"Son of a whore," Markus said. "It's Jules."

When it came to detail Ted's night vision wasn't too good. From what he could make out there was a dark flat place where the guy's nose should have been. One leg was bent clear up sideways, the ankle almost touching his ear.

Jules coughed again, spit to the side then asked Markus why he'd hit him.

"Didn't see you, Jules. Didn't know it was you. What you doing walking in the center of the road?"

Jules had no answer for this. Markus and Ted bent his leg down, tolerating his screams, then picked him up and carried him to the car, where they put him in the back with Philip. Jules tried protesting being in back with a guy who'd blown his own head off but didn't have the energy to do anything about it. He told Markus and Ted that he was paralyzed from the waist down and the rest of him didn't feel too good either.

"It's raining blood back here," Jules said.

"Not on your side it isn't," Ted told him.

"And it smells like crap."

"I don't have control of what Philip did after he blew his head off."

"Damn, that's Philip?"

"That's right. It's raining Philip."

They started up the road again. Staring out the side window, Ted thought about how he'd told that asshole Philip not to aim that shotgun up towards his own head. Christ, hadn't the guy learned anything in his years of this kind of work? Obviously not, the dumbass.

Markus noticed something strange at the bottom of the windshield. At first it was hard to make out what it was, then once he figured it out he didn't know whether to laugh or throw up—Jules' nose. He wondered how it had gotten such a clean cut. Flipping on the wipers Markus watched the nose slide up the glass then stop in the left corner. He put the wipers at full speed but they wouldn't touch it, and even with lots of wiper fluid it stayed where it was. Markus sighed, then in one swift motion he rolled down the window, reached out, grabbed Jules' nose and flung it onto the road.

"I feel awful," said Jules.

"So what happened to you?" Ted asked, then added, "Other than you've been hit by a car?"

The Day the Leash Gave Way

"Broke outta jail. Gave one of the guards my sister's number—God, she's a whore—and he didn't notice when I slipped through a little hole in the fence. The hole's been there forever. Guards and the warden kept meaning to have it fixed but could never find the time." He laughed pathetically. "This should be a lesson to them."

"Damn, Jules, I'm sorry." Markus got onto I-25 and headed back to town. "What do you need? What can we do for you? I mean, if there's anything at all, just name it."

Jules thought a moment. "Well," he said, "I could sure use a burrito. One without onions." Then he coughed and asked, "You still see Jose? How's old Jose doing?"

"Actually, he was killed about two minutes before we hit you."

"That sucks."

When they got back into town they took the quickest route to Taco Bell, opting for the drive-thru rather than going inside, since Jules couldn't walk. Markus emphasized no onions on the burrito, "and I mean not a one," he said.

Waiting in line Ted suddenly remembered that Philip was still in the back with no head. Others might frown upon seeing him. Good thing no one was behind them in line, given that the back window was half smashed and dripping with blood, brains and skull fragments. Thinking quickly before they got up to the window, Ted reached into the back and grabbed both his cyclops mask and Philip's *Creature from the Black Lagoon* mask. He snatched Jose's Dracula mask from the floor and stuffed both cyclops and Dracula into the Creature, giving it a bit more form. Turning around again he fitted the mask over Philip's neck, pulling it down to the shoulders and wanting to throw up. Boy, he thought, if Rose could see me now. Of course one never knows; maybe Rose was into kinky stuff like rubber masks.

At the drive-up window the pimpled-faced teenager looked curiously into the back at the crippled man with no nose and the dude with the monster mask who didn't seem to have a neck. He either didn't notice the blood in the back seat or wasn't saying anything about it. He handed Markus their food and told them to have a good night.

Jules spit. He couldn't move enough to roll down his window so he just spit into Philip's lap, losing two teeth. Philip didn't seem to mind. Actually, with the mask on, the guy looked rather chipper. Ted thought it was an improvement.

Markus parked in the parking lot away from the other cars. The food helped cover up the coppery smell of blood, which was appreciated by all. Ted fed Jules his burrito, every so often turning back to eat some of his Double Decker taco. Both couldn't help worrying that the burrito might have an onion lurking in it somewhere.

"Well," Markus said after some time had passed, "what do we do now?"

"I'm thinking," Ted said with his mouth full, "maybe we should just go home and never see or talk to each other again. Forget we ever did any of this stuff and forget we ever knew Philip or Jose."

"Can't believe Jose is really gone."

They chewed their food in a moment of silence. Ted chewed with his mouth open because Philip didn't deserve no damn silence from him.

"What about Jules?"

"How you doing, Jules?"

"Uhh," said Jules.

"I guess we could take him to the hospital," Ted said. "But if they fix him they'll be throwing him right back in the slammer."

Markus remembered being in the hospital with a broken leg when he was a kid. His mother was pushing him down the hall in a wheelchair and a nurse came from out of nowhere and tripped over his busted leg, simultaneously smacking him in the head with her clipboard. No, he couldn't live with himself if he put Jules in that kind of situation.

Ted finished his taco and realized he was still hungry. Jules still had half a burrito but Ted didn't feel right eating any of it. Not when the man was in the shape he was, with no nose and all. He was debating whether he wanted to go inside and get another taco when Jules coughed blood against the back of the seat in front of him and said, "Gimme another bite…quick."

Ted turned around and granted Jules' request, then watched as Jules' eyes rolled up into his head and the beans, beef, cheese and tortilla oozed out of his mouth, most of it clinging to his chin.

Turning in his seat, Markus saw Jules, then cursed and wiped a tear from his eye as he'd wiped Jules' nose from the windshield. "Can't believe of all people, Jules was the one who happened to get in front of our car."

"It's a damn shame," Ted said, seeing the bright side of the moment as well because now there was half a burrito no one else was going to eat.

"All the guy ever wanted was to be a painter," said Markus, thumbing another tear. "Just wanted to paint and eat Taco Bell every day." He looked at Ted. "I went to visit him one time in prison. Said they never served Mexican food at all, and the only paints he could get were finger paints."

"A damn shame," Ted said again, and looked anxiously at the burrito in his hand. He wondered how tacky it would be if he were to eat a dead man's burrito.

"Man, he loved this place." Markus looked through the brains and bone shrapnel to the Taco Bell behind them. An idea crossed his mind. Yes, the more he thought about it, the more it seemed like the right thing to do. He had to do it. Jules would want it this way.

"At least he died with burrito in his mouth," said Ted, then decided to hell with it, and started eating the burrito. Hell, no one else was going to.

Markus wiped away one more tear then started the car, climbed out, opened the back door, checked for onlookers, grabbed Jules by his orange shirt and flopped him to the pavement. Before the body had settled on the asphalt he got back in and drove away.

"I think he's happier there," Ted remarked, finishing the last of the burrito. He wondered if Rose would want to see him again if she knew all he had done tonight.

"What about Philip?" Markus asked. "He's gonna start stinking before too long."

"Maybe we should go put him with Jose and that other guy."

"No way. I'm not going anywhere near that place again."

"Well," Ted thought a moment—"Is he married?"

"I believe so. Yes, I'm sure of it."

"You know where his house is?"

The Day the Leash Gave Way

Markus turned the car around and started whistling. There was no Jose to tell him to shut up anymore and Ted didn't seem to mind. It took a little time to remember where Philip's house was because he'd only been there once and it was a while ago.

They parked alongside the curb. Ted saw a gray Toyota with a bumper sticker on the back that said *Make New Friends But Keep The Old* parked in the driveway. He only now recalled that sticker being on the back of Rose's car.

Climbing out, they took Philip out of the back, making sure to keep the mask around his neck. They carried him up to the porch and sat him down in one of the chairs. Even with a rubber monster mask on he looked very much at home. His shirt was soaked with blood but it seemed to add to his disposition.

Ted went back to the car and collected all the Taco Bell wrappers, put them in the bag then brought the bag to the porch and tossed it into Philip's lap, figuring they might as well clean out the car a bit while they were at it.

As they drove away Markus struggled with the guilt of hitting Jules with his car. He was also angry because cleaning the inside was going to be a pain in the ass, and he was gonna have to replace the rear window. It was nice of Ted to take the Taco Bell wrappers out at least. Ted was often considerate with things like that.

Ted thought about seeing Rose's car at Philip's house. Markus could have had the wrong place, given he'd only been there once before; but either way, Rose was there. If indeed it wasn't Philip's house then Rose merely had a big surprise coming to her next time she stepped out onto her porch, and Ted didn't like the potential shame he might feel over that. On the other hand, if Rose was married to Philip, it meant she was a cheating whore, while on the bright side, she was now truly available.

Markus dropped Ted off at home. Ted offered to help clean out the car but Markus said no thanks and he'd do it in the morning. He just wanted to get to bed for the night.

Right then and there, they agreed to never speak again, and admit complete ignorance of one another's existence.

They said goodnight and Markus drove down to the corner and ran the stop sign. A siren blared and lights flashed and pulled Markus to the side of the road.

Ted inserted his key into the lock, turned it, then went inside and got ready for bed.

Hope Is an Inanimate Desire

It had ceased. After what had seemed an eternity the pain was finally gone. Now there was nothing for him to do but wait until someone spotted his car and got some help.

He wouldn't deny that he'd been drinking. If he did, he knew that the only person he'd be lying to would be himself. But it hadn't been his fault. The spare tire had flown from the wheel. On his way to the bar he'd run over a nail, though it wasn't until he'd come out, drunk off his ass, that he'd noticed the flat and had to change it with blurry eyes and fuzzy mind. Tye and Frank had tried to stop him, telling him he was too messed up, piss drunk; but as usual, Calvin refused to listen, and now it was obvious that he hadn't put the tire on tight enough. And because he didn't listen he was now stuck, strapped upside-down in the driver's seat of his car.

Dusk. The sun was creeping away and soon he would be waiting in darkness. The chances of somebody seeing him at night were slim. No one had seen him since he'd crashed two hours earlier. Why the hell should anyone see him in the dark?

Worse yet, he couldn't move.

He hadn't been able to move for over two hours now and was horrified that he might really be paralyzed. So he hung, immobile, upside-down and held up only by the safety belt that had saved his life, or had possibly just ruined it; in which case he would hope for death. But there was no point concerning himself with any of this at the moment. It was best to just wait. Somebody would come for him. Someone would have to see him eventually.

The sun crept away behind the hills. He felt himself swaying gently, back and forth, back and forth, like a clothesline dancing in a lonely breeze. His view was little more than a dashboard, a few weeds and stones peeping through a shield of cracked glass with blood all over it. The upside-down clock told him that it was five of eight. If no one saw him by nine then most likely it wouldn't be until daybreak that he'd be spotted and rescued. If he could make it through the night.

There was nothing for him to listen to other than the sound of his own dying breath. The few parts of his body that he could still feel were tingling, and his head still spun from shock and from the alcohol he had consumed earlier, along with the amount of blood which undoubtedly had made its way to his brain.

Why had he been so stupid? What kind of an idiot changes a tire while drunk, only to go out driving on it?

It didn't matter. What was done was done. It wouldn't do him any good to beat himself up over it. He already seemed to have crippled himself beyond repair. There was no sense in adding the mind into it, if it could by chance be avoided.

The Day the Leash Gave Way

It was a long and winding road, up and down a mountainous terrain. He had been in the outside lane—the lane with the twenty-foot drop off on the side. And as he wouldn't deny that he'd been drinking, he wouldn't deny that he had been speeding. Taking a fast left turn, there was a popping sound from the back and the car jumped, spun out of control, fish-tailed, right, left, right, left, then off the side and down—down the rocky slope, round and round. And for a very brief moment he could have sworn he saw himself outside the vehicle, watching, screaming bloody murder.

It had simply been a dumb move all around. And now he was paying for it; and he would pay for it until he died, be it in five minutes or fifty years.

You did it this time, Calvin, he thought to himself. You finally pushed yourself over the edge…literally…over the edge. You knew this would happen some day. Your family and friends kept telling you that someday you'd kill yourself if you didn't stop. But did you listen? No, of course not. Do you ever listen to what other people say? Sometimes it really is a smart thing to do, y'know. Oh well, maybe this will finally teach you.

He told himself to shut up.

And now you won't even listen to yourself.

His head ached like someone was stirring stones in his skull. Hanging upside-down for as long as he had been was really getting to him, and he was starting to feel as though his head might soon explode.

The wind was picking up and the dusk-shrouded weeds began to move a bit more than before.

Why hasn't anybody seen me? I think that I even smashed through a side-rail. Yes, I know I did. Someone would see the damage and then look down here and find me, wouldn't they? But why hasn't anybody stopped? I've heard cars go by. I'm sure I've heard cars go by. But that's all they do…go by.

Drip, drip, drip. There was a subtle dripping sound below, above his head. Since he couldn't move, he used his mind to probe the parts of his body that he could until he had found its source.

Well, well, well, my head is bleeding in back.

He looked at the blood-covered windshield.

Front and back—way to go, Calvin.

He could only imagine what he looked like.

He hung for a while, listening to the steady rhythm of his own dripping gore. Drip-drop, drip-drop. Be-bop-a-drip-drop. Be-bop-a-drip-drop…Thoughts only, he began to sing songs of no meaning, creating melodies in his head as he went along, trying to think up words, trying to pass the time until someone saw him and the carnage he'd created. Many of the words were not words at all, though they began to come together in their own way. The darkening weeds swayed back and forth, as if dancing to his tunes.

Be-bop-a-drip-drop…
I feel something funny in the back of my head.
I hear something that's funny, something funny
someone said. I turn the clock past zero, but
it still keeps my time. The allegories hero

never thinks about time.
Be-bop-a-drip-drop…

He sang it through his head, over and over, trying to think up another verse. But no other would come.

Though his body was almost completely deprived of sensation and motion, he realized—with unpleasant decisiveness—that he had to relieve himself. And he was immobile. Would he be able to control it? Or would it just come when it was time? This was, though in some ways it seemed near unimportant, the major priority at the moment. Images of his car seat acting as an upside-down urinal began to enter his mind and refused to disappear. In reality, he knew that if the unimaginable happened, his own strung up body would be acting as the receptacle for his urine. He was never into golden showers. There were things that he found far less appealing, but this was close to the top of the list, and he had no interest in experimenting, especially with his own, or in this particular situation.

The sun was now entirely gone. There was nothing more than black. He was alone in the dark. He could still hear the slight breeze outside, serving as his only companion. It brushed across his face through the broken driver's side window.

"Hello, wind," he said as best he could, which was very weak.

"Swooosh," said the wind.

Calvin thought for a long span of time. Then, with the same weak voice he asked: "Am—am I gonna get out of this? Am I gonna live? Survive, I mean? Or is this my time? Is it my time to leave this world I've known for so long? Thirty-two years? Have I really…been alive for thirty-two years?"

"Swooosh …"

The wind's answer left Calvin filled with drunken hope. It continued to swoosh and swish its words of comfort, mixing with the rhythm of his dripping head.

Be-bop-a-drip-drop…

"If I get out of this," he told the wind, himself, or anyone who might be listening, "I promise." He paused. "I promise to give all this shit up." His lungs refused him any more words. They felt like wet sponges, soaked through and through.

I'll give all this shit up. Yes, sir, yes I will. No more drinking, no more driving, no more not listening to people when you know you should be. No more goddamn pride ruling over smarts.

"Calvin, if you'd just listen—"

"No."

"Why do you always have to be such a stubborn jerk?"

"Fuck you! You don't tell me what to do. You don't run my life!"

—*That's pretty typical of you, Cal. Your standard talk, your standard conversation with any friend or family member. Your standard defense, when defense is unnecessary. You just can't stand to think of someone else being right. Because we all know that you are always right, ain't that the truth of it? Mr. Calvin with the last name I forget. The man who is never wrong and always right…What the hell is my last name…?*

The Day the Leash Gave Way

He wanted to shift with discomfort of this realization, but was unable. His body still refused movement. His body simply swayed, back and forth, back and forth. Even the wind seemed to have lost interest. All was silent. He could no longer remember the song he had been singing either. Something about heroes, though nothing more could he remember. But the steady dripping of blood continued.

—*Be-bop-a-drip-drop...*
Fast rush, train brush, throw wet on dry
and fly into a cherry pie. Flying notebook,
I wanna go home. I is high if the eye is high.
If I had a dollar for every time I puked,
that would sure as hell make me puke.
Be-bop-a-drip-drop...

With the new song of nothingness, he found that his eyelids were beginning to slip closed. Open, close, open, close, and then they closed and remained so.

He was at the bar.

The wind sat beside him in near swooshing silence.

Both had beers in front of them. The wind did not have to worry about driving drunk, for it could be anywhere and everywhere all at once, if it so desired.

"Shon't shrive," the wind said. "Shon't shrive shrunk."

It told him that if he got into that car, revved up the engine and pulled onto the road, he could kiss his ass goodbye. And though he knew he shouldn't, and he knew that it was too late, he refused to let even the wind tell him what to do. "What is this? Some kind of fucking public service announcement?" Flinging his beer off to the side, he stood up and half stumbled, half stormed out of the bar—out into the sky and its preparation for evening.

"Goddamn wind." He inserted the key into the ignition, turned it. The car started.

Calvin woke up, still upside down, swaying gently, blood still dripping from his head, though much slower than before. He figured that it was because he was still upside-down, the blood would still not cease to flow. Drip...drip...drip. The difference between now and before was that he could now feel pain, crawling through his body, but only through specific areas, through his head, and dripping from somewhere near his brain. Drip...drip...drip...

Outside the night was blacker than Death. He wondered what time it was. It was too dark to see the clock. The wind blew through the trees outside, singing silent songs with their swaying branches. There was no moon out tonight. If there was, it was sure doing a great job of hiding.

Then, he noticed. What he'd hoped wouldn't happen had, while he was asleep. His crotch and shirt, all the way up his back and front and sides, as the shirt pressed against his stomach and chest and back, he realized that it was damp. He smelled the urine. It wasn't as bad as he thought it would be. Maybe it was because he had been fighting with the wind when he had done it, and he hadn't been around for the experience. Didn't matter—there was nothing he could do about it. It would dry up. If nothing else, his bladder felt relieved. Plus, he had more important things to consider. As he thought about his bladder, his stomach entered into his mind. He was hungry. Though it was not audible, he could sense growling sounds coming from within. Doing his best to forget about it, the more he tried, the more he thought about forgetting it, which caused him to think about it more.

Sing another song, he told himself, think of another song that can help you to take your mind off it.

No song would come to him, and he realized that the dripping sound had stopped. There was no more beat to follow. No more drip, drip. No more rhythm. He knew that it would be best if could simply sleep—sleep and leave all his troubles behind until morning. For all he knew, morning may only be an hour or so away. It would be preferable to just slip into a deep slumber until he was discovered. Or better yet, just sleep for a while, and wake up to find that nothing had actually happened. That the situation he was in was really nothing more than a bad dream, and that he would wake up in his own bed.

For the moment, though, he knew that all he could do was hope. Hope is a word that should always be used in quotes, he thought. Hope is a desire accompanied by expectation and anticipation. And what if…what if no one found him until it was too late? The hope would all be for nothing. To him, at the moment, hope seemed the most trivial thing in the world, inanimate, pointless, though he found that he could not expel it from within himself. There was nothing more for him to do than this very human thing—perform the trivial, inanimate, mind bending desire that is "hope."

He heard another car pass by, up high above him, without even slowing down as it passed by the unseen wreckage. Yes, he knew that in the night, he was invisible. No one was going to find him until daybreak, maybe not even then.

Of course they would find him. There were enough people in town who knew his regular routine, who would notice when he didn't show up here or there. They would start asking around, and then there would be a search. The search would not take long, for it was a small town, and he had driven his car off the road—the road which led to his home. They would most certainly check, and when they found the broken side rail, they would stop, and they would see him, and rescue him. Maybe it would be later in the afternoon, or even in the evening, but he would be found, he was certain of that. He would be found, rescued, and taken to the hospital. It would be a two-hour drive to get there, and he would be lying in the back of an ambulance the entire way, with paramedics staring at him, poking him. But he would most likely hear his last name, and he would be safe. The doctors would help him. They would rid him of the small pains, and give him back his movement.

If only he could move.

If he could move, it would be as simple as bringing his right hand to the buckle of his seat belt, pressing the little red button, with the word "PRESS" embossed on it, and he would drop

down. Maybe then he could, if nothing else, climb out of the car, and lay in a patch of dead weeds and hard stones. Anything would be better than swaying back and forth, upside-down, with most all of his blood pooling in his head.

I've gotta get down, he told himself. Gotta get down…get out of the car.

The Day the Leash Gave Way

But he knew it was impossible. The few parts of his body that he could feel were filled with nothing more than weak, numbing pain.

There was nothing for his eyes to see. Nothing but black lay before him, a dark cover wrapped around his world—nothing but a void. His only company being the wind, which had grown sleepy. He felt, in some ways, as he did when he was six or seven years old. Back a quarter of a mile behind his house he had climbed down into a pit: a pit too steep and deep for him to climb back out of. His brother had been witness, and ran back to the house to fetch his father. In that fifteen minutes of waiting he had never felt so alone, so scared, so helpless. This time, however, he knew that his father would not be coming to his aide.

His father had been dead eight years now. An aneurysm while in bed. Apparently he had woken Calvin's mother in the middle of the night and told her that his head hurt, then he simply dropped down onto his pillow. If only it were that simple for Calvin, to have just one quick moment of pain, then have it all end. There was a chance that it would be that simple, and he wanted it to be so...he hoped, even though he didn't want to hope.

Hope is an inanimate desire.

Swaying like the sleepy breeze outside, through the silence and darkness, he heard footsteps. Too quick to be human, they made their way around the car, and halted at the driver's side window. He could only see to the side what his eyes would allow, for he could not turn his head. What he could make out in the darkness was a pair of pointed ears, and the sound of panting breath. Then he heard its eerie howl, ripping through his ears.

It was a coyote, inquiring about him, discovering him. And all Calvin could think was that he wanted it to go away and leave him alone. Far off in the distance, he heard a return call. Then the loud, ripping howl pierced his ears, once again. He wasn't sure how, but he suddenly knew that the coyote's eyes were fixed upon him, and the wild dog began to growl and snarl. Just go away, he tried to say, unable to say it. Leave me alone. The first time he had ever been bitten by a dog—he must have been four—he thought of the blood, the pain, and how he now had no interest in reliving such a situation, especially at such a disadvantage as this.

There was a great moment of silence, then the dog turned away, walked to the back of the car, and then his world was quiet, still; and after the calming momentary pause, he could hear the animal gnawing on something. A juicy old bone, possibly, or a recent kill. His heart eased a bit, but tension was still there. At least now that the animal was not directly before him. What was it gnawing on? Maybe when his car had come crashing down—through the small trees and rocks—some poor animal had been in the way, and was now the midnight snack of this lonely coyote.

The gnawing was not too loud, but with little else to hear, it began flooding into his ears. Now, more than ever, he wanted to get out. There was a crunching sound, and the dog's breaths deepened. The sounds grew more and more violent, then quieted down again, continuing on as before.

It was the thought of what he may be like if no one were to find him soon. Could he be one of the coyote's next meals? Even if he were to die, strung upside-down in his car, smelling like urine, covered in blood, it was likely that, at some point he would become a beast and bugger banquet. It is a natural part of the decomposition process.

And what happens when you die? Where do you go? Is there a real Heaven and Hell? Or is it nothing like what we've all been told about? What if, when you die, you simply stay in your body? What if you can feel certain things? Feel things like your body decomposing, cremating? What if you don't go anywhere, and all that happens is you simply lose control of your body, you stiffen up, but you are still there, completely aware?

The lazy breeze washed over him, again.

His mind snapped back to reality when he heard the sound of the coyote's footsteps. The animal was coming back his way. His heart tensed up. He saw the wild dog pass by, trotting along happily with something in its mouth. He only saw it for a brief moment, as it passed by and vanished into the blackness, but a rush of horror hit him. He wasn't sure if what he thought he saw was real. An arm? A human arm in the clenched jaws of the wild animal. No, that couldn't be right, could it? Surely he would have seen, even in the chaos, that there was someone down the slope. Surely he would have seen a man or woman, as his car slammed into them, ran them over. He would have heard a scream. No. That couldn't be right, there hadn't been anyone there. His imagination was just running away again. If it was a limb, it was probably from a dead animal: something he had possibly hit and run over as his car descended the rocky slope.

That was how it happened, right? The memory now seemed fuzzy, like a dream. Five minutes ago he would have been sure, but now, he didn't quite know.

Yes, that's right, his car had…what had happened to his car? All recollection of the event was quickly vanishing, obscuring into nothing.

It didn't matter.

All the memories in the world weren't going to change the fact that he was still stuck in his car, strung up by a seat belt, unable to move, caught in pitch black darkness. The only thing that really mattered was getting out. It didn't matter how it happened. He just needed to get out—get out or have someone find him soon.

How many hours remained in the night? There was no way of telling how long he had been asleep, or how time was moving. The dashboard clock was invisible. It might be minutes, it might be hours before the sky would begin to lighten and bring forth the day. It might be an eternity, or several of them before anyone found him. And he was helpless to do anything about it. Even the dull pains he had been having were gone now. His entire body was without sensation. All he had was slow movement of his eyes, and weak maneuvering of his tongue and jaw.

I'll give all this shit up, he said to himself. Yes, sir, no more drinking, no more driving. I just wanna get out of this and be okay. Please, make this all end. Just kill me, if that's what's going to happen. Just kill me, get it over with. Why am I being punished like this? What have I done? Just kill me, get rid of me, let me go. I can't take this! Can't take this any longer!

More than anything he wanted to twist and turn, throw a tantrum of some kind, but his body wouldn't allow it.

The Day the Leash Gave Way 95

Stop! Stop it! Just kill me! Let me go! I don't deserve this! I don't want it, not this way! I was always right, yeah, ain't that the truth of it? Mr. Man with the name . . . He could no longer remember his name. Didn't it start with a B, or maybe a D?

Suddenly, he felt very calm. Everything which had been running through his head had stopped, and he was sleepy, so sleepy. His eyes began to close. His mind felt at rest, at peace. It was time, he decided, time to go.

Into eternal sleep.

All was quiet.

A loud sound startled him into wakefulness.

The sun was up. The birds were singing. He was still in the car.

He hadn't died. He was still alive, and now he heard voices.

"I can't believe this," one voice said. It sounded familiar, like an old friend. "Frank, it's him." It was Tye's voice. With his slow moving eyes, he focused them on the rear view mirror. It was Tye, and after a short moment, Frank entered into the reflection.

"Man," Frank said, then he turned and called up the hill: "Yeah, It's Calvin Sawyer alright."

Calvin?! Was that his name? Yes, but somehow it didn't seem quite right. He didn't feel like a Calvin at all. But what other name could he have? No, his name couldn't be Calvin. If they were talking about him, they would be standing before his car, looking at him, trying to figure how to get him out. What were they looking at, back behind his car? He had to be Calvin, so what did they find? Why weren't they coming over to help him?

"Looks like some dog got at him in the middle of the night," Tye said. "Let's get him out. He's long dead."

Dead? No, I'm still here! I'm over here! What are you guys doing? Come get me out! Help me!

He continued to watch the reflection. The two guys were busying themselves, just out of the small mirror's view. There were a few huffs and puffs from the two men, followed by the sound of something dropping.

"Let's get 'em out," one of them said. The two men entered back into the reflection, this time dragging something . . . someone.

Who is that?

The familiarity was amazing. It took him a moment to realize that it was him, or rather, his body, the left arm gone, ripped apart, bitten off. It had been a human arm he saw last night.

It was the remains of Mr. Calvin Sawyer.

But it can't be me! I'm over here! Why am I over there when I'm here? What the hell is going on? He watched the two men ascend the hill, carrying Calvin's body with them. There was nothing for him to do but wait.

About an hour passed and he heard the sound of a tow truck.

In the mirror he saw his car, only briefly, and only a part of it as it slowly climbed the hill. Once the car was towed up, there was nothing, and the world was still. The wind blew through the window, causing him to sway back and forth, back and forth.

Divadavidavida

David had noticed.
    David wondered. "I'm sorry, David."
        David had plenty. "You awake, David?"
  You're trapped, David.
"David, you—"
    "David…" *C'mon, David.*
    David asked, "Becky?" "Becky?" Right. Right.
Yeah, yeah, David! David didn't answer. (Kiss me, David)
        Remember: survival, David.
  David asked.
C'mon, David. STOP LYING, DAVID! *C'mon, David. Everything's crazy, David.*
Forget it, David. Becky! Yeah, David thought. *David?*
David? Please, David.
David paused.
Hey, David? Please, David.
    Dead David, dead David, rah-rah-rah!
Now listen, David…
    Now David…
    GODDAMMIT DAVID!   David…
    (David)
Right?
Right?
    David?
David knew. Becky's voice.
    "David?"

Lovely Day for Beating an Old Guy

For Brian Knight, recalling a kindness.

"Ever seen a horse take a leak?"

Tony shook his head slowly from side to side, then stuck his finger up his nose, whittled it, and wiped the booty on his jeans. Tony had never seen a horse at all, let alone one taking a leak.

"It's like a goddamn fire hose," Mark said, whose favorite word in the world was goddamn, and he could hardly go more than a sentence without using it. "Save a goddamn burning house if you got a goddamn horse to piss on the thing."

Using his nails, Tony scraped the nose plunder from his jeans and mushed it into the sidewalk, then looked at the grime that had just collected on the tip of his finger. It was something to do to pass the time, anyway. He whittled his finger in his nose again, dirt and all, and wondered if he was to do it long enough if he could start a fire. If he caught his head on fire there wasn't any horse to put it out. Fear overtook him and he removed his finger.

Both Mark and Tony were losing patience. Clarence, or Hawk, as he preferred, had told them to meet him outside his house at four o'clock; and here it was twenty minutes past and neither Mark nor Tony had seen so much as a goddamn shadow moving around in any of the goddamn windows.

"Old Man Ford's got a horse," Mark said. "Way out at that goddamn ranch."

Tony brought his finger to his nose again but stopped before it entered, remembering there wasn't any horse to piss on him if he caught his head on fire.

"If Hawk don't get out here in another five minutes," Mark said, "I say we go out to that goddamn ranch and watch the horse."

Tony was intrigued. If they went out there then he could whittle all he wanted because the horse would be there if an emergency arose. And anyway, he was getting tired of waiting for Hawk, too.

Hawk was 24 and still lived with his folks, which was probably for the best because the guy could talk the talk well enough, but when it came to walking the walk it was like he had something shoved up him.

Five minutes passed. It was actually two and Mark just wasn't any good with time or counting. They stood up from the curb and just as they did, the front door of Hawk's house opened and out stepped Hawk, wearing ripped jeans and combat boots and a Slayer T-shirt with holes in it. The hair on his head was messy and bald in certain areas because he'd tried cutting it himself a few days earlier and had trouble with his perception in the mirror.

As a chicken on Ritalin would walk, Hawk made his way to his troops. He took out a cigarette, and making sure his friends were watching, ripped off the filter and stuck the smoke between his lips.

"Howdy, boys," he said, fumbling with a pack of matches; and after the cigarette was lighted, he smiled wide. "Lovely day for beating an old guy, ain't it?"

Tony scratched his arm. Mark looked longingly at Hawk's cigarette, and was impressed that he opted to remove the goddamn filter.

"Glad you guys could make it," Hawk said, puffing away.

"We were about to leave," said Mark. "We were gonna go to Old Man Ford's place and watch his goddamn horse."

"Good thing you waited," Hawk said. "You can watch that horse any time. Not everyday do you get to help someone beat an old guy."

"What the hell took you so goddamn long?"

"The old lady didn't want me going out in a shirt full of holes," Hawk explained. Then with a smug smiled he added, "But she can't tell me what to do no more. I'm old enough to have my own way."

Mark and Tony nodded.

Then Hawk's smile crossed and he said, "And anyway, she still calls me Clarence, like I haven't given up that sissy business. I ain't no sissy. Just my dick alone is enough to prove it."

Mark and Tony smiled because their friend was so cool and tough and important.

Flicking ash from his cigarette Hawk clacked his tongue, then said, "Never did like Old Man McGregor. Bastard."

"From what I understand, you sure liked his dog," answered Mark.

"Those are lies and you know it." Hawk pointed his cigarette like an extra finger. Tony thought if he whittled *that* up his nose his head *would* catch on fire. "People love spreading rumors in this town. If it wasn't for rumors, everyone would sit around here with their thumbs up their ass."

"Is that why we're gonna beat Old Man McGregor?"

"Partly," said Hawk. "And partly 'cause he hit me with that broom stick."

Mark shrugged. "Shouldn't have been fucking his goddamn dog."

"I told you those are *lies*, you bastard. I ain't never even sniffed a dog, let alone gotten it on with one."

"Not what they're saying around town."

"And that's the problem with the shit town. And that's also why I'm gonna beat the bastard."

Understanding, Mark and Tony nodded.

"Now let's get going," Hawk said, flicking his cigarette away half smoked. Mark was irritated because he wanted to finish it.

They walked two blocks up the street and went right, up another three and they made a left. Old Man McGregor's place was at the very end. Mark and Tony noticed that when Hawk was in the shade the bald spots on his head didn't look so bad.

The Day the Leash Gave Way

Almost all the paint had chipped off of McGregor's house. There was a screen on the ground beneath one of the windows and the weeds were so overgrown an entire army could've been hiding in it. Hawk liked the idea of an army, and looked gleefully down at his boots.

Mark and Tony thought that they were gonna sneak in and surprise the old guy or something—say boo and then pound the wrinkly fart until he was the consistency of oatmeal. That's what Mark and Tony thought, though they also couldn't help feeling sorry for the guy because he was so old; and shit, he hadn't hit either of them with a broom stick. McGregor had never done anything to Mark or Tony that they could remember.

When they got to the front of the house Hawk marched right up to the door and pounded five times, then shouted at the top of his lungs. "Come out, you old bastard! Come on out and take your medicine!"

Mark and Tony shied away, their faces turning a bit red.

The door did not open and there was no sound from inside the place. Hawk turned to his companions, hoisted his ripped jeans up to his gut, then let out a sigh, turned back and pounded on the door again. "You old bastard! Open up! Not so tough when you're outnumbered, are ya? You old blister!"

Still, there was no reply.

"Goddamn, Hawk," Mark said. "You aren't very goddamn subtle."

"Shit in my eye," Hawk said. "We ain't here to be subtle. We're here to beat an old guy." He turned and pounded on the door again, muttering a different cuss each time his fist struck it.

"Maybe he's not home," Mark said.

Hawk was prepared to agree but decided to try the doorknob anyway. It turned easily. He pushed it open and all three peered inside. The place was dark, the shades down. Tony figured they could see better if they had a torch, but didn't wanna offer his head, especially without a horse around.

Hawk stepped inside. Mark and Tony followed. The first thing they noticed was an unpleasant odor. They all exchanged glances, each with a funny who-farted face.

"Smells like something died," Mark said.

"Smells like rotten pussy," Hawk added.

"You wouldn't know pussy *unless* it was rotten," Mark told him, then thought on it and concluded, "or maybe if it was doggie style."

Shame touched upon Hawk's face and he didn't answer. Instead he followed the stench, his loyal companions trailing behind. Tony thought about how cool Hawk was, having done it doggie style.

Slowly, they made their way down the hall. The smell intensified with every step and Mark thought of a time when he was a kid at camp and he fell through the outhouse shitter on account that the hole was too goddamn big.

Hawk stopped at a partially open door and listened. Chewing sounds slipped out from the other side like someone stepping on soggy breakfast cereal. No, that wasn't right. It was more like gnawing.

Removing his cigarettes and matches from his pocket, Hawk lipped a smoke and gently pushed the door open; and the next thing anybody knew Hawk was on the floor in the hall and Old Man McGregor's goddamn dog had its teeth thoroughly clamped on Hawk's crotch. The cigarettes and matches fell to Mark's feet. Mark picked them up and stuck them in his own pocket, then looked back at Hawk, who was chewing on the smoke he'd put in his mouth, filter and all. No matter how Hawk tried, he couldn't get the dog detached from his crotch, and finally he resorted to screaming for help, his voice climbing higher in pitch with every cry.

Mark and Tony looked at Hawk, saw all the blood that was dripping onto the floor. Then they looked into the room the goddamn dog had come out of, and saw Old Man McGregor, pants down, arm practically gone and eyes rolled back, sitting with one wrinkly bun on the toilet and the other hanging over like a half-moon chandelier. He looked like he might be a bit bloated, but it could've just been the light.

Hawk grabbed hold of the dog's ears and tried pulling it away, but all that did was piss the animal off more and make it sink its teeth in deeper. Tears rained from Hawk's eyes and spit with bits of tobacco ran down his chin like a mudslide.

Mark turned to Tony. "What do we do?"

Tony thought if they could whittle a finger up the animal's nose maybe they could set its head on fire; but given that was the best he could come up with, he didn't verbally suggest it.

Not knowing what else to do, Mark stepped forward and kicked the dog in the ribs, causing the animal to let go for a second, bark at Mark and Tony, then dive in and latch onto Hawk's throat. Hawk's screams began to gurgle more after a moment. His eyes wobbled back and forth in his sockets, and Tony noted that with the light the way it was, the bald spots on Hawk's head were hardly visible at all.

The drool that enveloped the tobacco on Hawk's face became red, and Hawk struggled a little less with each second that went by. Mark and Tony saw something that looked like a curled hot dog resting in a pool of blood between Hawk's legs, and Mark felt bad for the cracks he'd made earlier about Hawk getting it on doggie style.

Tony thought about how the Slayer T-shirt had more holes than before, and wished they'd gone to see Old Man Ford's horse take a leak instead. Beating an old guy didn't seem like so much fun now.

Finally Hawk was still, his face frozen in his own personal who-farted face. The dog looked at Mark and Tony, barked a couple times, then went back into the bathroom and began biting on Old Man McGregor's overhang.

Mark and Tony exchanged glances then looked down at Hawk, whose face was still in a vulgar expression of pain and confusion. Mark said Hawk's name then let out a groan and concluded that he was dead.

"Aw, his mom's gonna be pissed," Mark said, and Tony thought it was because there were more holes in the guy's shirt and his mom didn't want him wearing shirts with holes in them. "We gotta get him outta here. Gotta bury him or some goddamn thing." Mark moved in and stuck his hands under Hawk's arms. Tony reached for Hawk's feet then stopped and pointed at the curled hot dog lying on the floor.

The Day the Leash Gave Way 101

"He doesn't really need it anymore," Mark said—"but I guess every man should be allowed his manhood in the afterlife."

Tony picked it up and wiped some of the blood off on his jeans, then tried sticking it in one of Hawk's pockets but couldn't get it to go in. He looked up at Hawk's twisted carnival face, saw his mouth was hanging open, and stuffed it in. With one hand under the bloody tobacco chin and one on top of the bald-spotted head, he pushed Hawk's mouth closed. Mark did not express the indignity he felt in seeing Tony perform this goddamn action, though an unspoken agreement passed between the two that Hawk didn't seem quite as cool as he did before.

Tony picked up Hawk's feet and just as they got him hoisted up, Old Man McGregor's dog barked ferociously and scared them both so bad that they dropped him back to the floor. The dog charged and both Mark and Tony fumbled backwards and tripped, falling to either side of Hawk, ready to lose their own manhood.

Instead, the animal stood on top of Hawk's body and snarled, causing Mark and Tony each to back away. When there was a good amount of distance the dog buried its muzzle into Hawk's mouth and retrieved its flaccid prize, chewed it up happily, then sank its teeth into Hawk's throat again.

Another unsaid agreement passed between the two that it was time to get the hell out of there. They couldn't do Hawk any good anyway, not with his pecker gone and his life somewhere else. Slowly, they crept away, out of the hall then out the door they'd entered from only minutes before, when Hawk was still alive and well and endowed.

Outside the world seemed quieter, smaller. Neither spoke for some time as they walked, then as they rounded the corner and Hawk's house came into view, Mark said, "You think we should tell his folks what happened?"

Tony shook his head, then wondered if Hawk's dick would have fit up his nose.

They walked passed Hawk's house casually. Mark even whistled a tad.

When they passed and were in the clear, Mark said, "What's say we go see Old Man Ford's goddamn horse."

And that's what they did.

Old Man Ford's truck was gone and the ranch was quiet and still. Mark and Tony sat up on the fence and watched the horse. Tony was particularly impressed. He was also pleased that he could whittle his finger up his nose again.

"Still wonder if we maybe should've told his goddamn folks," Mark said.

The more Tony thought about it, he was glad he didn't try to put Hawk's dick up his nose, because in the end Hawk wasn't as cool as he'd thought. If he was gonna have any dick in him, it had to be a cool one.

They sat for a while; just the two of them, watching the horse stand around and occasionally smell things. When it finally took a leak, Tony bounced up and down on the fence and clapped his hands. It *was* like a fire hose, and the puddle on the ground was immense, reminding Tony of when his neighbors plumbing went to hell and flooded the entire street.

"Aw shit," Mark said. "His folks will find out in time any-goddamn-way. No sense in putting it on *our* goddamn shoulders when we don't have to." He stuck his hand into his pocket and removed Hawk's cigarettes and matches, thinking about how cool Hawk had seemed when he'd ripped off the filter. Pulling two out of the pack he lipped one and handed the other to Tony, who thought about his nose but put it in his mouth.

"Hawk wasn't so cool anyway," Mark said. "*Smart* people are cool, and smart people know that filters on cigarettes save lives." He struck a match and lit his smoke, then brought the flame over to Tony and got his going as well. "Smart people, yeah. That's what's cool."

Without really thinking about it, Mark tossed the match, not into the dead weeds he aimed for, but right into Tony's hair, which went up like a Roman Candle. Tony flailed around and fell forward off the fence, then kicked and batted his hands at his head. Mark scratched everything he'd just been saying about smart people and climbed down to the ground with his heart pounding because, shit, Tony had never done nothing to no one.

Through the crackling of flames around his head, Tony was shouting something, but Mark couldn't quite make it out.

"Hoasish! Hoasish!"

Mark remembered that a way of putting out fire was to beat it. He was afraid, however, of burning himself if he hit him with his hands. So he grabbed a bushel of dry weeds and hit it several times over Tony's head until it caught fire and he got scared and threw it away into the dead weeds he'd tried throwing the match into.

"Hoasish! Hoasish!" Tony shouted. Then a little clearer—"Hoas piss! Hoas piss!"

The horse had wandered to the other side of the field and was drinking water. Mark saw this, and he grabbed Tony by the belt and pulled him in that direction. If he could just dunk his head into the goddamn water—but Tony was flailing so much that he fell to the ground; and as the thought of throwing dirt on Tony's head occurred to Mark, more of the dead weeds caught. Tony's shirt was burning now also. Mark had to back away because otherwise he was gonna catch on goddamn fire too. And as he backed away he watched the fire spread out in every direction on account of a breeze was picking up and pushing the flames goddamn everywhere.

Tony kicked around, getting himself burning worse, thinking how it wasn't on account of his finger that he got his head caught on fire.

"Hoas piss! Hoas piss!"

Not knowing what else to say, Mark told him, "The horse already pissed, Tony." Then, not knowing what else to do, seeing the place grow brighter and brighter, seeing and hearing the horse get frightened, the crackling of the flames, and feeling the heat, Mark hopped over the fence and ran. He heard Tony cry one more time for horse piss, and then there was only the sound of the fire and the terrified horse.

Once he'd gotten a good distance away he turned and watched as the flames licked Old Man Ford's house, then caught it and began eating it, shitting the remains into the sky. And when the house was good and bright, he turned and walked away, thinking how Tony was never all that smart, and how when he'd closed Hawk's dick in his mouth, it had really cramped Hawk's style, and maybe that was why Hawk didn't seem quite so cool

The Day the Leash Gave Way

anymore. Because Hawk had always seemed so cool, even with his hair the way it had been. Maybe it was always Tony that hadn't been cool, with his finger up his nose and all.

"Aw hell," he said.

When he got into town he walked casually through the streets, eyes shifting from one side to the other. He even whistled a tad.

Opportunity Knocks

"So what good is a closed business going to do for you?"

Jared switched the phone from his left ear to his right. "Hopefully it'll open," he said. He had to admit there were certain advantages to being unemployed, such as being able to sleep as late as he wanted and not having to answer to anyone—at least not since Monica left. Taxes had gone up so he was saving on what the government would be taking away, and no more dreaming about work, only to wake up and find that he had to get ready and go to work. These were a few of the perks to being laid off, but Jared didn't want to stay in this rut forever. The bookstore was a place to start, and a chance for him to get back on his feet. As much as he hated that his uncle had taken his life Hemingway style, what he left behind was quite possibly the blessing he had been hoping for.

"Have you talked to Monica?" Rob asked.

The taste of Jared's next words were bitter. "Not since she called to tell me she wasn't coming home."

A pause. Then, changing the subject, sensing he'd touched upon a sore spot, Rob asked him what he was going to do with his new found opportunity.

Jared shrugged at the phone as if Rob could see him. "Guess most of the inventory is still in there. Need to get more of the new releases, of course, but I wanna check it out. Take a look around and see what needs to be done if I wanna get the place up and running."

The next pause was so quiet Jared heard the clock ticking on the wall. Then Rob said, "How you doing? I mean, other than…y'know."

"I'm doing fine, Rob, thanks." He didn't bother to mention his struggle the night before in the bathtub, actually holding the razor blade in his hand and touching it to his wrist before changing his mind and agreeing to give himself one more try. "How are *you* doing? How's Mary?"

"She's doing well. Six months along now."

"That woman's gonna pop before you know it."

Rob chuckled at that, then said, "Listen. You want me to go down there with you? I know that place might hold some weird memories."

"Yeah, that would be great, thanks."

Two years earlier, it hadn't been the first time that Jared's Aunt Karen had locked up the bookstore only to discover a customer still lurking in one section or another. The store itself was not huge, though there were enough little nooks where people could tuck themselves away without being noticed. Authorities figured that's what had happened. Either that or someone she knew had stopped by and she'd let them in, having no idea

The Day the Leash Gave Way 105

what was in store for her. Whoever it was, they had been kind enough to leave the key in the bolt when they left, after raping her and stabbing her with a pair of scissors.

Jared turned the key in the lock and opened the creaky door to the dark place that had once been a successful independent bookstore. All things considered, the store was in good shape. The thick layer of dust could easily be wiped away, and the boxes could either be packed or emptied and moved out.

Jared flipped a light switch and the fluorescent bulbs on the ceiling crackled, then crept to life. "Man, those things last forever," said Rob, running his finger along the edge of a shelf and checking the dust buildup. "Jeez, they hardly touched anything when they shut down."

Jared walked slowly through the aisles, taking in the different categories, authors and titles, many he'd read, more he'd only heard of, and even more he hadn't. It was true. The place was practically untouched, almost like it had never closed down. He pictured himself sitting behind the counter, reading a book and only setting it down to give assistance or to ring up purchases. If indeed he got the place going, it would be *his* business and he could do it however *he* wanted. Not all the perks of being unemployed would be gone. He'd probably hire a couple people, most likely college students, and leave a lot of the usual day to day stuff for them. At first, though, he would want to be around as much as possible, figure out the best way to do things and see if this was something he could really pull off.

"It smells like my grandfather's garage," Rob said.

"Beautiful, isn't it?"

Weaving through the aisles, Jared saw a spider skitter across the floor. For now he let it go. He'd get an exterminator before too long. No point in doing unnecessary harm, he told himself, which was something he'd said to himself the other night—*No point in doing harm when something good might be waiting right around the corner.* Something that he had told himself before. Possibly the one thing that kept him going. Only this time it had been true. This time opportunity knocked.

Hearing Rob remove and replace books from the shelves, Jared made his way to the back room, where two years earlier his Aunt Karen had been found sprawled in a pool of blood with a pair of scissors in her mouth. Now all that remained was dust and the occasional spider and randomly fallen book. Some of the books had been nibbled by mice. He crouched down to pick up a chewed copy of *Moby Dick* when a chill raced through him. For a brief moment he thought he saw his own breath, but wrote it off as imagination and went back out to the front of the store, leaving the book where it was.

The chill lingered.

Rob noticed right off. "You okay, man? You look pale as hell."

"Is it just me, or is it cold in here?"

"It's a little cool," Rob said, "but I'm all right. Is there something you can put on? You got a sweater or anything in the car?"

There wasn't anything like that in Jared's car but he didn't really mind. The chill would pass. He rubbed his goosebumped arms and went to the counter, where the empty register sat open next to a jar full of pens and pencils. Half the pens had Disney characters printed on them. Jared remembered how Karen always insisted on using them instead of the others because it, quote, "makes writing this kind of stuff a little more fun." Karen had been odd that way and it was a part of her personality that Jared had loved so much. The same kind of oddities and quirks he'd later found in Monica. Beneath the counter were rolls of register tape, paperclips, rubber bands and a variety of other office supplies.

"So what do you think?" Rob asked, then scratched the back of his head. "Sweep it up, get rid of a few bugs, add some more current titles to what you've already got here—place will probably be looking pretty good. Ready for business in no time."

"Yeah, well, there's still all the paperwork to go through. Not really looking forward to that part of it." But he was going to go through with it because he needed this. Goddammit, he needed this. He was given an opportunity to get himself together again and he didn't want to blow it. No more nights like the one in the bathtub, and so many others before. It was time something good came to Jared Richter, and he now had the interest to keep it going.

"Well," Rob said, "I don't know much about that end of it, but if you want some help cleaning this place up, I'm more than happy to give you a hand."

"Thanks, Rob."

"No thanks necessary."

Rob had a heart of gold and a lovely wife to match. Rob and Mary were the perfect couple in every way as far as Jared could see. No lack of affection between them, always supporting and encouraging each other in everything they wanted to do, both together and as individuals. More in love than really seemed possible. And now, as another product of that love, they were going to have a baby together. In some ways Jared couldn't help being envious. It was one of the main things he wanted in life: a good relationship—but he'd messed that up again. He wished he could have done things differently. He'd gotten rid of Monica. Now he wished she would come home. He'd do his damnedest to change if she would be back at his side. But she never would. He hated facing reality like that, but he knew it wasn't going to happen—not the way things had been at the end.

"Well," Rob said. "You up for starting now?"

"Huh?"

"We brought the brooms and vacuum and all that cleaning stuff. Wanna have a go at getting this place ship-shape?"

Jared looked around, feeling the emptiness left by thoughts of Monica, then feeling loss at the memories of Karen. He and Aunt Karen had been close. Not blood relatives, but it often seemed like they were brother and sister, rather than Karen being a woman who had married his father's brother. It was strange to be in the bookstore again knowing that Karen wouldn't be coming out of the back with an armload of books, or that she wouldn't be sitting behind the counter doodling on a notepad or ringing up purchases. Jared hadn't been here since he'd last seen Karen, and he hadn't seen Karen since he'd last been here. Two years now, and yet it felt like yesterday.

"What do you say, Jared?"

"What?" Jared had been completely lost in his thoughts.

The Day the Leash Gave Way 107

"Should we start cleaning this place up, or what?"

Before he could answer the front door opened and Mary's voice rang with a "Knock-knock?" She stepped in, a fast food bag in her hand. Her belly was big and round and she wore her smile on her face as naturally as she wore shoes on her feet. Her auburn hair was tied back in a ponytail and it looked to Jared that carrying another human being inside her hadn't altered the rest of her slender body in the least.

"Hey, sweetie," Rob said. "What are you doing here?" He planted a kiss on her lips and she giggled like it was the first time.

"You said you guys might be here awhile, so I brought you both something to eat." She held the bag out to Rob, who took it and paid her with another kiss. Like before, Mary giggled, then turned to Jared and said hello.

"Hi, Mary. You look great. Haven't seen you for some time."

She agreed, thanked him for the compliment, then placed her hands on her round belly and told him that the baby had been really kicking lately. "And now it doesn't want to stop." She moved to Rob and snuggled against him and Rob wrapped his arm around her, kissed her cheek, then asked Jared to excuse them for a moment. He handed Jared the bag and told him to go ahead and tear into it. Mary added that his was the one with the sticker on the wrapping because she knew he didn't like pickles, so she made sure to get him one without any.

Jared thanked her and opened the bag, then watched them exit the store, arm in arm. Seeing them together, seeing Mary with her belly so full of the love she and Rob shared enhanced the emptiness already inside him. Even Monica, after a year and a half, couldn't remember that Jared didn't like pickles. Mary had known without having to ask. She just knew. When he thought about it, Mary knew him better than Monica ever had, and he didn't like the subtle shift of feelings this thought raised inside him. From emptiness to longing. A fine line to cross but he noticed, and couldn't help feeling ashamed of himself. Mary was Rob's girl, and Jared didn't feel he had any right to even think the thoughts he was. Of course, he'd been down that road before. It wasn't the first time he'd felt something for someone else's girl.

Setting the bag on the counter, not quite hungry yet, he looked around the place again, hoping to find something to distract him from the thoughts swishing in his head. The coldness came back. It had never entirely gone away. He walked to the nearest section of books, Self-Help & Inspiration, reached out and pulled one from the shelf at random and dropped it as a cold electrical charge shot up his arm. He shivered, tensed his shoulders. Then, once over the worst of it, he looked down at the book he'd dropped: *All the Power You Need, All the Power You Want*. He couldn't help laughing at the irony. Here he was feeling powerless, thinking thoughts he didn't want to think, shivering because it was so cold; and the book he'd chosen from the shelf was exactly the kind he would have picked had he been consciously looking for self-help and inspiration.

A small laugh that didn't sound like his own escaped him. He crouched down to pick it up, thinking that maybe he *should* take it home and give it a look. Halfway down he stopped and straightened at the sound of someone sliding a row of books along one of the shelves then flopping one to the floor. From where he stood, Jared couldn't see anything unusual. He called out a courteous hello, then took a few steps around the Self-Help section and looked down the next aisle. No one there and nothing out of place.

"Rob?" he said, wondering if his friend had gotten inside and was sneaking around. Despite his heart of gold, there was a tendency in Rob to have a poor and childish sense of humor sometimes.

No, impossible. Rob couldn't have gotten into the store without Jared noticing. The only way in was the front door, which Jared would have easily seen from where he was standing—practically right next to the damn thing. And even if he'd somehow managed not to see it, he would have heard the creakiness of the door.

Moving to the next aisle he saw a single book lying on the floor halfway in. Another laugh slipped from inside him, more his own than before. All the stuff in this place had been untouched for two years now, then he and Rob came in and started poking around, disturbing the settled placement of everything and kicking up dust where it had been still. No surprise that a book would fall from the shelf. It happened in just about every store he'd ever been in, some precariously placed object that finally can't hold on any longer.

The paperback on the floor was lying face down with a blank cover. The same feeling of icicles spidering up his arm came when he picked it up, but this time he didn't let go. The ice crept into his neck and shoulders and head, then crawled down his back. Jared almost lost the book from all his shivering but held on to it, turned it over and saw the title, *Karen*, written across the top in raised red letters. No cover art, no author, just one simple name that called up many odd and uncomfortable feelings. The cold extended from the tips of his fingers all the way down to the ends of his toes. His lips quivered and his teeth chattered as he opened the book to the first page and read.

A cold day in June—strange that it would be so cold that time of year, even in Maine—when I was fourteen I saw my father for the last time. Being a fisherman, his primary resource was lobster. It was thanks to the lobster that we had a roof over our heads.

Karen had spent the first seventeen years of her life in Maine. Jared looked up from the book and read the sign at the top of the shelf: Biographies. The coldness in his body took on an excessive amount of weight, particularly in his stomach and chest. Turning to a random page halfway through he read a little about Karen meeting Uncle Ted, Ted in the process of starting up his own bookstore.

He was the last person I ever though I'd get involved with. Kind of a mousy man, and neurotic. Not as bad as Woody Allen, but he could be frustrating. And yet, there was something about him. He had charm beyond what I thought possible. And that charm had no ulterior motive. Maybe that's why he wound up being such a good businessman.

With every word Jared read the book grew colder. He half expected to see frost. The thought hadn't even occurred to him that his aunt had never written a book. Poetry from

The Day the Leash Gave Way 109

time to time—she'd published a few pieces in local literary journals—but never an entire book of any sort.

He flipped further in, his fingers numb, and suddenly the cold inside him turned to icy fear.

Ted's nephew, Jared, was a very nice boy, if not a little strange. But then again, Ted's brother was strange. Every afternoon Jared came to the store, hardly ever bothering to look at books. I have to admit it was cute to see this young man infatuated with me. He helped with everything, always wearing a smile on his face...

Jared closed the book. Intrigued as he was, there was something very wrong about it all. Something unnaturally wrong that frightened him. The book was now too cold to handle, and not sure he could read any more of it, he placed it back on the shelf just as the front door opened and Rob and Mary entered, giggling.

"Jared, where are you?"

"I'm here," he said, noting that his voice sounded strange. He rubbed his arms then joined his friends up front and saw Rob placing *All the Power You Need, All the Power You Want* back on the shelf. Next to the door there was now a broom and a dustpan, a bucket filled with cleaning products, rubber gloves and rags.

"The vacuum's still out in the car," Rob told him. Then, "You haven't started eating? The stuff's gonna get cold." He opened the bag and removed two wrapped cheeseburgers, handed the one with the sticker on it to Jared, then reached in again and pulled out two cardboard containers of French fries. "You didn't get anything for yourself, honey?"

"I already ate," Mary said, then looked at Jared and smiled.

Jared smiled back but it was a strain on his face. He did not feel like smiling. What he felt was a mixture of icy fear and lonely desire, as he watched Mary place her hands on Rob's shoulders. As she gave her honey a massage, Jared felt his own tension, his muscles, tight and knotted and throbbing in agony. Cold fire flared in his lower back and shot up into the base of his skull.

Another shiver. A big one, large enough to chatter his teeth again and attract Rob and Mary's attention. They turned and looked at him. Jared was pale and chilled, trying to unwrap the cheeseburger in his hands.

"Jared, you okay?"

"Fine."

"You look like you might have a fever," Mary said.

"I'm fine, really." After a few deep breaths, the chills subsided. He removed the burger from the paper and took a bite.

"You sure?" Rob asked. "I mean, we can do this another time. There isn't really a rush, is there?"

"I'd like to start today, if it's all the same to you."

Rob hesitated, then nodded and said okay. "Let's just finish eating." Then he stuffed a French fry into his mouth and turned to Mary.

Mary was watching Jared like she might watch a cripple trying to get up a flight of stairs. Sensing an uncertainty in her, Rob reached out and took hold of her hand. After all, it was only Jared. Maybe a little under the weather, possibly a bit weirded out by being in a place with so many memories attached to it. But still only Jared. His hand seemed to comfort her, because her smile returned and when it did, Jared thought she was the most beautiful woman he'd seen in some time.

Quickly finishing his burger and nibbling a few fries, Jared took the rubber gloves, a rag and a bottle of Pledge from the bucket. "I'm gonna get started," he said. "Take your time." Then he chuckled. "You're right. There isn't really a rush."

Cleaning utensils in hand, he made his way back to the section he'd been in when Rob and Mary came in. Searching as he slipped his hands into the rubber gloves, he located Karen's book, removed it from the shelf, and couldn't shake the cold feeling rushing throughout his body. It was still cold, even with the gloves on, but nothing like before. Though it was hard turning the pages with flimsy rubber at the tips of his fingers. He heard the mumbling of Mary and Rob's conversation.

Flipping through the pages, Jared located a random spot close to the back. He was compelled, had to know more about what this book said, and had to know now.

Mary giggled somewhere off in the distance and a lump developed in Jared's throat as he read from a page near the end.

> *I closed the store alone last night. I wasn't often alone at this time because Jack was usually closing up with me, but some nights it was just unavoidable. The last customer I had was a shady character buying erotic novels. He kept looking at me, grinning, his demeanor like some sort of psycho beneath dark curly hair and a pale complexion, as if he hadn't seen the sun in years. His look was very different from the way Jared looked at me. Jared's goofy look was always rather cute. This man's was anything but. This man was scary, and I wanted him out of the store.*
>
> *Ringing up his purchases I saw the man lick his lips and then slide a hand over his crotch. My heart pounded. At that moment the only thing I understood was fear—and I understood it very well. The store had no alarm, so unless I could manage a phone call to the police—which was very unlikely—I was stuck.*
>
> *Fortunately, I hadn't yet locked the door. Just as I felt myself on the verge of panic, Jared walked in. The man at the counter changed his attitude instantly, paid for his books, and not wanting a bag, took them from the counter and rushed out. Thank God.*

Jared felt the coldness hardening around him like a shell. The lump in his throat swelled and his muscles ached. He heard Mary giggle again, then he continued with the words on the page.

> *I passed the keys over the counter and asked Jared if he would lock the door and as he did, I told him about what had just happened. He nodded from time to time but I got a sense that he wasn't really listening to me.*

The Day the Leash Gave Way

I opened the register and removed the cash drawer and walked into the back, uncomfortable and confused.

Setting the drawer down between the adding machine and a jar with pens and pencils and a pair of scissors in it, I felt Jared's presence looming behind me. I turned around and there he was, staring at me with a blank expression on his face. In an odd monotone he told me that he was in love with me. Said seeing me with Uncle Ted drove him crazy and he was tired of it. He wanted me, and I think it was when he removed a small square package from his pocket that I came closest in my life to throwing up solely out of fear.

"Jared?"

He approached me. There was nowhere I could go. He blocked the only route of escape. I told him to stay away but he kept coming, his fingers tearing away at the condom's packaging.

"Jared, what you doing back there?"
"What? Nothing." His voice sounded like a child's. His head spun and his eyes hurt and he was so cold. So goddamn cold. But he had to keep reading, as though he didn't have any choice. All the words printed in the book were mind boggling. Unbelievable. Insane. An overriding force kept him going, though, held his eyes on the pages. He hated it. But he couldn't stop.

Finally I spoke my first word. It felt like I'd never spoken before in my life. My voice sounded distant and muffled, like my face was buried in a pillow. "Jared," I said, and there was a long and tense silence between this word and the next. "No."

His expression did not alter. Saying this did not seem to effect him. I think that had I said yes right then his blank face still would not have changed. It was as though he was being controlled by some power stronger than he could handle—but I guess that's what jealousy and lust do when experienced without caution.

He had not touched me yet. Just stood there with the condom in his hand, staring at me with hollow eyes. Then, disregarding what I had said, he told me to take off my clothes.

That's when I reached for the scissors...

A hand touched upon Jared's shoulder and startled him. He dropped the book. Rob and Mary were standing beside him. Jared felt silly crouched down like he was, reading a book, shivering and wearing rubber gloves. He must have looked like the craziest man alive.

Rob looked down at the book on the floor. His eyes narrowed and he said, "Jared, are you sure you're...maybe we should do this another time. You're shivering like a madman. You should probably just go home and get in bed."

"I'm fine. Really. I'm sorry. I don't know what's gotten into me. But really, I feel fine." He picked up the book and rose, trying to conceal the title but Rob saw it, and as he did his face cracked up into a smile.

"Didn't know Calhoun could get you so uppity."

Baffled, Jared looked down at the book in his gloved hands. *John C. Calhoun and the Price of Union*, by John Niven. Flipping through the pages he couldn't find any of what he'd just read. Like the cover now said, it was about John C. Calhoun. He put the book back on the shelf, embarrassed, then looked at his friends before looking back at the book, which was still a biography of Calhoun.

"You know," Mary said. "No offense, Jared, but if you're getting sick, I don't wanna risk catching anything. Especially at this time." She placed her hands on her stomach, as though trying to protect it.

"Yeah, sweetie," Rob said. "Why don't you run along. No sense in risking that."

Jared agreed, though he insisted that he was fine. He thanked her for the food and offered to reimburse her but she refused, and said in exchange she would just use the bathroom. Jared pointed her in the direction and when she closed the door behind her and the bathroom fan switched on, Rob turned to Jared.

"Okay, what's gotten into you?"

"Huh?"

"Jared, you're sort of freaking me out. Not just me. Mary too. If you're not sick then something's got you wigged. I mean, really *wigged*. So spit it out."

"I'm fine, Rob."

"Is it just being here, in the bookstore?"

"Maybe. No, it's... Look, just drop it, man. I'm fine."

"You're not fine."

"I'm fine, Rob, so why don't you just leave me the fuck alone?"

Rob hesitated, then his head nodded, he said fine, and told Jared he was going to go get the vacuum out of the car. "I'll stick around and help, if you want. But I'm getting this feeling you wanna be alone."

The two of them walked to the front. Rob stepped out to get the vacuum. Just as the door closed Jared heard the toilet flush. A moment later Mary came out, looked around, smiled, and then asked where Rob was.

"He's out getting the vacuum," Jared told her, and with no chance to stop them, the feelings bit into him like a million sets of teeth. Looking at Mary, he wanted her now more than ever, almost to the point of insanity. The thing that kept him from doing or saying anything about it—the only thing—was his sense of right and wrong. The value system that still lingered somewhere inside him. The only thing that prevented him from taking action. He knew it was wrong. He'd known it when Mary had first shown up, and he knew it now. That road was paved with hell, and there was enough hell in his life without having to look for more.

Monica flashed before his eyes, her tongue lolling, eyes rolling into her skull. He hated the feelings he was having because that was the kind of thing it led to. Loss of control. The value system gone and everything else exploding.

The Day the Leash Gave Way

The front door opened. Rob fumbled his way in, vacuum cleaner commanding both hands. He set it just inside the door, then straightened up and regarded Jared and his loving wife.

Seconds passed like minutes. Unspoken words flowed between all three of them. Then Mary nodded her head. "Right," she said. "I'm gonna get going."

"Thanks again for the food, Mary," Jared told her, fighting against the voices in his head telling him to take her.

"I think I'm gonna go with you, honey," Rob said, then turned to Jared and raised his eyebrows. "That okay with you, Jared? Maybe tomorrow or next week?"

Jared nodded, fighting the chills, fighting the voices, the screaming voices in his head. "Yeah, that's fine. Thanks for your help." But the voices told him that he couldn't let this happen. He couldn't stand by and watch her leave with the man she loved. It drove him crazy, seeing them together, how much they were in love. He struggled to hold on to that value system, though, and hurried them out as though the place was on fire, touching Mary on the shoulder as he did. And as his hand touched upon her he experienced, in complete contrast to all else he was feeling, extreme warmth. Heat, snuggling and comforting, and he hated it more than the cold, more than the chills, more than what he'd read in the book only five minutes ago. He hated it. He wanted them gone.

And a moment later they were. Jared closed the door and turned the bolt, drew in a deep breath and cursed under it. He saw Karen again behind his eyes, saw her as she begged him, as she pleaded, tears running down her face. And then it was Monica. Jared brought his gloved hands to his eyes and rubbed, hoping it would all go away.

Something in front of him dropped to the floor. Removing his hands he saw a book lying face down. He half expected it to move, but after a moment when it did not, he approached it and picked it up, turned it over and looked at the cover. *All the Power You Need, All the Power You Want.* Maybe he hadn't noticed before, or maybe it was different. He didn't recall much in the way of pictures on it, but now there was a single razor blade on the cover, sparkling like a gemstone. The book was colder than the other one—the coldest thing he'd ever touched, even with gloves on. But the oddest thing about it was that the author credited on the front was himself. He flipped it open to a random page and saw the same sentence written over and over again:

Time to say goodbye, Jared.

He closed the book, dropped it on the floor and, leaving everything where it was, left the store, not bothering to lock it up. It didn't matter. None of it would matter ever again.

Bathing Beauty

The reason Jake's wife had become a pool of meat was because she'd stood up in the bathtub and slipped while Jake was away on business.

When he came home and found her the first thing he did was turn on the overhead fan and open the window. Then he sat on the toilet and thought about what to do with her. Jake had been gone nearly ten days, and from the look and smell of her it had to have been a good week or so since it'd happened.

He couldn't deny that he loved her. He also couldn't deny that dealing with police this late in the game (even though he'd been out of town) would be a downright pain in the ass. They would wanna know why he didn't call sooner, and if he explained he'd been out of town, they'd wanna do a check, and that could send him into some serious crapola. Goddammit, Donald—drunken bastard with his drunken ideas; and Jake had been stupid enough to listen to the guy. So sloshed that he was thinking about ass hair when he agreed to Don's proposition.

He swatted at some of the flying pests around his head and watched as some of them flew in and out of his sweetheart. He couldn't help thinking of a National Geographic special he once saw, where they sped up the film and showed a dead grasshopper get gnawed down to nothing by other insects.

He loved her, rest her soul, even as he looked at her there in the tub, all blanched and swollen and wrinkled, a layer of sticky soup skin on top of the water, red, black and blue, and an extra large blotch of mess up near her head. Come to think of it, she almost looked more like a blistered, bloated mass of orgy residue mixed with sewage than she did a woman, but Jake knew better. He'd recognize those rolled back eyes anywhere, even if they were retracted and opaque. Yes he loved her; but dammit, he had to get rid of her.

A buddy of Jake's, Syd, had once said that water was the thing to ruin an otherwise fine dead body. "Lotta trouble they got in Louisiana," Syd said, "it being beneath sea level and all."

As far as Jake was concerned, his wife was ruined. There didn't seem much chance of bringing her back, and she probably wouldn't have been in the best mood even if he could.

And damn, the smell, like demons dumping fiery loads in his mouth and nose, and he had no choice but to sniff and swallow. Dry heaves came upon him. He went to the kitchen for a breather, splashed some cold water on his face, then got the bucket, as well as the mop and a can of air-freshener from the pantry.

The problem was going to be getting her out of the apartment building without anybody catching on. He wiped a hand across his brow and sighed. Apparently the crazy lady upstairs hadn't noticed any sort of aroma, nor had that four-eyed geek directly below

The Day the Leash Gave Way 115

him. Good thing she died in the tub, he thought, otherwise Doofus downstairs might have had a dead woman leak in his ceiling; and if Jake remembered properly, their bathroom was just above the guy's stove. On the other hand, maybe things would have been easier. Someone could have reported the stench, the body would have been found, and Jake would've been sad and cried but at least he would have been out of town and there wouldn't be any other questions. Maybe Four Eyes would've become vegetarian. He marveled at the construction of the building. "Damn. One air-tight place," he noted. "You wouldn't think by lookin' at it." Then a half-guilty chuckle escaped him. "Seems a little more worth the money we've paid."

He went back to the bathroom and the first thing he did was spray a bunch of the air-freshener around. Unfortunately it didn't do as much good as he'd hoped. Now it was a strange aroma like burning shit and freshly picked raspberries. And another problem he was having were the flies that were finding their way in through the window because the damn screen had fallen out six weeks earlier and they'd never bothered replacing it. There had already been pests, but now it was a banquet at an insect convention, damn it.

Jake sat on the toilet a few minutes and thought about what to do. He swatted at the flies and studied what had once been his wife, saw that the washcloth covered her privates and figured that was probably for the best. The hardest part would be the bones, he decided. Some of the rest of her looked like he might be able to just scoop up in a bucket or sop up with a towel. But the bones—they were gonna be trouble. He sat on the toilet a little longer, used it once, and thought about how to do this.

There was still an inch or two of water in the tub. Jake didn't know whether it would be better to drain it or leave it, then figured it would be easier to scoop her out if there were some more water to help her along. So he turned on the faucet and let it run a good five minutes, hoping there was enough for her to become a creamy consistency and he could get a good scoop in the bucket. He didn't like the idea of feeling any strange fleshy sensations, passed from his wife through the bucket to him. The washcloth moved and he felt embarrassed and looked away, as if he'd never seen what was behind it before.

"Jeez," he said to himself. It really figured, after everything else that had happened that day, starting with the trip not going as planned; and of course the airport was more agonizing than fucking a cactus. His flight was delayed two hours and changed gates three times. With those long hikes through the concourses, he might have actually preferred fucking a cactus. Then on the flight back, with the help of some heavy turbulence, the overhead compartment had opened and a large bag had fallen on him. Smacked him right in the damn head. Spilled his whiskey and rabbit turd peanuts everywhere. And now, to come home and find his wife dead in the bathtub, well, things were turning out to be dandy. Oh yes, just dandy. "Cute as a catheter," he was fond of saying. Then he had a flash image of fucking a cactus.

The vile odor, the flies, the woman he was used to fucking now a rotted mess—all of it made him wanna puke. Scooping what he could, bits of her clung to the rim of the bucket and he had to wipe it off with a paper towel. After two scoops, with his eyes watering, he sprayed more air-freshener, still wondering why no one else had smelled her. Maybe the neighbors just thought she was cooking again. She'd never been too skilled in that area and he himself often wanted to gag when she had a go at it. Her folks had gotten them a fucking Grind-O-Matic for their wedding, and damn if the bitch didn't decide to try it out on more than one occasion. Neither of them even ate sausage; and it sure as hell wasn't any fun making it at home. The Grind-O-Matic had been sitting at the end of the fucking counter, untouched, for years now.

With another couple scoops he realized his plan wasn't going to work as he'd hoped. Something else had to be done. The bones were going to be a problem, but now he discovered the flesh wasn't gonna be no summer in the park. Sure, he could scoop and sop up some of it, but most of it was tougher than it looked. It wasn't as simple as pour some down the sink, flush some down the toilet and haul the rest out with the garbage.

Looking at her there in the tub, her eyes were open but rolled into the back of her skull, like she was reacting to something frustrating or stupid.

"Am I being that dumb?" he asked her.

He caught a fly in mid-air and flung it into the tub.

"Well," he said, "if you're so smart then just what the hell do I do?"

The fly struggled feebly.

"I can't call the cops," he told her. "They'd wanna know all sorts of shit. And now that I've tampered with you they'd really wanna be askin' me questions. Damn, why couldn't you just be the pool I thought you were?"

One final lurch and the fly was still.

"At least I know now why you never picked up the phone or returned any of my calls." He sighed, contemplated, said, "This ain't gonna be pretty," then added, "Shit!" One more scoop and he flushed the toilet. "I dunno what to do. I mean, hell, I love you, honey, so don't take this wrong—but I don't wanna touch you."

The bathtub drain clogged quickly. This didn't surprise Jake but it frustrated him all the same. Just one more thing he was gonna have to deal with, goddammit. Maybe he should've left it full. Fuck it.

The bones concerned him but it was the carving knife that disturbed him when he took it out of the kitchen drawer and ogled his narrow reflection in the blade. The task took him so long and it was so brutal; and the worst part was that it was only a test. If things worked out, he'd need to do it again, and that almost seemed worse than just leaving her where she was, even with the flies and that smell.

"Stupid klutz," he said, making the last few cuts, swatting at some flies. "Why couldn't you have waited 'til I got home to fall? Maybe I could've saved you." He pulled her left hand away from her wrist and what skin was still there peeled off like a glove. It was so foul that he had to fight a serious urge to retch, and sprayed more luscious raspberry around. Shaking his head in a tsk-tsk manner, he gagged, then said, "Things would'a been simpler, y'know? Sure as hell wouldn't be all this."

He brought the hand to the kitchen, turned on the sink disposal and shoved it down. It sounded like metal grinding against metal. Bone shrapnel and blood leapt from the drain in little gobs and the retching feeling came back, only this time he couldn't fight it. He covered his mouth and made his way to the bathroom, then stopped when he remembered what was in there, and if he was vomiting with his wife beside him like she

The Day the Leash Gave Way

was, he'd never stop. And of course the kitchen sink was right there. He turned back to it; but it was filled with bloody chewed-up hand. He paused uncertainly, like a discus thrower immortalized in a statue—and just as he pivoted indecisively he disgorged a hearty sum of chunky brown liquid all over the floor, his shoes, and his left arm. He saw a couple of the peanuts he'd had on the plane, and was glad he didn't get to eat the whole bag.

All said and done, he declared he wouldn't go through that again. If he had to keep doing that over and over he'd vomit 'til he turned himself inside out.

So then what? What could he do? He couldn't just leave her where she was. The smell would get to someone eventually—and it was sure as hell getting to him—and sooner or later somebody would drop by. He always felt people should call before coming over but there were a couple of his "friends" that did not hold this belief. Someone would stop by in the next few days, and what would he do then?

Then another thought crossed his mind and he trudged to the bathroom and poked his head inside. "And just what the hell am I gonna say when people ask where you are?" It hadn't even crossed his mind until now.

She looked like she rolled her eyes but they had been that way the whole time.

"What do I say? You decided to leave me? Wrote me a note or left me a message and then just skipped town?" He shook his head, tsk-tsking himself. He wished he were more creative. "I dunno what else to tell 'em."

Clearly, neither did she.

"Sometimes I wish we'd never gotten together," he told her. "I could'a just been a guy and done guy things. Women get ya into trouble." He paused and looked at her, as though she was listening.

"Well what the hell do you call this?"

He sighed the sigh of a man that didn't want to argue.

"There's nothing else I can tell 'em," he said, spraying some more air-freshener around, tantalizing his senses with decaying raspberry flesh. Then he added in a soft mutter: "Sorry about your hand."

He mopped up the water and some chunky bits from the bathroom floor and wished he smoked. He sure could've used a cigarette.

"So what do I do now?"

Her eyes were tucked into the back of her head.

The phone rang just then and Jake jumped, then answered it. It was Syd, not the brightest crayon in the box. Tuna fish in the skull, Jake thought. The kind of guy you could poke in the eye and he'd ask if you heard that.

"I's just callin' cause I'm hungry and bored, and wondering if you and the little lady wanna accompany me out to get somethin' to eat."

"Now's not a good time, Syd."

"How is the little lady, Jake?"

"We're having a bit of a problem, Syd. She's falling to pieces. I'll call you later."

"But—"

Jake hung up and went back to the bathroom. The first thing he did was yell at the festering mass in the tub. "Look at the damn trouble you're getting me in!" He punched a wall of air and shouted "Fuck!" then picked up the can of air-freshener again. "Syd'll be over in the next day or so now," he said. "It'll take his tuna a time to click, but then he'll be over and he'll see what's going on." He looked down at himself and saw, along with some of his vomit, soft sinewy bits of meat clinging to his pants, particularly on his left leg and his crotch. One piece at a time he picked them off and flicked them back into the tub. "Take a look at us now," he said, and chuckled at the thought of what she would say.

He sprayed more air-freshener. Practically half the can was gone and it wasn't doing nearly as much good as he'd hoped. He went back into the kitchen and rinsed the carving knife and considered what to do next. He thought about Allen and Chuck, the fag couple down the street, sweet as could be but they owned a real mean rottweiler named Juju. That dog would eat just about anything. Jake almost got his balls bit off once while he and his wife were visiting, and Jake wondered whether the dog was queer too. If only there was a way to get Juju over without having to explain anything to Allen and Chuck, but Jake couldn't see how. He'd expressed his dislike for the animal when it tried to bite off his balls by kicking it in the ribs. Neither Allen nor Chuck had quite forgiven him for that.

The phone rang again. It was Syd. His voice was taut but it didn't make him sound any smarter. "Jake," he said, "I'd *really* like to hang out with you and your lady and get somethin' to eat."

"Double-wide Jesus, Syd. I told you, now's not a good time. Don't call me again."

He hung up.

Immediately after there was another ring and Jake picked it up, shouted into the receiver, and discovered it wasn't Syd. It was a telemarketer, which made Jake feel better for yelling.

In the bathroom his wife was quiet and still. Acid crossed his mind, but he didn't know what kind he would need or if he could even get it; and even if he got some good strong stuff, there was a possibility that the bones would stick around "…like in that movie," he mumbled.

If only she were a woman without bones.

He looked down at her. "You're a mess," he said, then flicked another chunk off his pants. "You're absolutely disgusting, and you smell. I'm sick being in the same damn room with you."

His opinion on her hygiene never bothered her before, and it sure as hell didn't bother her now; but what did it matter, anyway?

"It's odd, y'know? You being in the bath all this time and you're worse off than before."

A fly flew out of her nose. Jake wondered how long it had been up there.

Taking a bathroom break he thought again about the sink disposal. Then he considered the blender. Chucking both options out the window he sat on the toilet and sprayed more of that exhilarating raspberry air-freshener. Damn, it just wasn't helping like he wanted it to.

If only she was in small pieces things would be simple. She wasn't, however, and he knew damn well he couldn't stomach the process of turning her into finger food—not after what he'd done with her hand. There was enough of her in the water to make a thick stew, but even if there was enough to feed Ethiopia, he'd still have the bones to contend

The Day the Leash Gave Way

with, and all of this was making him sicker by the minute. Worse yet, he was starting to believe he didn't have any other options. The carving knife was in the kitchen but he'd just washed it and didn't wanna mess it up again, at least not in the way he was thinking.

Closing his eyes he imagined her other hand crumbling in the blender. When he opened them he saw it was still attached to her wrist, the fingers curled into the palm. It was the same hand she used to stroke him with, back in the day. She hadn't stroked him that way in a few years now, and he longed for the old times. But those times had ceased shortly after they'd moved into this amazingly airtight apartment. Jake never understood why, but it didn't matter anymore because that hand was putrefied and gross and he didn't want it stroking him anymore.

Softly, Jake muttered how he never should've gone on that stupid trip, and vowed it was the last time he was ever gonna get drunk with an old college buddy. A guy never knows what he'll find himself doing. Goddamn bastard-ass Donald with his wild *Crime Can Pay* bullshit. Knocking up some teenage whore and not wanting to deal with it, figuring Jake could help him for the right price. And now Jake could never show his face in that damn hick town again—as if it was some great loss and he really cared. Still, killing someone wasn't nearly as easy as it looked; though Jake reminded himself to kill Donald if he ever saw him again.

To hell with it, to hell with it, other fish to fry.

A little more of that raspberry fragrance and he went back to the kitchen, not knowing what else to do. Again, the phone rang. Jake didn't exactly know why he answered it, because when Syd asked him if he and the little lady were okay, Jake got so pissed he smashed a dish on the floor, then went to the sink and grabbed the carving knife. He raced into the bathroom and stopped before the pool of meat, dropped the knife then dropped to his knees, and regarded his wife with a strange mixture of emotions. Even though he was angry he was able to understand what it was about her that he loved. He saw her beauty, both on the outside and within. Looking into her rolled back eyes—such a bathing beauty—he felt the intensity of his love, and would have done anything for her.

As if it was a big surprise, the phone rang again. Jake said to hell with it and let the answering machine pick up. This time it wasn't Syd, nor was it a telemarketer. It was Allen from down the street, and when he spoke his voice was laced with heavy sympathy.

"Hi, Jake. By now you know and I'm sure your world is upside down. I'm sorry. Someone should've told you. I mean, everybody's known about it for a long time now. It was dishonest...on everyone's part. I'm very sorry. Anyway, I just want to let you know that we're here for you. We love you, Jake, even though you kicked Juju in the ribs. Take care, and call if you need anything. Ciao."

Allen clicked off and Jake wondered what the hell he was talking about. He walked over to the answering machine and, for the first time, saw that there were messages waiting. Jake started them and listened.

Message One:

"Hey, little lady. It's Syd. I just wanna confirm the plan with you. Somethin' to eat. I'm assumin' that's what we're still doin' unless I hear different from you. Love you, baby."

Jake rubbed his chin and narrowed his eyes.

Message Two was Jake's voice. "Hey. Arrived safely. Hate airplanes. Call you soon. Miss you. Bye." There were a few more calls from Jake, each sounding much like the first, only he wondered a little bit more as to where the hell she was each time.

Then came Syd again: "Hey, Sweets. Where are you? You didn't return my call. You okay? Two more days 'n' Jake'll be back. We goin' with the somethin' to eat plan or what? Lemme know. Hope you're okay. Love you."

Click.

Jake turned to the bathroom and took a step forward. He stopped and clenched his hands when the answering machine beeped and another message began.

"Where are you? I stopped by your place earlier and you wasn't there. I waited nearly an hour. We *are* still goin' through with this, ain't we? Maybe you just need a little time, I understand. I'll let you have it. Just know that I love you, babe. Jake's a good man. He'll be understandin', I'm sure."

Syd clicked off and there was another message from Jake. "Hey, babe. Be comin' home today and, really, I can't wait to see you. A little time away and I realize how much I miss you. You haven't returned a single goddamn call so I hope you're okay. Don't be pissed at me. Things went for shit..." A heavy block of silence, then, "Can't wait to see you. Love you. See you soon."

Jake heard himself click off.

The last message—before the one Allen just left—was, of course, Syd, in his wink-wink, nudge-nudge tone of voice. "Hey, cutie pie. Sure as I am, I'm gettin' *hungry*." And there were no other messages. There didn't need to be.

Jake went into the bathroom. The carving knife was on the floor and he knew that it just wasn't gonna cut it, so he took it back into the kitchen; then he checked the time. The hardware store was still open for another thirty minutes.

She was stacked neatly in the tub, about twenty pieces in all. If Jake wanted to, he could've had sandwiches for a month. He scooped some of her from the floor and put it on top of the pile.

"Hell of a saw, wasn't it, honey?" waving his hands at the flies.

She'd never wag her tongue again, and sure as shit, Jake couldn't even tell where her tongue, lips, teeth or eyes were anymore. Somewhere in there, but he didn't much care to look.

It took strength and patience but as far as he was concerned the smell wasn't any worse than it had already been. Not a womanly deed, he thought, feeling better than he had in quite a while. It was about time the Grind-O-Matic was put to use again; he'd been getting ready to throw the damn thing out.

Thinking back on cutting off her hand, it didn't seem so bad now. He just didn't have the stomach for it initially. Grinding her for a second time to make sure she was very fine, he was pleased to discover that she was quite pliable.

Maybe Donald was right after all, thought Jake—maybe it's just a matter of the right motivation.

The Day the Leash Gave Way

After a while, with all said and done, Jake picked up the phone and told Syd he'd be happy to get something to eat with him. "Why don't you come on over and pick us up," he said. "The little lady just got outta the bath."

"Hot dog!" Syd exclaimed, then hung up.

Yes, Jake thought—

Hot dog.

The Disappearance of Experimentation

I love my girlfriend because we fuck all the time. We hurt each other. We bite each other. We whip each other. We piss and shit on each other and then we fuck some more. We fuck and fuck and fuck, and when we're finished fucking we give each other hand jobs. I fuck her in the ass and then she straps one on and fucks me. When she's not around I fuck myself in various ways. Sometimes I just jack off and other times I find things around the house. Like I fuck the couch, or some of her clothes. Sometimes my own clothes.

But I'm always fucking. And so is she. She tells me about what she does when I'm not around and what she puts inside her and I get all hot as hell and then we fuck. And when we're finished we fuck again until we can't fuck anymore. Then it isn't long and we're at it again, fucking each other and ourselves in different ways.

I take an unopened bottle of beer and shove it into her pussy backwards and open it and drink the beer from the bottle while it's up her. She has a big gaping cunt and I love to eat it—and when I'm not eating it I'm fucking it.

She ties me to the bed and whips my cock as hard as she can, then she sucks it until I cum then she whips it some more, then climbs on top of me and slips me into her and we fuck, me tied up and her in control. When we're finished I tie her up and spank her cunt, sometimes until it bleeds, then I go down on her and bite her clit, and if she's bleeding I drink the blood.

I jack off while I do this.

I'm always jacking off. Even at work I jack off. I must jack off nine times a day just while I'm at work, and I like to stick my finger up my ass when I cum. It makes me cum harder. And I can always cum.

My girlfriend says that we should bring somebody else in. Have a threesome. A guy or a girl, it doesn't matter, as long as we're fucking. I'm not sure I like the idea. I don't want to share my girlfriend with anybody. I wouldn't mind being shared myself, but I can't stand the idea of someone else touching her. Still, she wants to bring someone else in, and so I tell her okay, and the next day there's another girl with us. And we all fuck like crazy. We fuck and fuck and fuck. The new girl doesn't like pain quite so much. A little is okay but not too much, and I'm thinking how pain is part of the pleasure. But my girlfriend says okay, not so much pain. So we all feel less pain, and I don't like it quite as much. But we still fuck a whole lot. We still fuck like it's the last time we'll ever get to.

Next time: she brings a guy over, and we fuck and fuck but this guy isn't into all the stuff we're into. He's a bit of a sissy and I can't help wondering if he's queer. But I fuck him anyway. He fucks me up the ass as I fuck my girlfriend. Then he fucks my girlfriend and I stick my dick in her mouth, but she pulls my dick away and says she just wants to try it

The Day the Leash Gave Way 123

with him for a minute. That pisses me off but I don't say anything. I sit there and jack off and watch this other guy fuck my girlfriend. And all he's doing is fucking her. He isn't spanking her or biting her or anything. He's just plain old fucking her, and missionary style at that. And she keeps smiling and making these little ohing sounds, like she's really enjoying it. But she isn't screaming. I make her scream.

When they finish fucking I grab my girlfriend's tits but she pulls my hands away and says she needs to take a break. She goes into the bathroom and takes a shower as the guy gets dressed and leaves. When she comes out of the shower I try to fuck her, but she isn't in the mood. She lets me jack off in front of her, though. When I cum she says she's tired and she gets into bed and turns off the light. I climb into bed next to her and jack off again, hoping the sound of me fucking myself will wake her up and turn her on and we'll fuck. But she starts snoring and that pisses me off and I feel ashamed of myself. Still, I jack off until I cum, and I wipe it all over my belly.

The next morning I wake up and feel her ass. She slides away from me and continues sleeping. I get up and take a shower and when I come out she's gone. I jack off, then get dressed and go to work. I only jack off three times that day. When I get home my girlfriend isn't there. I'm feeling horny so I start masturbating. My girlfriend walks in on me and says oops, then races past and goes into the kitchen and makes herself some dinner without making me anything. Suddenly I don't feel much like making myself cum. I just sort of feel strange.

She finishes her dinner then says she's going out. I ask her where and she says out to have a good time. When she's gone I cry because I don't understand why she's not fucking me. I turn on the TV and watch a fucking movie.

A few hours later she comes home with a guy—the same guy we fucked the other night. They're making out as they walk in, taking off their clothes. I get excited and unzip my pants and start working my dick back and forth until I'm hard, but they don't even notice me. Making out the whole time, they go into our bedroom and close the door. I'm confused. I go to the door and try turning the handle but it's locked. I can hear them fucking on the other side. They're just fucking, and the softer, quieter moans are coming from my girlfriend.

I make her scream. He makes her moan. I'm pissed.

I bang on the door but they don't pay any attention to me. It's like they can't hear me at all. They fuck for a long time and when they're done I can hear the sound of their lips as they kiss. I haven't kissed my girlfriend for a long time. Not just a plain old kiss—we've been too busy fucking.

They never open the door and I sleep on the couch, angry and hurt.

The next morning the door unlocks, and they walk out together, arm in arm. They make breakfast together and don't hear a thing I say. I don't feel much like jacking off this morning.

As they sit and eat breakfast, my girlfriend tells the guy that she used to be a little crazy but she's over it. She just wants someone to love her. She's tired of fucking and fucking and not doing anything else. She wants someone to talk to and someone who will love her. She wants someone who will do things with her, and also do things for her. She wants someone she can do things other than just fucking with. She says she's done a lot of experimenting and a lot of it she isn't proud of. As she says this I look at my dick but it's gone. My whole crotch is gone and I can only see the couch where it should be.

She says she knows what she wants. She wants more than just a fuck, and I don't have legs anymore. She loves making love but she's tired of fucking just for the sake of fucking. She's over it and wants to move on and enjoy the other things in life. Things other than fucking.

My stomach is gone and so is my chest. I'm nothing but arms, shoulders, neck and head.

She looks into the man's eyes and tells him she's falling in love with him. She never told *me* that. Of course, I never told *her* that either. We were too busy fucking and it never came up. I just assumed it was love because we fucked all the time.

My hands disappear, now my arms and shoulders are gone and I can't see myself at all. But I can still see them, holding hands across the table, looking at each other and smiling. Then they talk about things that have nothing to do with fucking. They talk about all sorts of things; and when they finish breakfast they wash the dishes together. Other than fucking, we never did anything together.

That night the bedroom door is locked and I hear the bedsprings squeaking and I can hear her moaning. I can't jack off because I don't have hands or a dick anymore, though I'm not sure I'd feel like it even if I could.

An Angle for the Angels

Jeff set down his beer and thought about the pussy he didn't get. It depressed the hell out of him. With persistence he wasn't even able to cop a feel, and then Rebecca left the party with what's his name—the guy on the football team. And as she left she cut Jeff one of those glances that told him she was gonna go all the way with this one, cause he was a jock and had a letter on his goddamn jacket.

Twenty minutes later, Rebecca gone with what's his face, all Jeff could do was sit and drink beer and think about Rebecca's crotch, which made him mad because he kept thinking about what's his name thrusting his football hero lance into it. It made him wanna puke; but instead he drank some more beer and felt sorry for himself.

It wasn't as though Rebecca was the only girl in the world. Hell, there were plenty around. Problem was none of them would so much as look in his direction, let alone spread wide and invite him in—so he continued feeling sorry for himself, and kept on thinking about Rebecca's snatch.

Travis came over with a fresh beer for him.

"You still upset about Rebecca?" Travis asked.

It wasn't so much Rebecca that Jeff was sad about—it was what she had under her skirt, and the fact that what's his name had either gotten it, or was getting it as Jeff sat there. That's what really got him.

"Don't worry none," Travis said, who had one stray eye even when he wasn't drunk. After a few bottles it was as though he was looking in two completely different directions. "I hear Daniel's sister's got the hots for you. Of course, I also heard she'd spread 'em for a tube of toothpaste. Daniel said she offered herself to him on more than one occasion."

Maybe there was some form of comfort in there but it wasn't quite enough to raise Jeff's spirits. After all, when a retard likes you, sure, it's a bit flattering and all, but there's this other horrible feeling, knowing that the only one who likes you is a retard.

Jeff rubbed his shin, which he'd smashed the day before and still hurt like a motherfucker for the most part. He looked across into the kitchen at his friend, Daniel.

It was Daniel who was throwing the party, and who was also throwing up in the kitchen sink. His parents were out of town but his sister was lurking about somewhere. Jeff recalled one time being over and going into the bathroom to take a leak and finding Daniel's sister, Scuba, on hands and knees, drinking from the toilet. The frightening thing was the smell, whether from the toilet or from somewhere else, Jeff didn't know, nor did he care to investigate. Jeff was about to step out and leave her alone when she looked up at him, her face dripping toilet water, and said, "Scuba, Scuba." Her name was Danielle, but everyone knew her as Scuba because she liked "Scooby-Doo" but couldn't say it right.

Living in the desert the poor girl most likely didn't know jack about underwater exploration. "Scuba, Jeffee, Scuba."

Jeff, sipping his fresh beer, scouted the room. Daniel was still puking in the kitchen sink. Straightening up briefly, the poor guy wiped his mouth, laughed at something unknown, then leaned down and continued. Everyone was laughing at him, including Travis.

Travis had a good buzz going. Damn. For once it was almost like everything in the world was right and okay, and seeing people puke was cool. The way Travis was feeling he could have stumbled over and fell and banged his head on the goddamn coffee table and he still would've been having a great fucking time.

Jeff, on the other hand, was slipping more and more into depression. Thinking about what's his face banging Rebecca somewhere, while he sat and watched his friend vomit in the kitchen sink, really didn't leave him feeling too cheerful inside. Thinking about his life in general—thinking about how the only girls that ever really liked him were retards.

In some ways he understood why he never got any. He was good looking enough. One problem with this particular party was everybody already knew him. Girls had approached him in the past. It was the moment he opened his mouth that they usually ran the other way. If he could just learn to keep his goddamn mouth shut. A lotta the time when he opened his mouth it was like a big pile of shit dumped out, all moist and steamy; and the only ones that usually didn't run were the goddamn retards.

And then there was Lucia. Jeff used to have a crush on this girl named Lucia Mackendale, and she liked him pretty well too, until they went out on a date and Lucia found that goddamn dog collar still attached to his rear bumper. Jeff could've sworn he'd taken that off, or he'd looked and didn't see it or something. But Lucia found it all right, and the fact that the collar belonged to Lucia's neighbor and close friend, who'd cried three days after their dog disappeared, didn't score Jeff any points either. When he dropped her off at home and tried for a kiss she told him she'd just decided to start munching rug. That can hurt a man. It took Jeff a while, even with looking at magazines, to be a man again, and he felt ashamed of himself.

Problem was, Jeff didn't much like people. Even Travis, sitting next to him, drunk and jolly and all, was an idiot in Jeff's eyes. Jeff didn't much care if Travis stood up and stumbled and fell and cracked his head on the goddamn coffee table. Hell, Jeff had cracked his shin on a coffee table only the day before, and it still hurt like a bitch. The thing that really nagged him, though, was that he *wanted* to like people. He wanted to do good for others and all that, he just didn't really know how.

Travis leaned in close and looked into Jeff's eyes with one of his, and somewhere else with the other. "If you're wanting to stretch your pecker," he said, "I know Scuba would be more than happy to oblige." Then he leaned back and took a hearty swig and spilled some beer on his shirt without noticing. A tiny batch of foam clung to the end of his chin and it looked like a spider sac.

Thinking about giving Rebecca his hot meat injection, Jeff had to admit, made him want to give it to just about anything. Problem was realizing he was giving it to a retard would not have been the kind of thing to keep him rock hard. Being retarded wasn't his

The Day the Leash Gave Way

kind of foreplay, though he'd unwillingly acted that way himself in the past. He knew it, dammit. Yet, as he sipped his beer, the two things that kept coming to mind were that he was tired of acting like an idiot, and he had a pipe he needed to lay.

"Just saw her go into her bedroom," Travis said, and pointed in the direction like Christopher Columbus probably did when he first saw America, only Columbus probably didn't have a batch of beer foam clinging to his chin. "Ten bucks and my next beer say that if you go in there, you'll be shootin' your wad."

With all Jeff was thinking and feeling the idea of slipping it to Scuba didn't seem so bad now. Hell, at the very least he could imagine it was Rebecca. And hell, everybody needs to get some now and then, even a retard. He could look at this as a start to making good on what he wanted: to be a little better of a person and help others from time to time.

"All right," he said, and chugged down his beer and rose to his feet. He wasn't too drunk, but he was a bit wobbly when he stood up. There was a part of him that worried about just plain passing out while in the midst of it. Naw, he thought. Not the way he was feeling. He was gonna do it, and he would be able to look at Rebecca on Monday and give her one of those glances that told her he went all the way too—he only hoped he could keep that it was with Scuba *out* of that glance.

"You ready?" Travis said.

"Ready," said Jeff.

"How do you feel?"

"I—I feel ready."

"Ready to what?" Travis was overly enthused.

"Ready to..." He didn't know where to go with that. What the hell was he supposed to say? This wasn't a boxing match. It was a party where he was gonna try to get it on with his friend's sister—a girl who drank out of the goddamn toilet and occasionally ate grasshoppers.

"Are you a machine?" Travis said. "Are you a piece of iron? Are you a piston ready to..."

Jeff walked away and over to Daniel, who was now sitting on the floor below the sink with a ring of barf around his mouth. Daniel giggled every now and then, but other than that, he was like one of those vegetables that can't do anything but drool. Jeff put a hand on his shoulder, gave it a squeeze, then turned and headed for Scuba's bedroom, thinking about Rebecca as he went. Just as he got to her door someone turned up the music. One of those songs with way too much bass. The lyrics of the song helped get him in the mood though, and he straightened up in all areas as the song thumped:

I want your booty and your pooty, gimme poon-tang, yeah!
I want your booty and your pooty, gimme poon-tang, yeah!

Jeff closed his eyes, turned the doorknob, pushed it open and stepped inside. When he opened his eyes Scuba was on her bed, picking her toes. Her dress was hiked up and Jeff could see Scooby-Doo on her panties. He didn't know they put Scooby-Doo on panties for girls her size. Scuba had fat thighs and a fat ass, but Jeff knew he was only comparing her to Rebecca, who had the kind of flesh that could make a wolf howl.

Jeff closed the door and took a step inside.

"Jeffee," Scuba said. "Jeffee. Scuba, Scuba, hoochie." And with that she raised up her legs and smiled. "Hoochie. Scuba hoochie, hoochie." She kept picking at her toes with one hand, and a small stream of snot slipped out of her left nostril.

"Aw, shit," Jeff said. Suddenly he wasn't sure he could go through with it. If for no other reason, this was the same girl he'd watched drink right from the toilet. He'd never seen what was in the toilet, and was thankful for that much, anyway. But seeing her there, picking her toes and with the snot and all, it wasn't the kind of thing to make him hard as steel. And yet, Rebecca wouldn't leave his mind. He pictured Rebecca there on the bed, picking her toes with snot running down her face, and that somehow made it okay. Anything *Rebecca* did was okay in Jeff's eyes.

"Scuba snatch," Scuba said. "Jeffee unt Scuba snatch?"

Jeff wasn't sure he wanted any of it; yet something on a deeper level, possibly a primitive one, insisted that he take it. And after all, everyone needs a little oom-pah from time to time. Even retards. So he moved in and sat down on her bed.

Scuba kept on picking her toes. She removed a bit of toenail and put it in her mouth and said, "Jeffee unt Scuba snatch." Then she giggled.

Funny, Jeff thought, when she giggles she sounds just like any other girl.

A bit more toenail went into her mouth, and the snot was pouring in now, too. It was like there was a never-ending river of it. Some of it expanded into a bubble then popped and Scuba picked her foot some more and farted. "Scuba 'ake bubble," she said.

But it wasn't Scuba that Jeff saw there on the bed. Not right then. It was Rebecca, all snotty and picking her feet with her legs in the air and he loved it. He loved every damn second of it. He imagined what's his face from the football team in the corner, all tied up and having to watch as Jeff had his own go at stretching his long fellow in Rebecca's love box. What's his name would be crying, Jeff thought. Yeah, those tough guys are the ones who cry easiest in the end. Nothing but a damn sissy inside, once you uncover it. So sissy they couldn't even get a goddamn retard.

Jeff couldn't help puffing out his chest a little at that. Still, when he leaned in to make his first move, he wished to God he had a bag or something he could put over her head. The best thing, he reckoned, was to keep his eyes shut. As long as he couldn't see her, she could be anybody he wanted. Hell, even better than Rebecca, she could be that sexy blonde on TV, or that cute girl with the big eyes and the frizzy hair that worked at K-Mart. Jeff always liked shopping at K-Mart because that girl was always there, as if she lived there, big eyes and all, like one of those *Power Puff Girls*, except she always had a bit of an attitude, and those eyes usually looked like they hadn't slept enough. As Jeff slid his hand up Scuba's thigh, it was the K-Mart girl, even moreso than Rebecca, which got his blood pumping.

"Jeffee," Scuba said; and Jeff wondered if hearing her voice was gonna spoil the mood. He kept his eyes closed, though, and did what little he really knew how to do. The congestion of the snot in Scuba's nose sounded like someone grinding water. He just kept thinking about the big-eyed girl at K-Mart. It was the only thing he could do to keep himself up.

"Scuba," said Scuba. "Jeffee unt Scuba."

The Day the Leash Gave Way 129

Not really, no, but he was taking her anyway. In his mind he was with the K-Mart girl. She was smiling and cooing at him and telling him what a man he was. He doubted the K-Mart girl—or Rebecca or even the sexy blonde on TV—ever drank from the toilet. Of course, one never knows.

His leg started acting up. Of all things, it was thinking about a peanut butter and jelly sandwich and when his mom used to snuggle him that got his mind off of it.

Keeping his eyes closed was tough. His imagination was strong, and he'd convince himself that it wasn't Scuba under him, but rather the K-Mart girl, wearing her red vest and nothing else. Then just before he opened his eyes he remembered, and decided that if he ever did this again he definitely wanted something to put over her head.

Just as it occurred to him that he could use a pillowcase, an adult voice spoke his name. Sad as it was, Jeff opened his eyes, and briefly he saw Scuba's face, that river of snot covering her upper lip like a mustache, another big bubble growing out of it. Then he looked up, and standing across the room, in front of the closet, was a man in a nice black suit, holding a clipboard in his hand. He was very clean and seemed a happy sort, yet quite serious at the same time.

"Jeffrey Francis Chilcott?" the man said.

"Scuba," said Scuba.

Jeff didn't say anything. All he could think was that he was busted banging a retard. Oh the shame, dammit—what kind of trouble was he in *now*? Where had this man come from? Had he been in Scuba's room the whole time? Jeff hadn't seen him until now.

"Jeffee?" Scuba said.

"You are Jeffrey Chilcott, are you not?" the man asked.

"Who are you?" Jeff said, still moving up and down slightly on top of his friend's sister.

The stranger crossed his arms and sighed. Scuba picked her nose. The music in the other room got a bit louder: *I want your booty and your pooty, gimme poon-tang, yeah!*

Still on top of Scuba, the anxiety decreased that he was busted for boning a retard, and increased that there was a strange man who came from out of nowhere and was asking him questions.

"Scuba," said Scuba, picking her nose.

"All right," the man said, uncrossed his arms and regarded his clipboard. "Jeffrey Francis Chilcott, age seventeen, right?"

Jeff noticed he was still thrusting up into Scuba and pulled out. "I'll be eighteen in November," he told the man.

"A Junior at Desert High School. Correct?"

"Hey, is this about my last report card or something?"

The man did not acknowledge Jeff's question. "Born in Santa Fe, New Mexico, 1983?"

Someone stumbled against the other side of the door and coughed then attempted to sing along with the song playing. "Gimme poon-tang, dude, yeah, man. Word." This made Jeff paranoid enough that somebody was going to walk in, and he pulled his pants up and buckled his belt, forgetting to zip his fly.

Scuba sat up, finger in nose, and watched Jeffee talk to closet.

"What is all this?" Jeff said.

"Your mother is Christine Davidson. Father—Francis P. Chilcott."

"How the hell do you know all this?"

"It's our job, Mister Chilcott," the man said.

Job? Jeff wondered. What kind of job required voyeurism and intrusion? Was it a specialized field? Did he have a chance getting any kind of job like it when he was finally out of school in another year? Suddenly he was sorry that he'd ever come into Scuba's room. Hell, he was sorry he'd come to the party at all.

"Jeffee? Who talk?" Scuba asked him.

Jeff looked down at her, saw her picking her nose and looked back at the man with the clipboard. He'd had just about enough Scuba for one evening, and would rather be in most any kind of trouble than have to deal with her anymore.

"All right, okay, let's get down to business," the man said, and regarded the clipboard again. "Now then, it's twenty-two minutes after ten. That leaves an hour and...thirty-eight minutes until your departure."

"Departure?"

Scuba kicked her legs up and down and giggled. Her panties were wrapped around her left ankle and they brushed Jeff's arm every time they went by.

"Quite a bundle, isn't she?" the man said.

"Scuba," Jeff steadied her legs, "I think we need to stop playing right now."

"Hoochie," said Scuba.

"This man's asking me all kinds of weird questions. I think I might be in some kind of trouble. It could be important."

Scuba looked at the closet. "'Utt meh?"

"This man right here, Scubes, with the clipboard."

"Scuba!" she yelled, and her legs started flailing again.

"Forget it, Mister Chilcott. She can't see or hear me."

"Huh? Why? Cause she's a retard?"

"No. You can see me only if you're accompanying me."

"Accompanying you? Where?"

The man gazed down at his expensive-looking watch. "Your time is short, Mister Chilcott. Don't you think you should be getting things together?"

"What the—? Look, dude, I dunno what the hell you're talking about, but I just wanna say tha—"

"Mister Chilcott. Or do you prefer Jeff? You only have an hour and a half before we need to be leaving."

"I'm not going anywhere," Jeff told him. "I might, maybe, later, go home; but other than that, I'm staying right here. Frankly, right now, I don't trust myself to drive. I'm not stupid."

The man sighed, lifted his pencil and drummed it on his clipboard, irritating the hell out of Jeff.

"Scuba," said Scuba.

"I'm afraid you don't quite understand, Jeff. Jeez, you're just like everybody else." He set the pencil down on the clipboard, reached into his pocket and removed a stick of gum.

The Day the Leash Gave Way 131

"Everybody—" he stuffed the gum into his mouth— "especially you *kids*, think life is going to go on forever. It's doesn't, Jeff. You all think you're immortal, but like all things, life too must end."

A knot the size of a grapefruit tightened in Jeff's stomach. What the man was saying to him wasn't totally clear—it was just enough to make him feel that if he didn't get back on top of his buddy's retard of a sister, he'd never have another shot at getting laid.

"Hoochie," said Scuba, raking the snot from her lip into her mouth.

"Everybody goes sometime," the man told him matter-of-factly. "No one really gets to pick their time. It just happens."

"Go? You mean, like, *die* or something?"

"No something," the man said. "Die is the perfect word for it."

The music ended and a tense moment of silence followed before the next song came on.

Smoke a doobie, gimme pooty, get it on, get it on!

The man walked around the room, looked at all the finger paintings hanging on the walls. There were more finger paintings in that room than grains of sand on the earth. "Nice room this girl's got here. Reminds me of a kindergarten classroom." He stopped beside Jeff and looked down at Scuba.

"She's a retard," Jeff informed.

"Yes," the man said. "I'm well aware of Danielle's situation. A shame—but we don't get to choose our path. Most of the cards are just dealt out." He placed a hand on Jeff's shoulder. "The problem I see right now, Jeff, is that you aren't appreciating the way this is being handled."

"Scuba!" said Scuba.

"Think of all the people whose lives are violently terminated. Car crash victims, people who burn to a crisp in fires, or who are slowly tortured and skinned alive over several days, having their eyes gouged out and their fingers and toes cut off, one by one. We're not allowed to warn them." He spit his gum back into the silver wrapper and put it in his pocket. "You, on the other hand, lucky man, fall into a different category. You luckily get to go peacefully."

"Hoochie!" Scuba started kicking her legs again.

"What, exactly, do you mean by peaceful?"

"Well, to put it simplistically, Jeff, you're going to go by natural causes."

"Natural causes? You mean, like, old age?"

"I know you're not that stupid, Jeff. No." The man squinted at the clipboard. "Not because you're old, and no, you haven't caught any sort of sexually transmitted disease or anything. Can't catch anything like that from your hand."

"Hey." Jeff pointed down to the retard lying on the bed.

"She hardly counts either, Jeff—and that only lasted about two minutes."

Suddenly Jeff felt outraged. He didn't want to admit it to himself, but he was faced with the hard and painful facts, and someone else knew all about it: he'd just lost his virginity to a goddamn retard. Halle-fucking-lujah, if that wasn't gonna be eternal shit clinging to the hairs of his ass. Then he wondered if, technically, he *had* just lost his virginity—after all, he didn't, as Travis said, shoot his wad. Did that count as having sex or was it just fooling around? He certainly felt like a goddamn fool. What did one need to do in order to have it count?

"Jeff," the man said, "at midnight, your heart is going to stop. I recommend being asleep when this happens. You won't notice a thing if you're sleeping."

"Scuba!"

"But...how the hell can my heart just...*stop?*"

Again, the man placed his hand on Jeff's shoulder. Even through his clothing Jeff felt the coldness of the man's touch. "Yesterday," the man said, "you banged your shin. A good crack on your mother's coffee table."

"Stupid coffee table. The thing weighs like a million pounds. Thought I'd broken something for a minute."

"Yes, well, you did." The man straightened up and suddenly looked much more like a man who knew things. "What happened was, you slammed your shin in such a manner that it caused a very small—*very small*—hairline fracture." He looked down at his clipboard again, then back to Jeff's somewhat drunken eyes and pale face. "The damage is so small that there's a good chance a doctor wouldn't see it unless he was *really looking*—which doctors rarely do."

"Jeffee!"

"However," the man continued, "something else happened—something very rare indeed. A freak occurrence, if you will."

Scuba's legs kicked around and she farted again. There was snot smeared all over her face now and Jeff saw for the first time that her nipples were hard. Steadying her legs once more, Jeff got her attention and told her no more, it was time for her to stop and go back out to the party.

"Potty!" she yelled, and hopped off the bed, went to the door, her Scooby-Doo panties wrapped around her ankle. Jeff closed the door behind her, then gave his attention back to the stranger with the clipboard.

"Now, what was that?" Jeff said. "Something about me being a freak?"

"No, Jeff," the man said. "A freak *occurrence*." He straightened up again, which made him more serious looking. "With that small fracture you've suffered in your leg, some bone marrow has escaped into your bloodstream. It's been moving slowly but it's going straight to your heart, and it's going to stop it."

Jeff recalled the moment he'd bashed his leg. He'd made the informal exclamation of "Bitch shit!" and fallen to the ground grasping his shin. He'd wondered then if he'd somehow managed to break something. Sure as hell wasn't gonna break the coffee table, it being a million pounds and all. Now, as it turned out, according to this strange guy with the clipboard who'd come from out of nowhere, he <u>had</u> broken something—and now that small break was going to kill him.

Who was this man, anyway? It occurred to Jeff that he didn't even know the guy's name. The stranger had seen him with his rod inside a retard, and yet Jeff didn't know this guy from a dog turd. One time Jeff met a man in the park, who was sitting on the grass

The Day the Leash Gave Way 133

poking a fresh pile of grade A doggie doo with his finger. The guy had been crazy, and Jeff never got his name either.

Out the corner of his eye, in one of the few places on the wall where there wasn't a finger painting, Jeff noticed a big hairy spider the size of a quarter. It was just standing there, minding its own spider business, oblivious that it was surrounded by finger paintings.

"So what gives?" Jeff finally said. "You know all this stuff about me. You're invisible to other people. You like gum. Exactly who the hell are you?"

A bunch of people out in the other room laughed, and someone asked Daniel if he was ever gonna stop puking.

"Jeff," the man said, "how much clearer do I need to make it?" He walked slowly and casually over to the wall. "Sometimes it's astonishing how dense people can be." With one light touch gently against one of the spider's legs, the arachnid leapt off the wall and down to the floor; by the time it landed on the carpet its legs were curled into its belly and it looked two days dead.

Jeff opened his mouth, sensing steamy shit ready to pour. "Uh...like, you're, uh...Death?"

"Congratulations, Jeff. You may have turned the assignment in late but you got it right."

Suddenly Jeff felt like he would win if he were to have a puking contest with Daniel. One time they'd had a pissing contest and Jeff won by peeing nearly a foot farther.

The man looked at Jeff with a warm smile. Jeff felt weak and noticed the pain in his shin again. If all of this was real, then what was it really going to be like? Was he gonna go to Heaven or Hell? He didn't dare ask.

"Now," the man said, once again regarding the clipboard. "Back to business. Midnight tonight. That is in exactly...one hour and twenty-seven minutes. You are supposed to go while in your sleep. It will be painless and easy."

"Please!" Jeff shouted, trembling all over. "I don't want to go! I'm too young! I'm too young to die! Please!"

"Oh, Jeff," the man said.

"I can't even legally buy cigarettes or porn! I can't die yet, I can't!" One time he'd ducked into the pornography section at the video store but they'd kicked him out. Jeff couldn't wait for the day when they asked to see some ID and he could just whip it out and hand it over. That wasn't going to happen. That could never happen now, not if he was dead. Not if he was fucking dead. "Please! I can't go! I don't wanna go!"

"Hardly anyone *wants* to go, Jeff," the man said, then sighed and looked down at the crumpled spider on the floor. "I'm sorry."

"That's not fair," Jeff said. "Don't I get some sort of say in the matter?"

"Well," the man straightened up; "we do listen to appeals. But I have to say there is little to no chance for you. Now, for example, can you honestly say that there is going to be someone—anyone—who will give a crap about your demise?"

It took a long time thinking about it before Jeff said: "My folks. They'd give a shit. If I die they'll give a major shit."

"You really think so?" the man asked. "With your dad wanting nothing but women and your mom wanting nothing but TV? Do you honestly think they'd care? When was the last time you even spoke to one of them?"

Jeff couldn't recall.

"I mean, jeez, Jeff, you know it and I know it—you were an accident."

He hated hearing it, but again Jeff had to face the awful truth.

The man raised his eyebrows. "Yes, Jeff?"

"I was on the verge of getting laid, dammit! Hell, I was gettin' some when you showed up. Scuba will go crazy with no Jeffrey lovin'. I might be ready to go if I'd just been able to finish."

"C'mon, Jeff. Had you had an orgasm with Danielle, you really think you'd be ready and willing to go? Everything would be fine because, well Jeez, you got some tail?"

Once again, Jeff had to face reality.

The music whisked through the door like a breeze. *Smoke a doobie, gimme pooty, get it on, get it on!*

The man looked once more at his clipboard. "Do you have any unfinished business, Jeff? When I say that, Jeff, I mean unfinished business of a *major* nature."

Jeff turned and faced the stranger. "I've—I've never gone all the way. I mean, sure, I was on my way with Scuba, but I didn't score. I didn't get to go *all* the way. I'm sure you couldn't care less," he said, looking down at his shoes. "In a sense it's—"

"It's the exact same attempt you just made. The same damn thing."

"I'm seventeen," Jeff said. "You may not care but it means a hell of a lot to me. I don't know if you were ever my age, but if you were, you know what I'm talking about."

The man said nothing.

"It would be...one time in my whole life that I did something, y'know? One time that I was successful somehow." Jeff could see the man was losing patience. "For once, just one time on this freaking mud ball, I could be...proud of myself."

In the man's face, there was absolutely no expression.

"I'm seventeen, man," Jeff reiterated. "Most of the people I know have gotten some, and those who haven't will, eventually. I won't ever have a chance if I die now. All I want is one time. Not fair that anybody dies before gettin' a little."

"Jeff," the man said, "do you know what this means? This would require a delay."

"Only until I did it. Only until I went all the way—just once."

The man smiled, then sighed and shook his head. "Sorry, Jeff. Getting your rocks off hardly counts as business of a major nature." He looked at Jeff, saw the sadness that flooded through his face. Suddenly the man couldn't help it. He didn't like it one bit, but he started feeling teary-eyed. "Really means a lot to you, doesn't it, Jeff?"

"More important than anything else in the world," Jeff said, wiping away the tears that were finding their way out of his eyes. "More important than you could possibly imagine."

Tapping his pencil on his clipboard again, the man paced a few times around the room and stopped in front of the closet, on which the door stood open.

Jeff studied all the finger paintings on the walls, and thought about all the snot on Scuba's face.

The Day the Leash Gave Way 135

"All right, Jeff," the man finally said, still drumming that damn pencil. "Given your age and your needs, I *suppose* we can...grant you a delay."

Jeff thumbed away another tear and looked at the man. "For—for how long?"

"What do you think? Until you...you've gotten some." The man's face reddened.

"You mean, I—I can...stay around?"

"You can stick around until you get some, uh, lovin', yes."

A wave of relief washed over Jeff and he suddenly relaxed so much that he almost accidentally wet his pants. Then his eyes narrowed and his lips pressed tightly together and turned white. "Sounds like a fair deal," he said.

Just then Daniel barged into the room. He stood in the doorway, stared at Jeff a moment, then leaned over and threw up on the floor.

"Hi, Daniel," Jeff said.

Daniel moaned, eyes bloodshot, then left the room and closed the door, leaving the vomit where he'd put it.

"Now," the man said. "About this getting laid, Jeff—when can we expect it?"

Jeff, eyes slanted, shrugged his shoulders. "Oh, soon, soon. I dunno exactly when. These things can take time." Another shrug. "Guess that's okay, though. I've grown rather fond of my hand."

The man turned away and cut Jeff a sidelong glance. "Mister Chilcott, I suspect you're trying to pull a fast one."

"Really?" He giggled. "That's a trip." Then he lunged forward and, with all his might, shoved the stranger into the closet and slammed the door shut. "Fuck you, crazy man!" He took the chair away from Scuba's finger painting desk and propped it under the doorknob. "You ain't gonna take me that damn easy, you crazy death bastard."

He listened at the closet door but didn't hear a sound. Maybe the guy was unconscious. Maybe he was dead. That would be cool, he thought, to kill Death. He listened another moment; then, satisfied, he turned around to leave Scuba's goddamn finger painting covered room. After one step he stopped in his tracks. The stranger was sitting, clipboard in hand, on Scuba's desk.

"You don't get it, Jeff," the man said. "You really don't understand just how serious this is."

Jeff recalled a time when he was a boy and a magician made a coin disappear then reappear from behind Jeff's ear. It made him long for his youth then made him bolt to the door. He flung it open, and almost ran head on into the stranger.

"This is tough, what you've done," the man told him.

Jeff stared at the man, and had to struggle in order to keep his bladder from losing control.

"We've tried, Jeff. We just went out of our way for you. And what do you do? You shove me in a closet." The man shook his head and made a tsk-tsk sound. "Unfortunately, Jeff, for that there are consequences."

"Listen, pal, we made a deal. I don't go until I've gotten some pussy. You gotta wait 'til I get laid."

The man sighed. "True, Jeff, true. Sadly, however, on account of your reluctance, we've been forced into an alternative."

Just then Jeff heard Travis in one of the other rooms. "Scuba! Careful, like, what the fuck are you…?" Then there was a cracking sound and Travis shouted, "Fuck!" This was followed by a moment of silence as the songs changed. Jeff ran to the bathroom as the new song came on—*Pooty! Pooty! Bang it! Pooty!* —and found Travis standing by the sink, dumbfounded and staring down at Scuba, who was on the floor, her head resting in a pool of blood. Her eyes rolled around like Ferris wheels, and there was a red splotch on the toilet.

"She was tryin' to stand on her head on the back of the shitter," Travis said.

Jeff kneeled down and looked at her. Her face was still covered in snot and her panties were around her ankle. "Oh, Scuba," he said, holding back a tear. After all, she was the only one willing to let him park his car in her garage.

Scuba didn't reply. Other than the rolling of her eyes she didn't move.

"Have you called an ambulance?" There were other kids peering in, most of them too drunk to comprehend what was going on.

Daniel, standing directly above Jeff, shook his head. "Huh-uh. Don't want no ambulance. They'll find out about the party 'n' tell my folks, and they'll kick me outta the house like they said they would."

Jeff was tempted to push the idea, and then realized doctors probably wouldn't be able to help, anyway.

"Let's get her into bed, though," Daniel said. "Then she's at least outta the way." He crouched down and, with Jeff and Travis, hauled her to her bedroom. Jeff got some of her snot on his shirt.

Daniel removed the panties from her ankle and they got her into bed.

"Everything's okay," Jeff told her, and she opened her eyes and smiled at him.

"Jeffee," she said, then looked beyond him and said, "Who dat?"

Jeff looked over his shoulder and saw the strange man with the clipboard, standing between Daniel and Travis. A flood of sickness poured through him. He watched the man leave the room. "It's nobody," he told Scuba. Then he got up and chased after the guy, stepping in the puddle of Daniel's vomit.

"Hey, dude. Wait."

The man stopped and turned to Jeff, eyebrows raised. "Yes?"

"All right. Okay. I—I'll go."

"Excuse me?"

"I said I'll go. You can't take Scuba. Please. I've changed my mind. I'll go with you. My heart's gonna stop…I'll go with you."

The man looked down and shook his head. "I'm sorry, Jeff. A deal's a deal. You tried to cheat us on the deal. I'm sorry, we had to make other arrangements. This is the alternative. I told you there were consequences."

"Please don't take her. She's just a retard. She isn't hurting anybody." He couldn't help wondering if there would be a toilet for her to drink out of in the afterlife.

"No can do, Jeff. Sorry. Danielle will be leaving with me at midnight."

The Day the Leash Gave Way 137

Jeff looked at the clock hanging on the wall. It was 11:20. Damn but time was flying.

"And what if you're not here at midnight?" he asked.

"I'll be here," the man said.

"I know, I know; but what if, by chance, you missed it? Just missed that one minute?"

The man threw his head back and laughed. "Impossible, Jeff. I don't flake on my appointments."

"But what *if*?"

"Well," the man said, humoring the boy, "I suppose Danielle would live."

Thoughts and ideas started flooding through Jeff's mind like maggots through a corpse. Problem was, none of them seemed very good.

"That's not going to happen, Jeff. Like I said, I don't miss my appointments."

The man walked to the front door, then walked through it and was gone.

Jeff stood there a moment and thought, then went back to Scuba's bedroom. A few people were passed out in the hall. Just as he stepped in everyone else stepped out, save for Daniel and Travis, who looked at Jeff and couldn't help laughing and pointing at him. Jeff looked down at his crotch and saw Little Jeff poking out. He tucked it away and zipped up, then crouched down beside Scuba, who'd lost consciousness again.

He whispered in her ear. "I won't let him take you, Scubes. I won't let him get you."

Most of the people were leaving. Usually, an injury is the kind of thing to ruin all the damn fun at a party.

Travis placed a hand on Daniel's shoulder. "What if she dies?"

It was as though the idea had never even crossed his mind. His eyes grew wide and he looked down at his sister, then cursed under his breath as a tear slid down his cheek. The only time Jeff had ever seen Daniel cry was when Patrick Huntington had pulled down his bathing suit at the swimming pool as he tried looking macho for the girls.

Someone in the other room turned off the music and a few people in the hall got up and said they needed to leave and they hoped Scuba got better.

Before long it was Jeff, Travis, Daniel and Scuba. Travis searched his pockets 'til he located his flat pack of Winstons. He took one out, screwed it into his face and lit it. Smoking wasn't allowed in Daniel's house but Daniel didn't feel much like saying anything about it.

"Well," Travis said, "ain't gonna do her no good standin' here watchin' her." He turned to Daniel. "How 'bout another round?"

Daniel wiped away his tears, then used Scuba's blanket to clean some of the snot from her face. He nodded and all three left the room, turning out the light.

"What about the blood in the bathroom?" Travis asked.

With a shrug Daniel said he'd clean it in the morning, then went to the fridge and pulled out three beers. Now that he wasn't throwing up anymore, he was set to do it all over again. Ready to get fucked up to the point that he couldn't see—and maybe when he sobered up and his vision returned his sister would be all right and his folks wouldn't throw him out like they wanted to. He handed one beer to Jeff and one to Travis, who flicked his cigarette ash on the coffee table. Daniel went to the kitchen counter and grabbed the big bottle of Jim Beam, then sat down on the couch and started taking shots, chasing it with the beer.

"Hey, gimme one uh those," Travis said, taking a seat beside Daniel. The two of them passed the bottle back and forth and it wasn't long before they were both out cold, Travis with his head on Daniel's shoulder, Daniel with his hand resting high up on Travis' thigh.

Jeff wished he had a camera. He looked at the clock—11:53—then downed his beer. He still didn't have any idea what the fuck to do. If only he could get laid in the next seven minutes. Wouldn't that do it? Wouldn't things revert back to the original deal if he could get some before it was time? He didn't really know. All he knew for sure at that moment was that he had to take a piss. He went into the bathroom, unzipped, and as he positioned himself around the blood on the floor he saw an unopened Trojan, lying half in the blood. Someone must've dropped it during all the chaos.

Jeff hadn't been smart enough to use one before, but now he saw it as a sign, an incentive. He picked it up and wiped the blood off on his jeans, set it on the edge of the sink, then peed.

Yes, now he knew what he had to do—for Scuba *and* for himself.

The smell of puke in Scuba's room was stronger than before. At first Jeff thought she was asleep, the way her breathing was steady and clogged. Then he saw, in the light stabbing in from the hall, that her eyes were open, rolled back. They twitched from time to time but that was about it.

"You awake, Scuba?"

Her lips quivered and her eyes jerked, then she was still again.

Jeff climbed into bed beside her and placed his hand on her stomach. There wasn't much time. Damn, practically no time at all. He unzipped and pulled out Little Jeff, worked it a moment, then opened the Trojan.

"I won't let him get you, Scubes."

He pulled up her skirt and climbed on top of her. Just as he entered she smiled and mumbled one word: "Hoochie." Then her eyes closed and Jeff got busy. Even though it was much darker than before, Jeff still wished he had a bag to put over her head. That grinding water sound from her nose and the smell of Daniel's vomit was making it tough, but he only had about two minutes, dammit! Two minutes to get off—how lame. Damn, if only he had a bag for her head. Maybe something to plug his nose so he didn't have to smell Daniel's puke. He could sense Little Jeff wilting. And in that same moment he heard footsteps out in the other room and knew it wasn't Daniel or Travis. It was the man. Death.

He had to do something. He thought about Rebecca, tried to imagine himself as what's his name from the football team but all that did was make him mad.

Any moment now. Death was waiting right outside in the hall, probably checking his watch.

Jeff needed something—a new angle. A new slant on his imagination. He looked down at Scuba. And realized that it wasn't Scuba. Like something sent from up above, it was the cute girl with the big eyes from K-Mart. She had her red K-Mart vest on and nothing else, and she smiled wide and buck-toothed at him. Suddenly Little Jeff was standing at

The Day the Leash Gave Way 139

attention again. Jeff worked and worked and she told him what a man he was. He realized, only then, that more than anybody else in the world, it was the K-Mart girl he wanted most of all.

Scuba's bedroom door slowly creaked open.

Jeff worked harder. In reality, the whole thing took about three minutes. Just as the stranger entered the room Jeff let out a moan and exclaimed, "K-Mart!" Then he collapsed on top of Scuba. He could feel the stranger's presence above him.

"How you doing, Jeff?"

Jeff climbed off of Scuba and slid out of bed and looked at the man. "I did it," he said. "I did it."

The man nodded. "Yes, you sure did. Maybe you do like people, after all."

"I got laid before you could take Scuba away." He removed the Trojan from sagging Little Jeff and tossed it onto the bed.

"This is true," the man agreed. "It is exactly midnight."

Jeff, heart pounding, said, "Okay. I'm... I'm ready."

The man smiled. "That was a great and noble thing you did, Jeff. Big-hearted." Then he looked down at his watch and then at his clipboard. "If only you'd finished about fifteen seconds earlier."

A chill ran through Jeff like his veins just filled with ice. "Huh?"

The man reached down, his hand went into Scuba's chest and he extracted a flat, flimsy circular thing that looked like a shadow. Scuba's snot-clogged breathing stopped. A light raised from her body, into the air, then disappeared up into the ceiling.

Jeff watched the man fold up he shadow and stick it into his pocket.

"But," Jeff said, "I got laid. You're supposed to take *me*."

"Like I said, Jeff—if only you'd finished a few seconds earlier. I *would* have only taken you." Then he smiled at Jeff and Jeff thought he looked like an alligator. "You see, I was coming for Danielle at midnight; and I'm to take you whenever it is you get laid... which you just did. Had you gotten your rocks off before midnight, Danielle would have been spared. Conveniently, you finished right *at* midnight. Thanks. I get two birds with one stone, as the saying goes."

"You tricked me!" Jeff shouted, shaking a fist at the man, spittle flying from his mouth.

"I did nothing of the sort, Mister Chilcott. You just set yourself up. We were prepared just to take the alternative, but you've thrown in yourself to boot."

Jeff then understood, and realized what he had done. He closed his eyes in nausea but had no choice other than to nod his head. "You're right. Dammit—dammit, dammit, dammit. I thought I had an angle with the angels."

"You did, Jeff. It was just to better *them*."

The used condom sat on the bed like an orange dead snake.

"You ready to go, Jeff?"

In the other room, Jeff heard Daniel and Travis stirring, then heard Daniel tell Travis that he had very nice eyes.

"Yeah," Jeff said. "Get me the hell outta here."

A door opened up in the wall. Jeff couldn't see where it led though he could hear people screaming and chains clanking and whips cracking.

"After you," the man said, and they started towards the opening when Jeff stopped.

"Hang on," he said, and went back to the bed where Scuba's body lay. He looked at her a moment, then picked up the used Trojan and saw his own crippled body on the floor beside the bed. He hadn't even noticed. Quite painless. He took the Trojan with him back to the doorway.

"Just like to have the proof with me," he said. "In case nobody up there believes me." Then he paused and his eyebrows raised in a hopeful gesture. "Up there?"

The man shook his head. "Sorry, Jeff. It was close. But the thing with the dog—and of course, thinking of the K-Mart girl while you were with Danielle. Well, that sort of killed it."

"Aw crap," Jeff said; then after a moment shrugged. "Well, long as that dog ain't down there waiting for me."

The man couldn't keep the smile from his face.

The last thing Jeff heard as he walked through the doorway was Daniel groping Travis.

"How to Write a Short Story for Publication in the New Yorker, by Everette Sage Brown"

If you're anything like the five-something-gazillion other writers on the planet, you aspire to have one of your short literary masterpieces published in the world-renowned magazine, *The New Yorker*. And why not? Millions of people read it every week. It is the literary equivalent of having your name up in lights on Broadway. Everyone suddenly knows what a genius you are, and along with full-page ads for Altoids and double-page ads for Mercedes-Benz, you reach millions of billions of trillions of people. Who *wouldn't* wanna be published in it?

I want to help you get there. You may never be as prestigious or "literary" as I, but the fact that you are still reading this says that you're at least willing to inquire about such a scholarly endeavor.

As a world-renowned writer published in world-renowned magazines, I have come to the point in my reputable life in which I would like to bestow my world-renowned knowledge upon you, the illustrious hopeful.

Let's not squander any more time!

I shall start with a brief overview of what the editors of *The New Yorker* are generally looking for. These are things that can make or break your sale right from the start, so pay earnest attention, as your potential world-renowned author reputableness might very well depend on it.

First and foremost: you should be from Long Island. If you are from Long Island there is a chance you might get published on that merit alone. (Note: if you can't be from Long Island, an acceptable alternative is Staten Island, due to the fact that it is also an island.) Long Island is the chosen location for stories published in *The New Yorker* for two specific reasons:

It has history.

It's in New York and full of rich white people.

A surefire way to catch an editor's eye is to talk about the city and suburbs, or maybe touch on "The Boom Years." If you really want to *wow* them, make sure you throw in some mention of the birth of Long Island, Colonial Long Island, or the Revolution. Just a passing throwaway sentence involving any one of these things is certain to get your manuscript noticed.

EXAMPLE: *Daisy never liked the way she looked in black, even though she knew that the Italian explorer, Giovanni da Verrazano, was wearing black in 1524 when he hit the mainland at the wide hip of present-day Cape Hatteras, N.C., where he slowly moved north and found Long Island, a pleasant place, situated amongst little steep hills. Through deep studious, contemplative rapt, Daisy objectively achieved the solo privity: If I'm wearing black, the possibilities for adventure are endless!*

Wow! It just sucks the reader right in and forces them to continue—or persevere—from one invigorating sentence to the next. And note how, with my own world-renowned literary cleverness, I used the word privity. This brings us to the next matter at hand, which is:

MAKE SURE YOU USE A LOT OF BIG WORDS.

Even if you don't know what they mean, throw them in. The editors at *The New Yorker* will be extremely impressed that you thought to use them rather than make coherent sentences. So pleased, in fact, that you may actually have some trouble if you ever meet this editor in person and they happen to be of the opposite gender, or swinging with your own (very common). Yes, no matter how abstrusely recondite it may be, it is superior to consciously usufruct as many dispensable and superfluous words as humanly surmountable. This will definitely bring you closer to that big sale. They love it. I'm not prevaricating! And now that you know to use big words, whether you understand their meanings or not, the next step is knowing *how* to use them. Adverbs with –ly are pretty much the way to go. If you can construct a sentence that is powerfully moving, grimly true, and handsomely, gracefully, delicately cute, you are truly on the road to successfully and proudly succeeding at what millions of other desperately striving authors so yearningly hope to achieve. Consider:

Jerry laughed heartily, with genuinely clear, sincerely and purely defined amusement. Vigorously he turned the car precisely around in the steeply slanted driveway and casually started his wearily long drive home.

Rolls right off the tongue, wouldn't you concur? Also, any verb other than "said" is always preferable when dealing with speaker attributions. People don't "say" things, they "exclaim" them, or "demand" them. They "snarl" and "mutter" and "ejaculate." Find the biggest words you can and use them instead. "The bigger the word the better," I soliloquize.

If you're not having any luck by this point, if your story feels forced or like it might actually be going somewhere, just do what F. Scott Fitzgerald did when he found himself in a rut and had a deadline. Rip off an excerpt from *The Great Gatsby* and just send it out. A note of caution, however: if you do this, make sure you add a lot more –ly adverbs.

Last but certainly not least, it is time to discuss Plot, Character, Conflict, and Resolution. These are simple rules but I hope you will remember them, and take them to heart.

The Day the Leash Gave Way

PLOT: Don't have one. If you even see an inkling of plot creeping subtly into your story, get yourself a blank sheet of paper and start over. The secret is to make sure that absolutely nothing is going on.

CHARACTER: This was explained a little above. Rule of thumb is that all characters must be from Long Island. They should be rich and definitely white, and at least *one* should smoke a pipe. Also, every character should whine a lot.

CONFLICT: Be careful here. People who read *The New Yorker* don't want to read about people with problems, so make sure you don't give your characters any.

RESOLUTION: This is where it gets fun. Since there is no conflict or plot and your characters are all whiney bitches, you can feel free to end the story in any way you choose, as long as it's happy and involves upper class white people from Long Island enjoying their money. I suggest all the characters having a glass of Chardonnay outside by the swimming pool, or maybe have someone petting a dog, or waxing a fantastically expensive car. Pay off is essential. A story is supposed to be true to life, right? So after all this whining let's give the readers their money's worth. Don't be afraid to expand on my suggestions, or to come up with your own. But *do not*, under any circumstances, have the dog enjoying a glass of Chardonnay while waxing a car by the pool. This touches upon imagination, and what might have been a perfectly good story up to this point will be rejected outright.

Now that you've finished your first draft, go through it once or twice and ask yourself these questions:

Have I used enough big words?

Do I have as many –ly adverbs as humanly possible?

Am I certain there is no conflict?

Have I mentioned Long Island at least once, if not several times?

Once you've accomplished this, your manuscript is ready to go into the mail. Your name will soon be up in lights. You too will be a prestigious world-renowned lugubrious prevaricator, and the checks will start rolling in. I promise you, if you follow these cardinal rules of good writing, it will literally happen overnight.

The End of the Rainbow

Did I ever tell you about the time me 'n' Eddie Stockton went searching for the end of the rainbow and actually found it?

Huh? No, it wasn't quite that simple. It was a little more involved than that. You've asked me before how I got all my money. Well, if you're interested I'll tell you, though I'm not sure you'll believe it. It isn't your standard, run-of-the-mill story, though it's fitting for a night like this.

It started with my Uncle Joe. I don't think you ever met him, he died before you and I met, I think. He was a strange old bastard, lemme say that right off. He was fond of two things: scratching himself and beer. I'm not sure which of those two things took precedent, but that was pretty much it. His idea of living life to the fullest was sittin' on the back patio with a brew in one hand and his crotch in the other. Anyway, when I turned sixteen he pulled me aside at my birthday, out on the back porch, and told me something he thought I should know. It was a rainy day, though well behaved at the moment, and he cast his gaze out at a rainbow that leapt and arched in the sky, and came down in the nearby hills. "Billy," he said, "you know what a leprechaun is?"

"Sure," I said. "It's like the guy on the cereal boxes."

My Uncle Joe nodded and told me I was close enough. Then he placed a hand on my shoulder and said that when he was a kid he'd been told that if you found the end of a rainbow there would be a leprechaun sitting there with a pot of gold. If you caught him he had to give the gold to you. I, just like anyone else on this mud-ball, liked the idea of gold.

"Why are you telling me this, Uncle Joe?" I asked. "Because when I was about your age, *I found* the end of the rainbow," he said, then scratched himself and took of sip of the beer he was holding, making an odd grunting sound the entire time.

"Did you get a pot of gold?" I asked him anxiously.

"Naw, naw," he said, shaking his head. "I hiked a good two miles, I believe it was; and down in a small arroyo, I found it, and it wasn't no cereal box leprechaun with a pot of gold," he told me, giving me such an intense eye that I thought I was gonna wet my pants.

"What did you find, Uncle Joe?"

He scratched himself again, took a sip of beer and straightened himself up like a board. "I'm tellin' ya this, Billy, because you're at an age."

"An age?"

"You're at an age when strange shit starts happening to you, ain't I right?"

He was right but I didn't quite follow him, so I just gave a nod so he would go on.

The Day the Leash Gave Way

"What I found at the end of the rainbow was a small little woman all in green, and man if she didn't have the finest pussy you ever..." He saw my eyes widen and cleared his throat. "You know what pussy is, don't ya, Billy?"

I nodded. Of course I knew what pussy was. I had a magazine under my bed with pussy in it and I liked to look at it and stroke the snake, if you know what I mean. You stroke the snake, I bet, don't ya? Aw, yeah, right. Anyway, where was I?

Uncle Joe nabbed another swig from his beer, as though he was trying to hide it, then told me, "Don't ever tell your mom—and especially your Aunt Mary—about this. They ever found out I made it with a leprechaun, your mom and aunt would have my johnson on a skewer."

"*You made it with the leprechaun?*" I asked, not entirely sure what "made it" meant; but I had a pretty good idea. One time I'd gone to a movie with Sandra Golden. Halfway through the movie I slipped my hand under her shirt and stroked her belly. When I tried getting down into her jeans for the prize inside she slapped me across the face and walked out. I watched the rest of the movie alone with my cheek tingling. Still, from the magazine I had and from what all my friends had told me about, I had a reasonable idea about what "making it" was.

"Keep your voice down," he said. Then as if I wasn't there, Uncle Joe scratched himself good and thorough, and narrowed his eyes at the rainbow off in the distance. "I wanna hang onto my johnson," he told me, and he was as he said this.

Uncle Joe explained that he was anticipating gold the entire time he trudged through that arroyo. Finally he rounded a bend and there the rainbow was—and there was the fine female, dressed all in green with a drunken Irish smile on her gnome-like face. "I don't think I need to go into any great detail," Uncle Joe explained, "but lemme just say that on my way home, I had some trouble walkin'." At first I thought he meant something like either the leprechaun woman had kicked him in the groin, or being in an arroyo, he maybe managed to get a rock or something stuck in his man-sack. Then I understood, and as we watched the rainbow cut kaleidoscopically through the sky, my Uncle Joe was the greatest man alive, in both our eyes.

What was that? Why am I telling you all this? Well, it's better if you know all this first, so you c'n understand me 'n' Eddie's motivation. Eddie kept hopin' he was gonna get to see some green crotchless panties with the hole cut in the shape of a shamrock, but I'm getting ahead of myself.

Eh-hem.

So anyway, a few months went by and suddenly, before you knew it—Wham! It was summer. Hot as Hell and dry as old bones. We were in the midst of a drought, and the air was like dust to the mouth and nose. I had finally given up on this girl named Deborah I was going out with. After five dates I tried gettin' me the prize and received the same slap-in-the-face reward I'd gotten from Sandra some months earlier.

My folks weren't around all that often, and when they were home they were drunk. When they came back from wherever they were—whether it was after two hours or two weeks—they were inevitably tipsy and stupid and ready to pass out. The odd thing was that I couldn't ever recall seeing either of them with a drink, not at a party or anywhere else. But they were somehow always drunk, and as a result they never knew and never cared worth a shit about what I did. And what I did was drink beer. Eddie Stockton would come over with a six-pack he either stole from his parent's fridge or he got shoulder-tapping down at Hewet's. We'd sit on the back patio 'n' suck 'em down while we talked about girls and how cool it was to drink beer—then we'd talk about girls some more. Eddie wasn't too good with the girls because he was afraid of water and hardly ever bathed. Me, I didn't have much trouble getting the cereal; it was the prize inside that caused me problems. I thought to myself that if I saved the proofs of purchase from my previous four dates with Deborah, I might've been able to send away for it with only a small fee for the shipping.

Anyway…

Day in, day out, we gulped beer and hung out on my back patio. It was early July when it happened. I don't think you were livin' in town at the time. This was long ago.

The weather had been hotter than the devil's oven for months. Then one day, as me 'n' Eddie sat out on the patio drinkin' beer, dark malicious clouds moved in faster than in a movie. Lightning struck once, then the rain started pouring down in chubby drops the size of marbles.

"Bitch shit!" Eddie exclaimed, on account that he was like a cat and hated water, and almost before he had finished saying the words, we were both soaked through our T-shirts and our pants looked like we'd had several consecutive accidents.

I looked at Eddie and could actually see brown rivers running down his face and neck. I couldn't help wondering if there were plants growing under his arms and in his crotch. If there had been, they'd probably have sprouted being hit with all that water. We sought refuge inside the house and sat in the living room, drinking our beer and staring out the window at the fat drops of rain that exploded on the ground like little water grenades."Well," Eddie said, "what'd we do now? We can't play outside no more."

And that was when we saw it. Colorful brushstrokes in the sky, blue, red and yellow—all the colors of the rainbow. As quickly as it had come, the rain stopped, the sun shined and the birds were out again, chirping and flapping and gliding through the air. But there the rainbow was, beautiful and majestic, standing in the sky like a kid knee-deep in water.

"Sure is pretty," Eddie said, which was a very un-Eddie thing to say. Eddie usually liked to swear and talk about how everything was stupid. But it was true. That rainbow, on that day, brought to us by sudden rain, was truly the most spectacular display of color and nature either of us had ever seen. "Normally rainbows are for girls, hippies and queer-folk," Eddie said. "But that one there…Well, it's either an exception to the rule, or I'm a queer hippie chick."

We took our beers back outside and looked off into the hills. The air was cool and moist; a nice change from what we'd been experiencing over the past few months. It made my skin feel good and I've always loved the smell of rain—but that rainbow, man. If there was ever something so visually beautiful to the point that I almost cried, this was it.

The Day the Leash Gave Way 147

I didn't really think much about it at first. It wasn't until I was downing the last gulp of my beer that it came to me, like remembering you were gonna do the laundry while you're nodding off in bed.

I remembered what Uncle Joe told me.

I remembered the story about how he went in search of the end of the rainbow to get himself a pot of gold, and how instead of getting gold he'd gotten laid. I wanted to get laid. The idea of leprechaun snatch came at me from all angles. As I stood looking out the window, next to Eddie, who was still furiously wiping moisture from his face, all I could think about was getting' it on with a leprechaun.

I turned to Eddie, nervous that he'd think the bulge in my pants was meant for him.

"I got an idea," I said.

Eddie looked me up and down, saw my bulge and took a step back, eyes widening. "No way, man. I'm not into no—"

"Eddie," I cut in. "I'm thinkin' pussy."

Relief flushed his face. "Oh yeah?"

I told him the story about Uncle Joe, and the next thing I knew we were headed for the end of the rainbow. Jesus, man, we must've walked an hour or more, way out into the middle of fuckin' nowhere. Nothing but trees and rocks and dirt after a little while—the closest house was probably at least a mile away—maybe more. The entire time we walked Eddie kept on talking about green crotchless panties. "Yeah, man. Crotchless panties with the hole shaped like a shamrock. Yeah. I wanna see that, man, yeah."

Sure, I can't deny that I thought about it once he mentioned it, but I was more down to earth than Eddie. I knew that if we found the leprechaun and the luck of the Irish was on our side and she put out, well, chances were she wouldn't have anything kinky like that. That didn't stop my fantasies, though, and it didn't keep Eddie from talkin' about it.

"In the shape of a shamrock, dude. A fuckin' four leaf clover."

I let him have his imagination. And anyway, you never know, right? So I tuned Eddie out like he was a screaming baby at another table in a restaurant, and continued on with my own thoughts about gettin' lucky with the Irish. There were a few minutes in there when I felt ashamed on account that I couldn't get the bulge in my pants to simmer down. It was as if my snake was a part of Medusa's hair and she saw herself in a mirror. Casually, I glanced over at Eddie and saw he had one too, and I felt better for not being the only one.

Then, suddenly, like when the lights come on the stage at a rock concert, Eddie and I found ourselves surrounded by vibrant color. We were in the middle of a dazzling kaleidoscope. The air became sauna warm. A high-pitched voice sent a melody our way. We exchanged a glance, then rounded the next turn.

There, sitting on a rock, was a little man about two feet high. I never felt my stiffy wither quite so quickly as I did right then. He had a little green outfit on, with funny little shoes, a little green hat atop his head, red hair sticking out the sides and a red beard accompaniment around his puckered face. He was singin' some Old Irish song. On the ground, near his feet, was a tiny bottle of Irish whiskey, and next to that was a pot of gold. The gold didn't interest me just then, however, nor did it interest Eddie because the first thing he said was, "You ain't no hot leprechaun chick." He kicked the ground. "I wanna see crotchless shamrock panties. I wanted to slip my shaft into a lucky four leaf clover."

The leprechaun looked at us with a start. His brow pointed in towards his nose. He shouted something at us in what I assume was Gaelic, and I know wasn't friendly. Immediately following his screaming, he reached down to his little bottle, uncapped it and took a very large gulp for such a very small man. Bottle in hand, he shouted at us again, shaking a tiny tightly clenched fist. Whatever it was the guy was saying, I think I can speak for Eddie too when I say his threats meant nothing to us—not because he was so small but because we were still let down about the lack of Irish pussy. Our whole reason for going on this adventure, our entire motivation had been shot to hell and replaced by a drunken dwarf in a green outfit with a bottle of whiskey and a pot of gold. If the guy had crotchless panties on, neither of us cared to look.

"What about the pussy?" Eddie said, and turned to me. "You said there would be leprechaun pussy here, Billy."

"There—there was supposed to be."

"Well where is it?"

I looked to my right. I looked to my left. I looked up, then down, but none did I see. I saw a little drunk dude shouting at me in a language I didn't understand. It never occurred to me what he was doing so far from home. Why the hell do they import themselves then just shout and insult us? Hell, they don't have to come here.

Huh? Why not?

Well, did you believe in Santa Clause as a kid? Then I'm sure you believed in leprechauns at one time or another, too.

What's that?

Right, so please hold your questions till I'm finished. We're almost there.

Now, where was I?

There was no pussy to be found, just a damn leprechaun. The little guy did a sort of angry dance, shaking his fist. I was ready for him to click his heels together but he never did. It was odd. I was less awe struck at really and truly seeing a leprechaun than I was let down that neither Eddie nor I was gonna get any.

"Where's the pussy, Billy?"

I stammered, trying to find the right words; but it was like something was lodged in my throat, keepin' the words down and silent. Well, all but one:

"Uhh…"

Eddie, taking a step closer, said, "Hey, little man. We hear there's a someone like you in these parts, only they got a winker instead of a poker, if you know what I mean." He fanned his shirt against his chest to help the drying process along. "You know anyone like that 'round here?"

The leprechaun's face scrunched, turned bright red, then his eyes opened wide and he began shouting again, shaking that tiny fist.

I was about to have my own go at it when the little guy paused, finished off his bottle, then threw it at us, hard and fast, but off the mark.

"You little turd!"

The Day the Leash Gave Way

We moved in on him. He was fast—damn he was fast—but eventually Eddie got hold of his belt and held him at his side like a suitcase. The shouting didn't cease. In fact, it got worse. His arms and legs flailed.

"What should we do with him?" I asked.

"Let's beat him up, take his clothes and send him back up the fuckin' rainbow," Eddie suggested.

"Sounds pretty good," I said. But before we set our plan into action, a thought occurred to me. The thought of him getting home, or wherever, all naked and bruised and bloody, and telling his leprechaun clan about what happened. This thought immediately jumped to one of me and Eddie swarmed in wee folk. They were choking us, biting us, pulling our hair and gouging our eyes.

"Hold it, Eddie. How about we just take his gold?"

Eddie looked at me with dumbfounded surprise.

"Isn't that how it works anyway?" I asked. "Catch a leprechaun and the gold is there so he can ransom himself? Well, we caught him, the little bastard. Let's take the gold, maybe give him a swift kick in the ass, and be on our way."

"Ain't you forgettin' something, Billy?"

"What's that?"

"Pussy."

I shook my head with contempt. "We ain't gonna get any here."

"But maybe he knows where."

"Why would he? And even if he did, how's he gonna tell us? We speak different languages, for Christ's sake."

"But there's the international language."

"Shut up, Eddie. Let's take the gold, give him a kick or two and be gone. With all that gold—" I made a gesture to it with my hand "—you can *buy* yourself some pussy. Hell, you can pay to have it painted green, if you want. Can buy your own crotchless panties."

"With a shamrock?"

"Yes," I said. "With a shamrock."

Eddie began setting the guy down then hoisted him up again. "We should kick him in the ass first, huh?"

"The little fucker's fast," I said. "We should probably get his gold first, too."

I walked over and hefted the crock of gold into my arms. It was a lot heavier than it looked. I still don't understand how such a little guy could carry such a heavy load.

"Can I kick him now?" Eddie asked.

"Be my guest," I said, watching the two of them but glancing down at the gold in my arms every other second.

Eddie extended the little man out in front of himself then drop kicked him high and far. A long and dramatic Irish scream—"Och!"—drifted away along with the sight of him. He flew like a football.

Eddie and I headed home. Eddie kept giggling about how he was gonna buy himself a pair of green crotchless panties.

Me, I thought about how, now that I was rich, both Deborah and Sandra were gonna regret not letting me into their service stations. They'd be beggin' for it, and I'd be laughing, sitting on a big pile of money, with women winking at me even when they didn't like me. Yeah man, we were rich. We were rich like—

There was a heavy thudding sound and Eddie sort of dropped to the ground like a poorly placed mannequin in a store window, only there was a big splotch of gooey red stuff around his ear.

"Eddie?"

Something pelted me in the back and it hurt like a motherfucker. Turning around I saw the little bastard behind a tree. He threw another rock but this time I was able to dodge it, pick one up myself, and fling it back. It hit the tree.

"Go on now," I said. "Fair is fair. We caught you, we got your gold, now get outta here and go back to wherever the hell you came from." Then I looked down at Eddie, who was slowly starting to move, his eyes squinching and opening wide in some kind of Morse code. He brought a hand to his ear and cussed. Sitting up, he looked at the blood on his hand and another rock smacked him in the shoulder and sent him back to the ground.

I thought leprechauns were supposed to be clever, but this one was just plain brutal. He flung another rock, which I heard whiz past my head.

Quickly, I set down the pot of gold, collected a few rocks of my own, threw one and ran at him, then threw another and another, covering myself as I approached.

With one stone left in my possession we came face to face—or face to knee is more like it. The little man's expression hungered for blood but his hands were shaking, like he'd been using a jackhammer. Then suddenly his lips started quivering and the hunger went out of him like someone turning off the lights.

Sadness came over me. I began to feel for the little guy, and hell, I was so much bigger than he was. With teary eyes he looked up at me, and said the only thing I ever heard him say in English.

"Me gold…Me gold…" with sniffles mingled in.

"Oh, look," I said, in hopes of talking it over, maybe coming to some sort of mutual understanding..

Then he delivered an upward punch and hit me square in the groin.

That did it. Suppressing the pain I grabbed the little worm by the lapels of his green coat and smacked him against the tree, head first. It was a similar sound to when Eddie got the rock to the head, only mushier. I didn't let go of him. I swung him back and smacked him against the tree again, then again. I kept going. I couldn't stop.

"Och! Och! Och!"

The red of his beard darkened and his face matched it. Amazingly, the hat stayed on his head the entire time, only got scrunched, until finally I had a dead limp leprechaun in my hands. I dropped him to the ground and searched his pockets, found one gold coin, which I put into my own pocket. Setting him against the tree I'd battered him on, I adjusted his coat to look somewhat presentable, and pulled out a piece of bark that was stuck in his eye.

The Day the Leash Gave Way

Eddie was on his feet when I got back to him, his eyes crossing and straightening like a cartoon.

"What happened?" he said. "Where are we? What's going on?"

I thought fast. "You hit your head," I told him. "You'd just finished, uh, poking the leprechaun chick when you tripped and hit your head on a rock."

It was amazing—or maybe it was lucky—because he remembered right up to when we got to the rainbow, but all else was gone. It's pretty common, I guess, for people to block out traumatic memories. He smiled, and asked me what it was like.

"She thought you were a stallion," I said, and Eddie seemed pleased. His face was covered in dirt, making him look more like the Eddie I knew.

"Where is she now?"

"There's a, uh, curfew for leprechauns," I said. "She had to get back or, uh, she was gonna turn into a, uh, Irish setter."

Then he saw the gold sitting on the ground, near by and raised an eyebrow at me.

"She said we were so good she wanted to pay us." Eddie didn't seem to doubt it a bit. A damn right expression slapped onto his face, as though he knew the outcome of a movie from the very beginning. Still, I could tell that something unsettled him. He just wished he could remember the experience, I think.

As we walked back to my place Eddie asked me what kind of panties she had on.

"Green ones," I told him, "with a hole shaped like a shamrock."

He smiled.

What?

I swear it's true. You know how I know it's true? Cause I was there. That's how I got my money, believe it or not. I told Uncle Joe what happened and he laughed, said he always thought me and Eddie were queer, and said because we came back with a pot of gold instead of an ache in the loins, he was sure of it. But that's what happened, God honest truth. That's how I got my money, except for that gold coin I took out of his pocket...that turned to ash. An ace the little bastard must have had up his sleeve, fuckin' with me even after he was dead.

Anyway, you want another drink? Maybe one of the green beers they got tonight? Won't have another chance to get one until a year from now.

Yeah, same to you.

Beannachtaí na féile Pádraig.

THE MUSIC

Ah, the music...
It washes through me in waves, moves me this way and that.
I can't really explain it—
It isn't something that can be understood unless it's experienced. There aren't any words for it. Just have to listen and find it.

I listen to the music, oh the music. All I want is to dance, drift through the air, bang my head. The sounds envelop me in warmth and happiness unlike any other melody. It makes me want to sing along but I don't know all the words and it doesn't matter. The words are only part of it, and what I really hear is the music. The notes, the chords, the beat. Soon I'll sleep, but for now I want to dance. I want to drift around the room, free to let my body move as it wishes. Alone, dancing, listening to the music, feeling better than I have in ages, in my mother's house, and she doesn't know I'm here. She's out with friends, so I turn up the music, louder, so I can lose myself in it's beautiful wash—the piano, the drums, the bass and guitar. Twirl, twirl, twirl to the kitchen and open the drawer, the one beside the sink. Spin, duck, spin again, and grab the handle, study the blade. Oh, I feel so alive. I hope the music never ends. Music will always be inside me, wherever else I am. Just like memories. Memories that don't dance but sit in the corner and pout and don't want to talk to anyone.

Take up thy blade and dance. Dance and wait.
And remember—
Remember dancing with her, how she hugged too close, and asked for a hand. Remember the deterioration of soul, the moisture on my fingers.

But also remember the music and dance. There's always a reason to dance, and the reason is clear tonight. So clear it's almost crazy.

I twirl and wait, twirl and wait, dancing, dancing, dancing—remembering, feeling, reliving as I move.

The front door opens and I spin, jump in the air, listen to the bass and the steady beat. She steps into the house and looks at me, asks me what I'm doing.

I swing the blade, swing the blade, listen to the rhythm as it slashes, the music of her screams. One beautiful composition. I duck and cut, duck and cut, and watch the red jump from her, spray like the lights of a disco ball.

Then the song comes to an end. I break for a moment, look at her there on the floor in her blood; and though there is no more music, I dance again, freer and happier than ever before.

The music is better than it has ever been.

Sparkle Head

Elton looked up at the cold, dark bitch of a sky then drank down the rest of his beer and glanced over at Jasper. Jasper sat with his beer between his legs and an unlit cigarette in his mouth and seemed about as thrilled as a cinderblock giving birth. If this night turned out to be like the rest—and most likely it would—then they might as well just call it quits now. One more evening of guzzling $4.99 twelve-packs of Hamm's and it would probably be better if they just flung themselves in front of an oncoming truck. Thinking back to the night of their high school graduation, Elton recalled with a touch of nostalgia how he and Jasper and a bunch of other guys had taken turns banging old lady Bertha with the bag over her head. Back in her day she was probably one hot piece of ass. But a bitch ain't like wine, and the years hadn't been good to her, turning her flesh all scaly like a lizard and her ass so big it was like a garbage truck that shit rather than dumped. Not to mention the lower portion of her face was gone due to years of smoking. Had her fucking jaw removed. Everyone, including Bertha, figured it a good idea that she wear a pillowcase over her head.

That had been the only time in both Elton's and Jasper's lives that they'd gotten to successfully lay some pipe. Elton had to admit to himself that since that night he'd been a little frightened of pussy. Probably on account that after everybody was done with her and each had kicked in their five bucks, it was he who accidentally walked in on her in the bathroom, where she sat on the shitter with no bag over her head and no jaw on her face. Realizing what he'd stuck himself into, Elton was never quite able to get over it. Any time after that when he got close to a woman, which was only a few times, he couldn't help being slapped with the vivid image of Bertha, her ass pouring over the sides of the toilet and her jaw gone, the smell of shit so strong he imagined there was blood in it.

Elton wasn't sure that if he had the chance now, he could get his dick hard, but it seemed better to try than to sit in this fucking park drinking cheap beer and hoping something exciting was going to happen.

"What do you say?" he asked Jasper, who tossed his beer away, not finishing it.

"Honestly," said Jasper, "I'm thinking about going back to my place and watching some porn. Got this one where five guys ass-fuck this girl then cum in her ears."

That had been fun back in high school, Elton thought. Back before they were old enough to buy alcohol and were so horny they could get a stiffy at the sight of a cardboard box, that had been a good time. But they were older now, grown men, and Elton wasn't gonna let himself get stuck in his past. He wanted to move on with his life.

"No, man, you can watch that porn anytime. Let's do something different."

"Well, I wasn't gonna invite you 'cause I wanna jerk off. That's different."

"Hell, man, I've seen you jerk off before."

"When?"

"Back a few days before we graduated. Remember when we all played 'Shoot the Cookie'?"

"That was back in high school, man. I've moved on with my life. Now I do it in private."

"Well, whatever. I say we find something different to do. Something different from drinking beer and watching porn."

"Nothing to do in this town," Jasper said. "Way I see it, I'm lucky I can get porn in a town like this."

"We could probably get just about anything if we put our minds to it."

That was a problem in and of itself. So far in their lives neither had displayed much talent when it came to putting things together or making plans.

"What do you suggest?" Jasper said.

Elton thought long and hard on it. "Maybe we could get us a dog or something," he said.

"Where the hell did that idea come from?"

Elton shrugged.

"What the hell you want a dog for?"

"I dunno. I thought we could play fetch with it or something, and if that wasn't any fun we could set it on fire, maybe, or drag it from the back of my truck."

"I tell ya, you gotta be real fucking bored if you want yourself a dog. And you gotta be fucked in the head you thinking about burning an animal alive or dragging it on the road. That's just cruel, man."

"Well, do you have any ideas?"

"I'm happy with watching porn."

"Thought you'd moved on with your life."

Jasper was about to say something, but before he could he processed the hard fact and realized what he had become. Or what he hadn't; he hadn't changed a bit since high school, dammit. Who the hell was he trying to kid?

"Okay," he said. "But I ain't gonna torture no dog."

"Fine, then let's think of something. The night ain't getting no younger and neither are we."

Jasper clicked his lighter and got his cigarette going. He looked around in the darkness. There was little to see. The closest light was clear at the other end of the park. "Tell you the truth, I'm a bit cold."

"So what, you wanna go shopping for a new jacket?"

"No, no, I'm just saying, that's all. I could do with a little warmth about now."

"You trying to come on to me?"

"Fuck you, man."

"I always wondered if maybe you were some sort of faggot."

"I'm no faggot, I'm just cold. Why would I be a fag just because I'm cold?"

"You've always liked that anal porn. Maybe it's some hidden way of getting it in the ass yourself."

The Day the Leash Gave Way

"You've always liked anal porn, too. Hell, you're the one told me how cool it was."

"All right, all right, forget it."

"Asshole."

"No thank you."

Jasper smoked his cigarette. Nobody had ever called him a faggot before. The thought didn't sit well. It made him want to throw away all his porn and invest in something useful or educational. Maybe some books or a globe. He always thought South America was kind of shaped like a pussy.

"Well," Elton said, "I'm getting up off this bench, and I'm gonna go discover me some fun." He stood up and tapped his foot twice on the grass. "You're welcome to come along but don't try to tell me later that it was your idea."

Jasper looked down in shame, then got to his feet, stifled a yawn and said, "Okay, let's go."

They walked across the park. It *was* a little cold, Elton noted, but he wasn't about to say anything to Jasper. They got to the light at the other end of the park and stood under it a moment.

Jasper finished his cigarette and tossed it aside. "What you thinking?" he asked Elton.

"I was thinking," Elton said, "I got some firecrackers back at my place left over from the Fourth. Ain't no raging party but at least it's something to do."

"What kind of firecrackers?"

"Got some bottle rockets and Black Cats. Think I might still have a cherry bomb or two."

"Aren't cherry bombs illegal?"

"I've got my connections."

"Wanna get 'em and bring 'em back here?"

"Hell no. We get the firecrackers I sure as shit don't wanna come back here. We spend too much time in this fucking park."

"Then where you wanna go with them?"

"How the fuck do I know? Let's see when we get back to my place."

They made their way down the dark street. Elton's house was only two blocks away so he liked to walk. Jasper's car had blown up a week or so earlier after he drove it into an electrical box, so he was walking too.

"Can't see a whole lot in this darkness," Jasper said.

"That's because there ain't no light," Elton said, and puffed out his chest at the fact that he was smarter than his friend.

The darkness was strong, no doubt about it. There wasn't any moon and if they hadn't been on solid ground they wouldn't have been able to tell which way was up and which way was down. But they continued on anyway.

"You ever get spooked of the dark?" Jasper asked.

"Sissy," Elton said. But the moment he said it the image of Bertha on the toilet flashed behind his eyes and a chill ran up his spine. Had she not had the bathroom light on he would have only smelled the shit, but of course it had been bright and he was scarred for life because of it.

His mind wouldn't let it go. He kept thinking about it, and didn't pull himself back to reality until Jasper asked him what had happened to the sidewalk.

They stopped where they were. Even though he couldn't see them, Elton studied his feet as though there was something wrong with them, but the only thing wrong was that they were on dirt rather than cement.

"What the hell? Where did we get off to?"

"You're the brains," Jasper said. "I was following your lead."

Elton couldn't count how many times he'd made this walk. Two measly blocks, and measly was the right word for it. Maybe he wasn't no Einstein but he knew what measly was, and it was the two blocks between the park and his house.

"Well," he said, "we can't be more than a measly block away from one street or another. Let's just keep going."

And they did, kicking rocks every once in a while, stepping in shallow ditches and bumping into trees. Jasper scraped his ear on a branch and wanted to yelp but didn't for fear of being called a sissy again.

After a couple minutes a streetlight came into view. As they moved closer they saw a van parked beneath it. Elton and Jasper stopped in the darkness and saw that the sliding door of the van was open, and that someone was hauling something out while someone else sat behind the wheel.

"What's going on?" Jasper said.

Elton didn't say anything, just watched the man struggle with the contents of the van. The engine was running and the country music on the radio was just loud enough to be heard from where they were.

"What's that he's taking outta there, Elton?"

"Shut up a minute."

The man at the sliding door was in the way of their view, but once he'd succeeded in removing his cargo, he turned into the light. Elton gasped at the sight of the limp and naked woman in the man's arms. Jasper nearly wet his pants. They watched the man move under the light and out of it, then they heard a thudding sound and the man returned with his arms free and climbed into the van and closed the sliding door.

Seconds later the van sped away.

"Jesus Christ," Jasper said. "Jesus in my ass, did that really just happen?"

They made their way to the side of the road. It was the cross street that intersected Elton's. They were just a measly half block from Elton's house. It was late and most folks were asleep, so there wasn't any traffic at all, and the van was long gone. Under the light they looked around a bit, not finding anything. Then Elton moved out from under the light and searched as best he could in the darkness until he found her by tripping over her legs. He reached into his pocket and retrieved a book of matches, lit one, and stared down at the face of a pretty brunette. She would have been prettier, Elton noted, had her eyes not been rolled into the back of her head and her throat not slit from ear to ear. Her bare breasts were awash in blood and little scrapes and bruises and cuts covered her arms and legs. These things aside, she was a damn fine sight. Beat Bertha by miles. This, Elton said

The Day the Leash Gave Way

to himself, is a sweet piece of ass. He shook out the match, got to his feet and joined Jasper back under the light. Jasper, for some reason, had been looking in the opposite direction.

"I found her."

"Is she all fucked up and shit?"

"She's dead all right, but not too bad. Throat slashed, that's about the worst of it."

"What do you wanna do? Should we go call the cops?"

Elton thought for a moment. Sure, they could call the cops and tell them what they found. But the police would wanna know why they were out at this hour, two single men wandering around the empty streets. "No," he said. It was occurring to him that with all the millions of times he'd walked from the park to his house that he just happened to stray away from the path on this night of all nights. It was a sign. Someone was watching over him. Somebody had heard his cry of boredom and gave him an opportunity for change. This he explained to Jasper.

At first Jasper was hesitant to understand, but then he listened and nodded his head. Maybe it was a little creepy, but he had to admit it was better than jerking off to porn, even if five guys ass-fucked the girl and came in her ears.

"Let's go get my truck," Elton said. "We'll pick her up and take her back to my place. Then we can make a real plan and really have some fun."

They went back to Elton's house, making sure to stay on the street so they wouldn't get lost again. As they walked there was an energy in the air that hadn't been there before. Maybe, even if only for one night, something exciting was finally going to happen—and if not exciting, at least different.

When they flopped her down in Elton's backyard, Jasper complained about the blood on his hands. "Maybe we should hose her down or something," he suggested. "Give her a little shower, get some of that blood and dirt off her."

"You don't like it down and dirty, huh?"

"She's dead," said Jasper. "Ain't that down and dirty enough?"

"I suppose you're right." Elton went to the hose, turned it on, kinked it, then brought it over, released the kink, and washed away the blood and dirt as best he could. Jasper ran inside and got a towel, and when Elton was finished spraying he wiped her down. The throat was a little tougher to deal with but they managed okay.

When done they both stared down at her. If not for the huge gash across her throat she would have looked just fine. A little roughed up, maybe, but nothing worth worrying about.

"What do you say?" said Jasper. "Should we get us some tail now?"

Elton thought on it a moment. He checked her out from head to toe then said, "Y'know, Jasper, seeing her now, in this light, I'm not so sure I want any of it." As he spoke he didn't know if his words were out of revulsion, respect, or out and out fear. Maybe it had something to do with the fact that he hadn't been able to get it up the few times he'd been with a woman. Could have been that getting it on with a corpse was just going a little too far. Hell, what good is a woman if she's dead and cold and stiffer than you are?

"But Elton," Jasper said. "This is free ass. As much as you can handle."

"I'm starting to think this might be wrong," Elton said. "Something's not sitting right with me."

"I gotta admit I nearly wet my pants when I saw her in that guys arms," Jasper said. "I was scared outta my mind and wanted to run the other way. But—but then I got curious. And it was you who talked it up. We never get to work our meat. Well, here's our chance."

Elton looked at her face. Her mouth was slightly open. In his mind he saw her jaw drop off. "Nope," he said. "Count me out. There are other ways we can have a good time. Doesn't have to involve getting laid."

"I was gonna jerk it to porn. Now I got my chance at some real snatch and you don't want me to have it."

"Think about it, man. She's dead."

"All that means is we don't have to talk to her when we're done."

"Go on home, Jasper. Go home and jack off to porn. You wouldn't have nothing right now if it wasn't for me. You wanna be ungrateful, then go home and watch your movie."

Jasper stood quietly. He wasn't too hot on watching the porn anymore. Maybe because after such a close encounter with the real thing, he knew his five-fingered kootie-snorcher wasn't gonna have the same pizzazz. "All right, fine," he said. "What are you thinking?"

"I dunno," Elton said. "I just don't wanna fuck her."

Dammit, maybe Elton was right. What did it say about them if the only tail they could get was dead meat? Sure, they could play their own version of "Shoot the Cookie," but that would be an awful lot for the loser to have to eat. And where would it get them in the end? Maybe it was time they cleaned up their act, started brushing their teeth and wearing clean clothes, bathing more often. Maybe it *was* time to buy a globe, Jasper thought. Hell, he could still study South America when the urge came upon him. He could still jerk off, but he'd be learning his geography when he did. He could cum all over Canada if he wanted, or Germany, or France or Italy—even Europe.

"Well, okay," Jasper said. "But we gotta do something with her. We brought her all this way."

"One measly block," Elton said, then his face lit up and he almost drooled. Without a word he raced into his house, made some rummaging sounds, then came back with a plastic grocery bag full of something.

"What you got in there?" Jasper asked.

"Firecrackers," Elton said, and searched the bag. There were six bottle rockets, a couple dozen Black Cats and, right on, two cherry bombs. He took out the cherry bombs and a string of Black Cats that had an extended fuse tied into them. He twisted the fuse into the fuses of the cherry bombs then out again so there would be something to light. "I've always been curious," he said, and winced as he parted the cut across the woman's throat, feeling the larynx rip a little beneath his fingers. He stuck the two spherical cherry bombs in about halfway then opened her mouth a little wider and inserted the Black Cats.

"I get it," Jasper said.

The Day the Leash Gave Way

Elton stood up and regarded her a moment. With stuff coming out of her neck and face, she looked like an avant-garde sculpture. If only he had a Polaroid. He reached into his pocket and withdrew his book of matches.

"How loud are those cherry bombs, Elton?"

"About as loud a grenade," he said, then freed a match, lit it, and brought it to the fuse and backed away. There was an intense fizzing sound for about five seconds; then it stopped, and the back yard was silent. Elton and Jasper stared down at her, both let down and a little worried that maybe she had somehow managed to put it out with her breath or spit or something. If this was the case, everything was going to be very different.

"Maybe I twisted those fuses too tight," Elton said, and took a step forward, then hastily took three steps back when it suddenly flared up again.

The Black Cats started first, making a series of loud cap gun popping sounds, one right after another. Fast little sparks and tiny bits of paper jumped from her mouth. Then, in quick succession, the cherry bombs went off in two thunderous booms and her head snapped back twice even with the ground behind it. Pop-pop-boom-boom-pop-pop-pop, then a brief moment of silence, and a final pop, and before they knew it, it was over. Dogs were barking all over the neighborhood. The woman's lips and cheeks were black and gray, and so was part of her nose. The cherry bombs had done a number on her throat, tearing a large and gaping hole. What had been a pretty face was now ruined, though her body was still pretty much okay, all things considered. Sprawled there with the remnants of Black Cats in her mouth, Elton thought she looked more like a zombie than an avant-garde sculpture. He wondered if he'd have nightmares about her coming for him.

"Hey Elton?" Jasper said, and Elton looked at him. "Why do you think they killed her?"

"I dunno," Elton said. "The bitch probably had it coming for one thing or another. Most women do. I'm sure, had we known her while she was alive, she would have been just another filthy piece of trash." He went to the bag and got another string of Black Cats and tossed them to Jasper. "Think I'm gonna save the bottle rockets for this next coming Fourth," he said, then closed the bag and took it inside.

After Jasper had lit the next set of firecrackers, the neighbor's started complaining. "Cut that shit out!" screamed one. "It's two in the goddamn morning!" shouted another. And there were more dogs barking than before.

"Good thing that was it," Jasper said. "Your neighbors are getting pissed."

"Yeah," said Elton. "Let's go inside and have a beer, let things settle down a bit."

"Well, all right."

Once inside and each with a can of beer, they stared out the kitchen window into the back yard.

Elton sighed. "Jasper," he said, "do you think it's wrong, what we've done?"

"Aw shit, are you having scruples again?"

"I'm just wondering is all. I mean, hell, I know she maybe had it coming. That doesn't bother me any."

"And it was fun," Jasper added.

"Sure it was fun. We wouldn't have done it if it wasn't."

"So what's the problem?"

"I dunno. Guess I'm just wondering if we have the right to do what we did."

"It was your idea," Jasper said. "I was happy with going home and watching porn."

"I know, I know." "And we didn't kill her, did we?"

"No, but what we did *would* have killed her."

"But we *didn't* kill her, and we never would have. She was already dead when we found her." "I'm just feeling a tiny itch of guilt, that's all."

"Well, we didn't really do nothing wrong. Someone else killed her. You said it yourself: she probably had it coming. All we did was help seal the deal."

"Yeah, maybe you're right."

"So don't go getting moral on me. This was your idea in the first place. All we did was ensure the elimination of some trash."

"Yeah, I suppose you're right. Okay. But I don't want her hanging out in my yard. We need to get rid of her."

"Then let's toss her back in the truck and take her back to where we found her."

"No," Elton said. "That's too close. With all that's happened and all the noise we've made, we should probably take her somewhere else. Drive her out into the woods or something, or at least into a neighborhood on the other side of town."

"Y'know something, Elton?"

"What's that?"

"We have come a long way since high school."

Elton laughed a little and finished his beer.

Jasper said, "Remember when we all paid five bucks a piece to screw that fat bitch with the pillowcase over her head?"

Elton's humor disappeared. His memory flashed to when he'd opened the bathroom door and saw Bertha sitting there on the toilet, her surprised and jawless face staring at him. Even now he could smell the shit. It was because of her that he couldn't get it up with other women. And the women laughed at him. They called him "Shrivel Dick" and "Lazy Noodle." One said he'd do better as a bitch. And now, because of this, he was afraid to even talk to women. A calm anger set in, flowed through him, and he said, "Yeah, I remember." Then he crushed his beer can. "Let's get her the fuck out of here."

"You okay, Elton?"

"I'm fine." He paused, then said, "I'm sorry, man. I snap at you a lot but I don't mean anything by it. Hell, you're the best friend a guy could have."

"Same goes for you," Jasper said.

"Maybe," Elton said, "when we've gotten rid of her, we can go back to your place and watch that porn."

"Can't beat five guys ass-fucking a chick," Jasper said.

"No," said Elton, "you sure can't."

LaVergne, TN USA
03 November 2009
162978LV00001B/19/P